# THE TAMING OF Serge Dumont

## MARILYN LEE

ELLORA'S CAVE
ROMANTICA PUBLISHING

An Ellora's Cave Romantica Publication

www.ellorascave.com

The Taming of Serge Dumont

ISBN 9781419955730
ALL RIGHTS RESERVED.
The Taming of Serge Dumont Copyright © 2002 Marilyn Lee
Cover art by Willo.

This book printed in the U.S.A. by Jasmine-Jade Enterprises, LLC.

Trade paperback Publication September 2007

# Also by Marilyn Lee

**ഌ**

# About the Author

∞

Marilyn Lee lives, works, and writes on the East Coast. In addition to thoroughly enjoying writing erotic romances, she enjoys roller-skating, spending time with her large, extended family, and rooting for all her hometown sports teams. Her other interests include collecting Doc Savage pulp novels from the thirties and forties and collecting Marvel comics from the seventies and eighties (particularly Thor and The Avengers). Her favorite TV shows are forensic shows, westerns (Gunsmoke and Have Gun, Will Travel are particular favors), mysteries (love the old Charlie Chan mysteries. All time favorite mystery movie is probably Dead, Again), and nearly every vampire movie or television show ever made (Forever Knight and Count Yorga, Vampire are favors). She thoroughly enjoys hearing from readers.

Marilyn welcomes comments from readers. You can find her website and email address on her author bio page at www.ellorascave.com.

## Tell Us What You Think

We appreciate hearing reader opinions about our books. You can email us at Comments@EllorasCave.com.

# THE TAMING OF SERGE DUMONT

## Bloodlust 2

&

# Chapter One

ೋ

Erica Kalai entered the last grade into her terminal, sent the file to the school's mainframe, and sat back in her chair. "At last," she said. She stretched and glanced at her watch. Six thirty-five. She'd made better time than she expected. She had plenty of time to head home, slip into something sexy, and wait for Mikhel to come spend the night with her. Ah, sweet, considerate, Mikhel Dumont. She liked everything about him. Even his name was sexy.

Thoughts of him and their fairytale relationship during the last few weeks brought a smile to her face. Little had she known when she allowed her friend Janna to talk her into going to that Halloween party in Salem, that she would meet the man of her dreams. Although Mikhel looked thirty at most, he was actually sixty and he had been the best fortieth birthday present she'd ever had.

After she'd managed to get past the fact that he looked so much younger than her, their relationship had heated up big time. Since that first magical night when they'd become insatiable lovers, she'd been showered with flowers, champagne, jewelry, and long nights of love, during which they greedily drank each other's blood. Although a part of her was still dismayed by her behavior, she'd developed quite a taste for Mikhel's blood and for the unprotected sex neither of them could get enough of. There was nothing in the world quite as wonderful as feeling his cock surge deeply into her pussy while she slurped his blood from the end of his finger. And when he drank hers from her neck, he sent her straight to multi-orgasmland.

Still, there were things marring her happiness. First and foremost, she was in love with a vampire, or at least he was

11

part vampire. While his father was human, his mother was a vampire, making him a half-blood. Lately, Mikhel seemed different—darker. Although she didn't feel personally threatened, there was an undeniable aura of menace surrounding him these days. Nevertheless, she would think about that later—after she'd made the most important decision of her life. If only she could confide in Mikhel.

Mikhel. He was the last person from whom she could seek advice.

Sighing deeply, she walked down the quiet, deserted corridors of Kennedy Hall, the main building in the exclusive private girls school where she'd taught for the last ten years. There were some lights in other offices, but she didn't look in any of the doors she passed. The few instructors that were still around were obviously working to get their grades uploaded before the midnight deadline.

She left the building by the side entrance and paused only long enough to pull the hood of her jacket up over her head before starting down the path that lead to the rear parking lot. Halfway along, she felt a sudden, ominous chill run over her entire body—right through her down jacket.

She immediately knew the source of the chill. She darted a wild glance around. A hedge bound the path on one side and a high wall on the other. The fact that she seemed to be on it alone didn't reassure her. She knew she wasn't alone. *She* was there somewhere waiting for an opportunity to strike.

*Oh, Mikhel. Where are you? Oh, get a grip, Rica. You can't expect him to sit around and guard you like a baby.*

She had quickly learned that there were undreamed of dangers involved in loving a man with vampire blood. While staying with Mikhel at his hotel room in Salem, she had been attacked by Deoctra, a full-blooded female vampire who considered Mikhel her rightful property. Although stopped before she could do much damage, both Erica and Mikhel had known the vengeful fem would want revenge. Once they returned to Boston, Mikhel, who headed a security firm, had spent the next two weeks teaching her how to defend herself. As a result, she felt more capable of protecting herself from an assault than she'd ever felt before. *So, do it,* she told herself.

She glanced back at Kennedy Hall, trying to decide if she should turn back or make a run for her car. After the briefest of hesitations, she decided on the latter. The only people still around were nearing retirement and wouldn't be able to help her. If she went back, they might get hurt or worst. Clutching the small but sturdy wooden spike Mikhel had given her, she quickened her pace. She was on her own, but she was far from helpless.

She had nearly reached the end of the long walkway when Deoctra stepped onto the path. "Human whore, I've come to settle with you."

Erica had seen this small, slender woman easily lift the six foot seven inch Mikhel off his feet and toss him across the room with no apparent effort. Now she wanted revenge on Erica for having taken Mikhel, whom Deoctra considered her bloodlust or perfect partner. How the hell was she supposed to stop this woman when Mikhel hadn't been able to without help?

*Damn. Some days it just didn't pay to get the hell outta bed.* Okay, so she was no match for the fem, but damn if she'd go down without a fight. She dropped her briefcase and took the leather purse Mikhel had given her off her shoulder. With her back to the wall, she began swinging it slowly, letting it build momentum. The bottom of it was lined with a heavy metal that made it a formidable weapon.

"Discard the spike and come to me whore, and I will make this quick. Look at me."

She knew better than to look into the other woman's eyes. But the desire to do just as she directed was difficult to resist. "Oh, God, please help me."

"He can't help you, human whore."

"I wouldn't be too sure about that."

As if in answer to her prayer, a tall, dark man appeared on the path behind Deoctra. As the full-blood whipped around, the man wrapped one arm around her throat and the other behind her neck, gripping her in a headlock.

"Low breed! Let me go!" Deoctra snarled.

Struggling to hold on to Deoctra, the man looked at Erica.

Looking into the dark, smoky eyes, Erica recognized the man. She'd seen him in Salem outside the ladies' room of the restaurant where she and Mikhel had been having a meal. At the time, she'd been disturbed and ashamed because despite her growing feelings for Mikhel, this handsome man had looked at her with such lust in his dark eyes that she'd quickly become aroused. "You! What are you doing here?"

"I am here to help you. So, leave me to do it. Go. Now."

"But you don't understand," she said. "She's a—"

"I know what she is," he said. As Deoctra tried to unbalance him, the man used one foot to kick her foot, lengthening her stride so that she herself was off balance. He transferred one hand across Deoctra's breasts and fondled her. "Hmm. Small, but nice."

"What do you think you're doing?!" Deoctra hissed.

"Can't you tell?" He dipped his head and licked the side of the full-blood's neck. "I'll bet you're a tasty little morsel." He lifted his head and looked at Erica. "Why are you still here? Go. I'll hold her here while you reach your car."

"But what about you?"

The big hand moved from Deoctra's breasts, to span her stomach. "I can take care of myself. Go! Now!"

Picking up her briefcase, she ran the rest of the way down the walkway. As she neared them, Deoctra hissed and struggled to reach out and grab her. Erica tore her jacket on the hedge avoiding her. Fear lending her speed, she cleared the path and raced across the dimly lit parking lot.

She could hear a series of growls and hisses behind her and she feared for the life of the stranger who had come to her rescue. She shouldn't have left him. She had to get to her car and call the police. Maybe the sound of the sirens would drive Deoctra off. In any case, she had to go back.

A few feet from her car, a small, dark woman appeared in her path. "Oh, God, not another one!"

She dropped her briefcase and gripped the spike like a knife. "Oh, God, Mikhel! Where are you?"

"Mikhel is not here, but we are."

It took Erica a moment to recognize the woman standing by her car, wearing a dark cape like coat with a fur-lined hood. When she did, her legs nearly gave out. "Mrs. Dumont." She ran forward, her breath coming in ragged gasps. She clutched Mikhel's mother's arm.

"It's Deoctra." She stabbed a finger back towards the path. "She's going to hurt the man who tried to help me. Please. You have to help him."

Palea Dumont glanced towards the path, her dark eyes glowing. "Serge!" She looked at Erica. "Follow me."

Erica glanced around, expecting to see Serge. She'd heard a lot about Mikhel's younger brother, but had yet to meet him. She saw no one. Shrugging, she dropped her briefcase, clutched her shoulder bag and her spike. She had barely turned, albeit reluctantly, back the way she had come and already Palea Dumont had disappeared in a dark blur. Steeling herself, Erica quickly ran back towards Kennedy Hall. As she neared the path, low moans reached her ears. The sounds were unmistakable. Oh, no! Deoctra must be raping her would be rescuer, as she'd attempted to rape Mikhel.

"Mrs. Dumont! Please help him!"

She rounded the corner. Her heart thumped with fear when she realized that Palea Dumont was nowhere in sight. Then she turned her stunned gaze on the scene before her.

The man had somehow retained the upper hand on Deoctra, even though his pants were down around his legs, exposing a firm, hard masculine butt. He must have successfully fought off the rape attempt. The full-blood's small body was spread-eagled against the wall. The man stood behind her, his groin pressed tight against her bare bottom, his hands holding her wrists, his face bent towards her neck.

He drew back his hips and shoved forward. Erica stood gaping in stunned amazement. For she could clearly see part of the man's shaft quickly disappearing into Deoctra's body. And not into her pussy either. He was taking her in the behind!

The resultant shiver from the full-blood was unmistakable, as were the animal like growls coming from her throat. "Yes! Yes! For a low breed, you have a passable cock. More! Give me more! More cock! More cock! Give it all to me. Fill my ass with your big cock! Shove it in deep, hard, and fast. I can take it. I can take it all. Give it to me. Ooooh. Ooooh, yes!"

"You're a greedy little vamp, aren't you?" The man demanded as he slipped his hand down to cup Deoctra's small breasts. He quickly settled into a steady, hard rhythm, his butt clenching with every movement. The full-blood moaned, her small behind quivering with each thrust.

"Imagine a full-blood like you enjoying being fucked by a low breed," he taunted.

"Shut up and fuck me!"

Heat rose up Erica's neck and flooded her cheeks. Her whole body felt hot. She pushed her hood back from her head so the cold air could cool her cheeks. The icy air didn't seem to bother either of the other two. They were clearly generating their own intimate heat.

Without warning, the man drew back, pulling his cock out of Deoctra's rear end.

Erica, stared, biting her bottom lip. He was as large and as thick as Mikhel. No. Actually, he was bigger than Mikhel. His condom-covered rod glistening with bodily juices, he rubbed the big head of his shaft against the woman's behind.

Even through the condom, she could see the man had a lovely shaft. She licked her lips, her cunt twitching. But how in God's name had the small woman managed to take all that cock up her rear end?

Deoctra meowed and shoved her butt back against the man's groin. "Put it back in! Now! Please!"

Reaching around Deoctra's body, the man thrust his fingers deep into her pussy. She moaned and tossed her dark head back against his chest. "Oooooh. More. More. Moooore!"

The man suddenly turned his head and looked directly at Erica, a mocking smile on his face. She swallowed several times. She couldn't hide her reaction to the scene enfolding in front of her. He knew watching him fuck was arousing her.

"Put your cock back in my ass!" Deoctra screamed.

He fondled Deoctra's small behind and mouthed the words. "I'll be all right. Get out of here!"

"But...how can I repay you?"

He grinned at her, revealing a set of even white teeth to rival Mikhel's. "Easy. You owe me a long, slow night of fucking. One night I'll show up in your bedroom to collect. Deal?"

The thought of this handsome young man turning up one night when Mikhel was away to collect on his debt, made her cunt pulse and burn. "But...you don't...know who I am."

"Of course I know who you are and I assure you, I will collect."

"Stop talking to the human whore and fuck me!" Deoctra screamed. "Or I will kill you both."

"Kill me?" He laughed confidently and slapped her behind. "I doubt that. First off, I have no intentions of being killed by you or anyone else. And second, you're too fond of my cock for that." He looked at Erica again. "Remember. One of these nights, when you're lying in bed alone, I'll come for my fuck. Keep your sweet smelling pussy moist and ready for me. Now go."

With one last, lustful gaze at the thick cock sinking back into the other woman's body, Erica turned. She stumbled back to her car, aware of a disturbing sense of jealousy because the handsome stranger was fucking Deoctra. On a conscious level at least, she refused to allow herself to even think about letting him fuck her if he ever turned up. Still, to her shame, she allowed the thought to linger in the back of her mind, where it thrilled and titillated her.

She scooped up her briefcase from the parking lot where she'd dropped it and unlocked her car.

"Get home quickly and you will be safe."

She let out a small scream and held a hand to her chest. Palea Dumont had suddenly appeared on the other side of her car. "Mrs. Dumont! You frightened me."

Mrs. Dumont looked at her with dark eyes. "If you're really Mikhel's bloodlust, you'd better get used to the comings and goings of our people. Now go while Deoctra is occupied."

She cast a worried glance back towards the path where the stranger was presumably still pleasuring a very happy Deoctra.

"What about the man? He and Deoctra are…"

"I know what they are doing. You enjoyed watching their fuck. Yes?"

"No! Of course not!"

"But you stood staring, licking your lips. Every time he thrust his cock into her ass, you rotated your hips and shook a little, as if he were fucking you. You've developed an insatiable taste for vampire cock. Yes?"

The hot blood flooded her face. Did that mean the man with Deoctra was a vampire? "I…I was thinking of Mikhel and I was shocked."

"Ah. It was thoughts of Mikhel fucking you in your ass that made your pussy drip."

"My…drip?"

Palea sniffed the air, her small, square tipped nose quivering. "The air is fragrant with the smell of your pussy. You want some cock. Yes? Mikhel's or…" She titled her head in the direction of Kennedy Hall. "His. Yes?"

Okay so she was lying and the other woman clearly knew it. She shrugged. "What happens when he finishes…will she hurt him?"

"Not if she values her life. Now go. I'll stay and make sure he's all right."

"Thank you. I couldn't go otherwise. And thank you for coming to my rescue."

"We could do no less for Mikhel's bloodlust."

There was that "we" again. She tossed her bag and briefcase in her car. "May I ask you a question, Mrs. Dumont?"

Palea Dumont inclined her head slightly.

She bit her lip, trying to decide if she really wanted to know the answer to her next question. Deciding she did, she went on, "That night in Salem, in Mikhel's hotel room. After Deoctra left and…were you still in the room when Mikhel got into bed with me…when he…"

"You want to know if I saw him making love to you. Yes?"

At first, she had been horrified when Mikhel had slipped his big cock in her while she suspected his mother was still in the room. It hadn't taken long, however, for her to lose herself in his love making to the exclusion of everything else. "Yes. Did you?"

"Yes."

"I was afraid of that."

"Why? I enjoy watching my children make love." She frowned. "His cock is a little on the small size, but still rather pleasing. Yes?"

If she thought Mikhel's, whose big cock still sometimes hurt Erica when they made love, was small, her husband must be hung like a horse. She nodded numbly.

The other woman smiled. "His father taught him well. When a boy is not as well endowed as he should be, it's important that he know how to use what he has. And my little Mikhel is a pleasing lover. Yes?"

Erica's face burned. What had she gotten into? Mrs. Dumont's "little" Mikhel was an excellent lover, but she didn't want to discuss that with her. She could never imagine her own mother discussing the tightness of her vagina and then asking Erica's lover about her sexual prowess. "He's a...well..."

Palea frowned. "You hold his smaller cock against him? You find him lacking as a lover?"

"No! No, he's a fantastic lover," she said in a dazed voice.

"Yes?" She sounded like a thousand proud mothers everywhere.

"Yes."

"Ah, yes. Serge, with his bigger cock, should do as well." Her dark eyes deepened and she smiled. "Ah, but my little Serge, he has charms all his own. Yes?"

Erica blinked at her. How was she expected to comment on the charms of a man she'd never met? "I'm sure he has," she muttered. "But I've never met him."

Palea Dumont's dark eyebrows rose. "Serge is with Deoctra now. My little Serge is as handsome as Mikhel. Yes?"

Erica felt as if the air had been sucked from her lungs. She stared at the other woman. "He's with...the man with Deoctra is your son, Serge?"

"Yes." She smiled. "My little Serge rode to your rescue. Just like the so handsome Marshall Dillon from the fabulous Gunsmoke. Yes?"

The man she'd been lusting after and had half promised a night long fuck was Mikhel's brother? "Oh, God!" She cast a quick look back towards Kennedy Hall. "I don't understand. Why is he...with Deoctra?"

The question seemed to surprise Mrs. Dumont. "She has a willing ass. Although my little Serge loves his pussy, she wouldn't let him fuck her there. She wants to save that for Mikhel. But no manner, he occasionally enjoys how do you say...a nice piece of ass. Clearly, Deoctra loves his cock, but who can blame her? He has a nice cock. Yes? Small compared to his father's. But nice nonetheless. Yes?"

"Yes," she said weakly. "But why is he with Deoctra? She tried to hurt Mikhel."

"Hurt him? No. Deoctra did not want to hurt my little Mikhel. You were the one she wanted to hurt. She considers Mikhel her bloodlust—you an impediment. But we will not allow her to hurt you. Especially now."

Something in her tone made Erica pause. She licked her lips and met Palea Dumont's gaze. "You know?" she asked quietly.

The other woman nodded, her eyes softening. "Yes, my little one. I know. But my little Mikhel. He does not know. You have not told him. No?"

"Not yet. Please don't tell him. I haven't decided what I want to do yet."

The other woman's eyes darkened and she projected a sudden and unmistakable air of menace. "There is only one thing to do. Yes?"

Erica shook her head, refusing to be intimidated. "That's my decision, Mrs. Dumont."

"Only if you make the correct decision. Tread very carefully, Erica Kalai. I would not like to hurt my little

Mikhel's bloodlust, but I will do what I must. You understand me. Yes?"

Erica shivered. "Yes. I do, but I also will do what I must."

"Do not attempt to cross the swords with me, Erica Kalai. All will not turn out well for you if you do. You must do the right thing by my little Mikhel. I will leave you to make your decision. For a time, but I will not have him hurt or lied to."

"I love him! I don't want to lie to him or hurt him."

"Then see that you do not."

Erica swallowed. "I am already so afraid, please don't threaten me, Mrs. Dumont."

The dark eyes softened and the other woman moved quickly to come to stand next to her. "My little Mikhel's bloodlust has no need to fear any Dumont. We will all defend you with all of our considerate strength." She touched Erica's cheek. "But you must be honest with my little Mikhel."

"I know, but please? Allow me to do it in my own time. Keep my confidence?"

"For now, but you must decide soon to do the right thing. Yes?"

"I will make my decision — soon. Right now, I just need to get out of here. Thank you. Goodnight."

Driving back to her apartment, Erica was filled with doubts and insecurities. She loved Mikhel, but uppermost in her mind was the fear that she had made a monumental mistake when she'd gone back to him in Salem. Once she'd left his hotel room, she should have kept going. Now, should she decide she needed to leave him again, not only would he be angry, but so would his mother.

She knew Mikhel had a dark side, but she also knew he would never hurt her. She shivered. She wasn't so sure about Palea Dumont. Mikhel had told her that his mother was nearly four hundred years old. To survive as a vampire that long, she must have done some incredibly horrible things. What had possessed her to become involved with such a family?

She shook her head. Don't get crazy, Rica. Get through Christmas, then make your decision and then deal with the consequences. Mikhel will not let anyone hurt you—not even his mother.

# Chapter Two

**৯০**

"I see exciting things in your future...lust, passion, love, and danger are all waiting for you. If you dare to reach out and embrace them, you will soon have your wildest fantasies come true."

Derri Morgan's lips twitched and she attempted to keep the skepticism from showing on her dusky face. She had never shared her most secret desires with anyone. Her wildest fantasy was unthinkable and unmentionable in a modern, independent black woman who fully intended to marry an equally modern black male one day soon.

"I see you doubt my word."

She glanced across the small table at the slender, exotic looking woman with the long dark hair and vivid blue eyes. It was difficult to take a fortuneteller seriously who looked as if she were barely twenty-one. Beyond the door, a few scant feet away, people rushed up and down one of Philadelphia's busiest downtown streets, returning from or going to lunch. Not ten minutes earlier, she had been in that throng, collar turned up around her neck to ward off the unseasonably cold early December wind, intent on getting to her downtown office.

Why she had suddenly come into this small storefront dive to have her palm read was beyond her. Now that wasn't quite true. She vividly remembered her mother's frequent visits to various fortunetellers. As a know-it-all teenager, she'd been secretly scornful of her mother's belief in the supernatural. Now here she was, hoping that by some miracle this woman would offer her some insight into the psyche of the person stalking her. If she was really lucky, the fortuneteller would show her how to get rid of the nightmares.

She readily admitted the idea was silly in the extreme. If nothing, she was a practical woman. That practicality, along with hard work and intelligence, was responsible for her rise to junior associate in the fast-growing law firm of Lewis, Beckmen, and Associates. There was no room in her game plan for foolish nonsense. It was just as well that she was scheduled to spend a long weekend at The Retreat.

"It's not that I doubt you," she said smoothly. She certainly knew the danger part of the medium's words were true. "I came in hoping...I have a problem..."

"Ah yes. You want to know about the one who shadows you on the street and frightens you with phone calls in the night."

Derri's lips parted and she stared at the woman. "You know about that? How?"

She'd told no one except the senior partner of the firm and the police. She'd even kept it from Karl. Otherwise, he'd no doubt have felt honor bound to return to Philly and try to resume their relationship instead of pursuing that job in Phoenix. The decision to end their three-year relationship had been an extremely difficult one. Still, she hadn't wanted him to learn why she'd refused his marriage proposal—even though she'd been so tempted to accept.

The woman ran a slender hand over a crystal ball pushed to one side of the table. "I have seen your tormentor."

She sat forward, her heart thumping in anticipation. "You have?" Maybe there was something to this supernatural mumbo jumbo after all. "Who is it? What does he look like? Do you have a name? How can I reach him? Do—"

The woman's eyes narrowed, as if she were trying to bring something in the distance into focus. After several long, tortuous moments, she sat back, shaking her head in frustration. "All is not yet clear. The details elude me."

I'll just bet they do, Derri thought cynically. She treated the woman to a thoughtful stare. Perhaps she should mention this woman to the police. How did she know Derri was being stalked unless she was somehow involved?

"Thanks for the reading." She rose, pulling on her leather gloves. She picked up her briefcase and shoulder bag from the floor near her chair.

"The details of the one who torments you are not clear, but your secret fantasy is. The opportunity to have your fantasy fulfilled will present itself very shortly. When it does, reach out and grab it with both hands. Take it…live it…enjoy it."

Not even her closest friend, Cassy Thompson, knew of her most secret desires. No way this woman with a pretty bauble and parlor tricks knew. No wonder she insisted on being paid first. It would be a cold day in August before she came back. With her hand on the door, Derri turned to look at the woman. "My most secret fantasy is just that—most secret."

"Is it? Is it really?" She stroked one hand over the crystal ball and opened her other hand. "Take a look."

Despite herself, Derri moved across the room to look down in the woman's hand. A small golden charm approximately an inch and a half high and one inch wide depicting nude lovers, frozen in the act of mating, lay in the woman's palm. Although small, the lines of the carving were finely detailed from the male's clenching buttocks, and his rigid thighs pressed tight against the female's behind, to the female's full breasts, complete with hardened nipples.

Her lips parted in stunned surprised. This was the talisman that had brought Cassy and her finance Chandler together. She frowned. Or was it? The last time she'd seen the charm the male had been white, the female black. Now both were golden. But hadn't Cassy said something about the couple sometimes changing colors?

"Would you like to hold it?"

She glanced up at the medium. "I…"

"Here. Hold it. Feel it."

Derri made no protest when the small talisman was placed in her hand. The tingle that raced through her when the charm touched her palm made her gasp, as did what happened next.

The miniature couple began moving. As the diminutive cock tunneled in and out of the small golden behind, the color of the couple began to change. In a manner of moments, the female took on the color and contours of a well-built black woman and the male those of a muscular white male. As the change took place, the tiny dick swelled until it looked as if its girth would split the quivering ebony cheeks of the female in half. The male went through several color changes in rapid succession taking on the hues of an Asian, a Hispanic, a Native American, several other hues, before shifting back to Caucasian.

Heart thumping and desire stirring, Derri watched until the couple finished copulating. It was only when she saw tiny white droplets oozing from between the female's legs that she realized the not so tiny cock was in the female's vagina. The few times she'd seen it when Cassy had owned it, the male had always been in the female's behind. Or had it owned Cassy?

Just as the male drew an almost impossibly long, thick cock from the confines of the female's quivering body, the medium took the talisman from her and closed her hand over the couple.

A gasp of protest on her lips, Derri raised her eyes to meet those of the fortuneteller. "Oh, my God!" she whispered. "How…how did you know?"

"There are many things I know, Derri. Everything that you desire is within your grasp. When you are ready to take all that life has to offer you, come back and see me."

"Why?"

"This talisman will help give you the courage to seize your heart's desire."

"Where did you get it? It belonged to a friend of mine."

"It now belongs to the man who is your destiny."

She shook her head. "I know about that...thing. I'll shape my own destiny and choose my own lover."

"Did you not feel a surge when you took the talisman? The choice has already been made, Derri."

"Oh, no it hasn't. And don't call me Derri."

Shaken and confused by what she'd seen, Derri rushed out of the shop. Breathing deeply, she joined the jostling crowds on Chestnut Street. At the corner, she paused behind several people, waiting for a cessation of cross traffic. The light turned green and the people behind her surged forward. Her mind on the strangely erotic scene she'd watch unfold in her own hand rather than watching where she was going, she stepped down off a curb that was much higher than she expected.

The heel of her boot caught in a storm drain. Her momentum carried her forward and she knew she was about to take a painful and ignominious spill. Her briefcase and bag flew from her hands and she cried out. The asphalt rushed up at her with alarming speed, as she extended her arms in an attempt to break her fall. She closed her eyes instinctively, another low cry escaping her lips, but instead of the impact with the asphalt she expected, steel-hard hands wrapped around her body. One arm clamped around her waist, while the other hand slipped into her coat and fondled both breasts before cupping the right one. She could feel the heat from a big hot hand right through her blouse and bra. The feel of the hand, combined with the warm lips moving against her ear, shot a jolt down her spine.

"It's okay. I have you." He spoke with his lips pressed against her neck. His voice was smooth and deep. It might have been wrapped in crushed velvet. The desire that had begun to flicker just moments earlier threatened to blaze out of control.

Keeping his hand firmly inside her coat and on her breast, the man slowly lifted her into a vertical position. Then, heedless of the staring passers-by, he eased her onto the sidewalk and held her in his arms. "I have you. You're safe now."

He lifted her coat above her waist and pulled her back. He ground his hips against her. The feel of his erect shaft against her behind was unmistakable. He was big, thick, and hard. She closed her eyes and bit her bottom lip to stifle a moan of desire. Thoughts of her secret fantasy tantalized her and she felt the telltale moisture between her legs.

This was insane. A stranger on a busy city street was sexually assaulting her and she was not only allowing it, but becoming highly aroused. *Get it in gear, Derri.*

She pulled away and turned to stare at the man. He was tall and handsome with short, dark hair and a diamond stud in his left ear. A prickle of alarm and pleasure ran through her nervous system as she encountered his dark gray eyes. Their gazes locked and she was back in the fortuneteller's shop. She was the female, moaning with anticipation as a long, thick, white shaft tunneled through her dark cheeks on its way to repeatedly plow deep within her suddenly empty, aching channel. *This* man's cock in *her* pussy.

She licked her lips. Oh, God, it would feel so good.

*Better than either of us will ever feel with anyone else, my ebony beauty.*

Derri blinked, shaking her head. She'd been watching the man's face, so she knew he hadn't spoken. Yet, she'd heard his response to her thoughts.

*Okay, Derri. Get a grip, girl. He cannot read your thoughts. You're imagining all of this.*

Her gaze moved slowly over the man's body. He wore a short black leather bomber-style jacket that ended at his waist.

He had long legs and a hard, tight body. She had felt it. The term super-sexy came to mind. She dismissed it. There was nothing sexy about being groped by a stranger.

"Look, I'm grateful that you saved me from a nasty fall, but...how dare you grind against me like that?"

He smiled unrepentantly at her. "How could I help myself? You must know that you have an absolutely fantastic ass — big and shapely, yet firm and contoured. And your lovely breasts. What can I say about them except that they're perfection like the rest of you?"

"What?!" She worked out several times a week to keep in shape and he told her she had a big ass and she was supposed to be complimented?

"The first time I saw you, I knew your beautiful body was made for me, made for fucking. Your pussy will fit around my cock like a custom made glove. Damn, we'll be very good together."

The first time he saw her? And when had that been? A flicker of fear skipped along her spine. Was this man her stalker? Did he get a thrill out of calling her in the middle of the night only to breathe in her ear? Was his the shadow she saw when she walked on dark streets at night? Had he now decided to confront her?

The thought that this man, who looked as if he were fresh out of college, was responsible for weeks of sleepless nights enraged her. It would be a cold day in hell when she was afraid of some silly frat boy.

"Who the hell are you?"

Instead of answering, he walked to the curb to retrieve her briefcase and shoulder bag. "These are yours."

"Thank you." She snatched them from his hand. "I asked you a question. Are you the coward who's been calling me in the middle of the night?"

His gray eyes darkened. "No. Have no fear of that jackal. He'll live just long enough to regret his choice of targets."

"What?" She stared at him. "What do you know about him? Who the hell are you?"

"Someone who intends to protect you."

She shook her head. "And how do you plan to do that? By assaulting me? Get this straight college boy. I don't need your protection. Nor do I have time to play games with you."

"I've never been more serious in my life." He extended a hand. "Come with me and let me show you how good we can be together."

The look in his eyes, which were now a light, whirling gray, held her immobile. What had the fortuneteller said? That she would have a chance to experience her wildest fantasies if she just reached out and grabbed the opportunity. Was this that chance? If she took this man's hand, went with him, slept with him. Oh, who was she kidding? If she went with him, she was going to let him fuck her.

*Come with me, my ebony beauty. My cock will give you great pleasure.*

Okay. She had not imagined that. The damn man was somehow projecting erotic propositions directly into her mind. A quiver of anticipatory desire filled her. He had a nice cock. He would be a pleasant lay. It had been a while since she and Karl had last slept together. It would be so good to be filled with a really big one again. And this frat boy's cock definitely qualified.

She blinked rapidly and shook her head. Get it in gear, Derri. There's no way you're going to sleep with this stranger…this young stranger.

"Stay out of my way, college boy. And if you're the one who's been stalking me, you'd better think twice before doing it again." She leveled a finger at him. "The next time I see you…don't let me see you again. If you know what's good for you."

He smiled. "I like a woman with a fiery spirit and a hot but yielding pussy. I'm betting you have both. You will definitely see me again."

This was the idiot she'd feared for so long? Well, no more. She only just resisted the urge to slap him silly. "A hot but yielding pussy? Are you a complete nut case? What makes you think talking dirty gutter trash will get you anywhere with a woman but kicked to the damned curb? You want to score points and make an impression? Stop relying on your looks and your big dick, which you probably don't even know how to use properly, to get you what you want. Cultivate a little finesse. The way to my bed is not to tell me I have a big ass and you want to fuck my hot but yielding pussy! I'll tell you what, why don't you come see me when you've acquired some polish and grown up a little? Until then, you can go to hell, college boy!"

She turned and walked away. She walked the remaining five blocks to her office so quickly that her feet were killing her by the time The Brown Building loomed in front of her. Only then did she turn to look around her. An angry breath escaped her lips. Her college boy stalker stood on the other side of the street, watching her. How dare he keep following her? What he needed was to have his ass beat down and kicked to the curb. She was in the mood to accommodate him.

Leaving her briefcase with the watchman behind the visitor's desk in the lobby, she went back out the building, determined to confront him. He was no longer on the sidewalk across from the building. She looked up and down the street. Although there were a fair number of passers-by on the street moving in either direction, the man who'd broken her fall was not among them.

# Chapter Three

**ഇ**

Derri reentered the building and went up to her fourth floor office.

"Derri, what's wrong?"

She paused at the receptionist's desk and arched a brow at the small, pretty, brunette sitting there. "What do you mean, Betty?"

"You have murder in your eyes."

She took a deep breath. "I am feeling a little rattled." She glanced quickly at her watch. "Is Mark in the conference room?"

"Yes. And Derri there's this absolutely gorgeous man with him."

Twenty-year-old Betty thought everything in a pair of pants was gorgeous.

She smiled. "Gorgeous, huh? Then I'd better go freshen up before I join them."

In the small bathroom connected to her office, she studied her face in the mirror. Her short, dark hair, which she wore in a series of natural curls against her head, was neatly in place, the maroon lipstick still glowed on her full lips, but her dark brown eyes sparkled with agitation.

And no wonder. Some lunatic was stalking her, a strange man she'd longed to surrender to had sexually assaulted her on the street, and she'd been handed the biggest case of her career as a defense attorney. Her future prospects with the firm depended in large part on how well she handled the Smith-Barley case. It wasn't every day she was asked to defend the man accused of stalking and murdering the only child of a multi-millionaire newspaper publisher.

She raked a pick through her hair, blotted her lipstick, straightened the skirt of her dark business suit, and headed for one of the smaller conference rooms on the floor above her office.

This particular conference room was enclosed by floor to ceiling glass, so she could see into it as she approached. Mark Lewis, her mentor and the managing partner, sat at one end of the oval shaped oak table.

She gave him a quick look. Was it her imagination or did he not look as unhappy and uptight as he'd been looking lately? She hoped so because he deserved a little happiness, something he hadn't had for several years.

She turned her attention to the other people in the room. Several paralegals sat at the table with Mark. A tall, dark man stood looking out the window.

Her heartbeat increased and her temper rose. Although his back was to her, she knew he was the frat boy who'd propositioned her not half an hour earlier. But how had he changed so quickly? He no longer wore the bomber jacket or the dark silk pants. How had he beat her to her office? More importantly, why had be beat her there? He'd gone too far and he was about to see that he'd picked on the wrong woman.

She pulled back the glass door and stalked into the room. "Mark, I'm sorry I'm late. On my way back from lunch, I ran into this idiot who…"

The man at the window turned and she faltered. Betty was right. He was gorgeous with thick dark hair and handsome, chiseled features. But he was not her gray-eyed frat boy.

She encountered his dark brown eyes, which swept quickly over her. She felt a breathlessness that both shocked and confused her. She didn't often respond this way to a man. She'd felt this way when she'd first set eyes on Karl nearly five years earlier. Since their separation, she'd kept a tight rein on her emotions and desires. Yet this made twice in one day when gazing into a strange man's eyes made her think of sex. First, with the frat boy and now with this man.

"Derri?"

She turned and looked at Mark.

"Derri, this is Mikhel Dumont of Dumont Security. Mikhel, this is Derri Morgan, one of our associates."

The man crossed the room with his hand extended, a warm smile on his face. "Ms. Morgan. It's a pleasure to meet you."

She placed her hand in his and experienced a jolt of pleasure. She shook it off. "Mr. Dumont." She withdrew her hand and took one of the two empty seats at the table. The hairs seemed to rise on the back of her neck when Mikhel Dumont took the seat beside her. Damn, but the man was panty-wetting sexy.

"Derri, you still with us?"

Heat rushing up her neck and into her face, she met Mark's gaze. "I'm sorry. My mind wondered," she admitted.

Mark smiled, his dark blue eyes understanding. "Can't say I blame you. You have a lot on your plate lately."

"I can handle it," she said quickly.

He nodded. "I'm sure you can, but you don't have to do it by yourself. I didn't commit your time and this firm's resources to defend Charlie Smith-Barley pro bono because he's my best friend's son. I also happen to believe in his innocence."

She nodded. After several conversations with the young man, she was convinced the police had caved into pressure from Ralph Mariono and had arrested the wrong man. "I do too and I intend to do my best to prove it."

"With the way things stand, you'll need to focus all your attention on that goal. That's why Mikhel is here. He or some of his people will accompany you to The Retreat, so you can spend a few days unwinding. No real work, Derri. I just want you to unwind and relax."

She blinked at him. "What?"

Mark's brows arched. "Your mind really did wonder. When did we lose you? Never mind. Mikhel will accompany you to The Retreat."

The Retreat was a remote but luxurious cabin Mark and his late wife, Jennie, had owned in the Pocono Mountains. Since Jennie's death several years earlier, Mark had avoided the place. During the last two years, The Retreat had been used exclusively for business. Often, whenever one of the associates of the firm needed a quiet place to prepare for upcoming trials, they headed for The Retreat.

The thought of spending time alone there with Mikhel Dumont sent a thrill of pleasure through her. She shook off the thought of how nice being alone with him would be. She couldn't even sit in the same room with him without wondering what it would be like to be kissed by him. How could she do her client any good alone in the mountains with him?

Inexplicably, she thought of the man she'd run into outside the fortuneteller's. *Outside the fortuneteller's shop. That woman knew something.* As soon as she could manage it, she'd have to get back there and find out how much she knew and how she knew it.

"So it's all set, then," Mark was saying when she pulled her thoughts back to the meeting. "Mikhel will pick you up at home and drive you up to The Retreat. And Derri, I want you to stay at least four or five days. The trial isn't until next year and I don't want you to wear yourself out. And whatever time you spend at The Retreat will have no bearing on the two weeks you have scheduled off over the holidays."

She shrugged, trying to appear nonchalant. "Okay. I think I can manage that, but I will take my laptop and work on the jury questionnaire."

"Okay, but nothing too strenuous, Derri."

Even as she nodded, she was formulating possible defense strategies. It was all well and good to say the burden of proof was on the prosecution and that the defense had nothing to prove. She always gave her clients her absolute best effort and that started months before the actual trial. "Nothing too strenuous," she promised.

"Great. Then it's all settled." Mark rose. "We'll leave you two to arrange things."

She watched Mark and the others file out of the room.

"Tell me about this case," Mikhel Dumont suggested. "Do you think anyone connected to it has anything to do with harassing you?"

She thought of Ralph Mariono's demeanor every time they encountered each other in and around The Criminal Justice Center where all the pretrial motions took place. Although he'd never spoken directly to her, his dark eyes blazed with anger and what seemed to be hatred each time he looked at her.

"I have no reason to believe that," she said slowly, then told him about Ralph Mariono's demeanor toward her.

"I see." He nodded. "And what about you? Tell me about yourself."

"Is this business...or personal?" she asked, meeting his gaze.

"Both," he told her, smiling.

"I'm single and an only child. Both of my parents are alive, well, and living in Florida."

"You're alone in the city?"

"I wouldn't say alone. I have many friends and an uncle or aunt and a few scattered cousins."

"I see. So tell me, when did you want to go to The Retreat? Tonight?"

"Tonight? Ah…I can't leave tonight. I have plans."

He sat back in his chair, raking his fingers through his short, dark hair. "A date?" He had a warm, deep voice that seemed to drop a timbre with the question.

She nodded. "As a matter of fact, I do."

"Lucky guy," he said softly.

"I'm the lucky one. I feel so much younger when I'm with him," she told him, feeling a need to flirt that she hadn't felt in quite awhile.

"He's younger than you?"

She grinned. The guy in question was her neighbor's ten-year-old son, with whom she shared a rabid love of video games. Not that he needed to know that. "A lot younger."

His eyes danced with dark lights. "You like younger men?"

Okay, Derri, this is getting out of hand. Fantasy is one thing—business is another. You are not going to flirt with this guy. She picked up her legal pad and rose. "It rather depends on the man."

He rose too and was at the door before she reached it. When he made no move to open the door, she glanced up at him.

He handed her a business card. "Here are all my numbers. You'll call me when you're ready to head up to The Poconos?"

She nodded. "Actually, if you'll be available, I'd like to go tomorrow."

"Morning, noon? Evening?"

"When is best for you?" she asked.

"If you have no preference, I'd like to wait to the evening. I'd like to fly back to Boston, but I'll be back tomorrow evening say around five?"

"Okay, but, do you have a reservation already? The lines at airports these days,…"

He smiled. "I'll be using my family's private transport."

"Oh. A plane?"

He shrugged. "A small jet."

He said it causally, as if every family owned a small jet. "Okay. Then I'll see you tomorrow around five."

"If you feel threatened in anyway, you call me."

"You'll be in Boston," she reminded him.

"You call me," he repeated. "Someone will be watching out for you, but you call me. I want you to understand that I will do my absolute best to ensure that no one hurts or frightens you again."

For the first time in months, she felt free of fear. He couldn't do anything about the nightmares, but she felt confident he could handle any physical challenges placed before him. "Thank you, Mr. Dum—"

"We'll be spending a lot of time together. Please call me Mikhel."

"Okay, Mikhel."

"May I call you Derri?"

She nodded. "Yes."

"Good. I'll wait for your call, Derri. In the meantime, I, or some of my people, will be near. Always. Even when you don't see us."

She smiled. She could really get use to the idea of this handsome man being always near her. Just maybe he was the one who would fulfill part of her fantasy. The thought sent a fresh rush of moisture between her legs. The coming long weekend was going to be very exciting and full of delightful possibilities.

He smiled slowly. She looked into his dark eyes and found it difficult to look away.

Finally, he opened the door and stepped aside. She went out without looking at him. Back in her office, she sat staring at her computer screen. Whew! That had been intense.

She shook her head. She had too much on her plate to get caught up in fantasizing about the man assigned to protect her. She frowned. Why hadn't she told Mark or the police about the fortuneteller and the frat boy?

Because she intended to handle the medium herself and now that she'd met her stalker, she no longer feared him. Instead, thoughts of him created a delicious sense of wicked desire in her. She shifted uncomfortably in her seat, recalling the feel of the frat boy's cock against her behind. It had been nearly three months since she and Karl had engaged in a nightlong, good-bye, love session. She sighed, feeling the strain of being without a lover for the first time in years.

She thought of Mikhel Dumont and smiled. Maybe, just maybe, she would get to know him up close and personal very soon. A man that size must have a comparable sized cock.

In the meantime, she needed to talk to Cassy. She paged her and began working while she waited for her to respond. Her secretary buzzed her an hour later. "Derri, Cassy's on the line."

"Thanks." She picked up the phone. "Hi, Cass."

"Hey, Derri. I hope you buzzed me to set up a lunch or a girl's night out. It's been a while since we got together."

She smiled. "I know, but I thought you and your Chandler needed some time alone. You sound really happy, Cass."

"Oh, Derri, you have no idea. I can't wait to marry him."

"When?"

"Soon."

"Big wedding?" she asked, visions of Cass in an elaborate wedding gown momentarily distracting her. "You are going to be such a gorgeous bride."

"That's what Chandler says, but no. We want to do it in the early part of the next year. It's going to be very quiet with just my family, his nephew and niece, his best friend, and of course, my best friend—you."

"I wouldn't miss it for anything."

"Good. I can't wait for you to meet Serge."

"Serge is the best friend?"

"Yes. He and Chandler attended Temple U together. Derri, Serge's to die for."

She laughed. "That's what you say about Chandler."

"And he is. When the two of them are in a room together...well, let's just say they must be the two sexiest men in the world."

Maybe two of the three. Men didn't come much sexier than Mikhel Dumont. She frowned. The ill-mannered frat boy had been pretty hot also. Okay, maybe two of four.

"Okay, you know two of the sexiest men in the world," she agreed. "But Cass, I was wondering whatever happened to that talisman you had?"

"Chandler gave it to Serge."

She hesitated, and then told her about her visit to the fortuneteller and the calls she'd been getting.

"Is that why you and Karl separated? But why didn't you tell him? He was nuts about you. He would have helped protect you."

"That's not why we broke up. I told you Cass, I have...fantasies he wouldn't have understood or stood for."

"Okay. But let me at least tell Chandler so he can tell Serge."

That surprised her. "Serge? Why would he tell this Serge?"

"So he can help look out for you."

"Why?"

41

"Didn't I tell you? He's in security."

"Is he? Well, thanks. That's sweet, but I don't need Serge to look out for me. Mark has hired a private security firm. I met the man who runs it and Cass, he is absolutely…he's hot. I won't be needing any help from this Serge."

"Well, if you change your mind, let me know. Serge is different and…so, tell me about this hot guy. What's he like?"

"Hot," she said, laughing. "Oh, Cass, I could really go for him."

"Yeah?"

"Oh, yeah, but that's not why I called. How do you think that medium got a hold of your talisman?"

"Are you sure it's my talisman?

"Yes and Cassy, they were active, if you know what I mean."

"Really? What color were they?"

"Black female, white male."

"Oh." A short pause ensued. "So that's your fantasy? To sleep with a white guy?"

"Yeah, and a few non-white ones. I guess that makes me sound a little —"

"Adventurous. Wow. Why didn't you tell me?"

"It's not that simple, Cass." She paused and decided she wasn't ready to admit to the full scope of her fantasy. "While I have this fantasy of sleeping with men of different nationalities, I fully intend to marry a black man. I just want a fling or two before I settle down. Karl would never have understood or taken me back when I was ready to get married. Not that I'd have blamed him. If he'd told me he wanted to do the same thing, I'd have been an unhappy camper. I don't know why, but it's what I want. If I don't do it now, I'll spend the rest of my life wishing I had. So I'm going to."

"Derri, if you want to meet a hot white guy, I'm telling you, Serge is your man. He's good looking and charming and he loves black women. And Dare, he's really packing, if you know what I mean."

"Really?" She grinned. "Why, Cass, and you'd know that how?"

She could almost see Cass grinning sheepishly. "You can't help but notice. He makes no effort to conceal how big or thick he is. It just sort of sits along the inside of his leg saying *Here I am come and get me.*"

She laughed. "Cass, you're exaggerating."

"Oh, no I'm not. And Dare, he's almost always hard. Serge's almost as hot as Chandler."

She smiled. "That hot, huh? He must be red hot then."

"Almost. Men don't come any sweeter or hotter than my Chandler."

"I'm sure they don't. Well, I'll meet this Serge sooner or later if he's Chandler's best friend. In the mean time, I am spending a long weekend with another hot guy."

"So then this security guy…"

"Oh, Cass, I'd love to have him fulfill my fantasy."

"I'll keep my toes crossed for you."

She laughed. "Thanks."

"So did you want me to ask Serge what he did with The Talisman?"

She shook her head slowly. "No. Let me think about it for a bit." She glanced at her watch. If she was going to get home in time to challenge ten-year-old Ben to a couple of games of video football, she'd better get back to work.

"Cass, I've got to run and I know you probably do too."

"Yep. Talk to you again soon?"

"Yep. Soon. Give Chandler a big, juicy kiss for me."

It was only after she hung up that she realized she hadn't told Cassy about the frat boy. No manner. Who had time to think about him when thinking about Mikhel Dumont was so much nicer?

Two hours later, she got up from her desk, stretched, and made her way down the hall and through several corridors to Mark's office. She smiled at his secretary. "Myna, is he still here?"

Myna gave her a mock frown. "It's only five-thirty." She rose and removed her handbag from a drawer. "Of course he's still here, but I, on the other hand, am out of here."

She smiled. "I heard that. Is he alone? Can I holler at him?"

She nodded. "Sure."

"Night," she said and walked around to tap at the door, behind Myna's desk.

"Come."

She turned and waved at Myna and went into Mark's private office. She paused in surprise by the door when Mark turned from the window to face her. Instead of the dark somber suit with equally somber tie he'd worn earlier, he now sported a pair of black leather slacks and a casual dark blue sweater.

"I can see you're surprised by my attire," he said.

"No," she lied, then nodded. "Okay. Maybe just a little. I've never seen you dressed so...casually." Looking at him, she decided it suited him. Jennie's death had aged him well beyond his fifty-nine years. Although his hair was liberally sprinkled with gray, his pleasant face was unlined.

He grinned suddenly. "I've decided it's time to stop grieving and get on with life."

She nodded. "Yes. It is." She titled her head to one side, smiling. "Got a date?"

To her surprise, he blushed. "Not exactly no. But I sure wish I did have one."

"You mean you're not going out?"

"Yes. I am, but it's not a date. Exactly."

She stared at him for several moments before his meaning hit her. Then she was hard pressed not to blush herself. "Oh. Oh, well…"

"You're shocked."

"No," she denied.

"Of course you are. I was shocked a little myself the first time I decided to…but it's been a very long time for me, Derri, and like any man, I have needs." He gave her a self-depreciating smile. "But you didn't come here to discuss my extracurricular activities. What can I do for you?"

"Nothing. Actually, at the meeting earlier, I just thought you looked happy and I wondered if you were seeing someone special."

"I guess I can't actually call it seeing her, as I pay for the privilege, but I do enjoy being with her. She's not your average call girl. She's young, beautiful, and so exciting. There's an aura of power surrounding her that I find so incredibly exhilarating. And she makes it so damned enjoyable. I'd pay her three times what she charges without batting an eye."

Derri tried to keep her face expressionless. She didn't want him to know he was rapidly approaching the too much information stage. It was one thing to want to know he was happy. It was another to be told the intimate details.

"After Jen died I lost my…desire, but this woman…this lovely, lovely woman has… she looks at me and I feel like the most horny and desirable man in the world. Am I shocking you?"

"No. Everyone has their…if she makes you happy, that's all that matters, Mark."

"It's early days yet and she's all business, but I'm happy when I'm with her. I know that sounds crazy, but it's true. I've never met anyone like her. She's just wonderful."

She thought of her own fantasies. "I say grab happiness whenever you can."

He smiled at her before glancing down at his clothing. "What do you think? Give me your honest opinion? Is this too much?"

She grinned. "Nope. Actually, I think it makes you look sexy as hell. There are few things sexier than an attractive man in leather."

"You're just saying that because it's true," he deadpanned and they both laughed.

He sobered first. "God, where are my manners?" He waved to the leather sofa along one wall.

She shook her head. "No. I'm not staying." She grinned. "I have a date too. I just wanted to say good night."

"Okay. Listen, are you comfortable with Mikhel Dumont?"

She managed to keep a straight face. "Yes. I feel safer already."

"Good. I'm glad." He crossed the room and touched her arm. "You're an important member of this firm and we are not going to allow anyone to make you feel less than safe."

"Thank you, Mark. Ah,...oh, I almost forgot to mention, we'll be going to The Retreat tomorrow night."

He smiled. "Good. When you're there, Derri, you just relax. Good night."

"I will. Good night."

On the way back to her office, she passed Brad Harris, another attorney, in the passage.

He paused, his smooth dark face lighting up as he smiled at her. "How's it going Derri?"

"Hi Brad. It's going fine. How about with you? How's the Johnson case coming?" she asked of his current murder case.

He grinned. "It's coming." He glanced at his watch. "I'm about to head out for the night. If you're not busy maybe we could go discuss it over dinner."

Her gaze moved lightly over him. Brad Harris was the personification of tall, dark, and handsome. He was kind, funny, and considerate. He would probably be a great lover. But she had a feeling he'd want more than the occasional one night stand she was prepared to give him.

She smiled. "Thanks, but I have plans already."

"Maybe another time?"

She hesitated before nodding. "Sure."

He smiled at her, his dark brown eyes twinkling. "Goodnight."

"Goodnight," she said and continued down the hall to her office.

The first thing she saw when she opened her office door was a huge vase of red roses sitting in the center of her desk. Karl, she thought, crossing the room slowly. He'd never been much of a romantic while they'd been a couple, but he must have thought of her and decided to send her red roses, knowing how much she loved them.

Smiling, she lifted the small envelope nestled amongst the roses and read the message.

*Please accept this small token in lieu of the apology you so richly deserve for my less than gentlemanly behavior this afternoon.*

*Your gray-eyed college boy.*

Derri walked around her desk and sank down into her chair. She supposed she should be angry still, but it was difficult to work up the energy. He had saved her from a nasty spill and being groped by him had been a decidedly pleasant experience. She looked at the roses. Besides, he apologized so handsomely. She also had more immediate concerns—like how the hell he'd known she thought of him as gray-eyed.

She glanced at her watch and shook her head. She wasn't sure how she knew, but she did know that she had nothing to fear from him except his lust, which she could handle.

Handle? She frowned. He had said they would see each other again and she didn't doubt it. The reception he received the next time they met depended entirely on how he conducted himself. Who knew, if things didn't work out with Mikhel, and the frat boy played his cards right, she just might give the young stud a go.

For now, it was time she headed home. After a couple of games of video football with Ben, she'd have a salad, pack a suitcase for her trip to The Poconos, and hit the sack.

When she arrived home, she found another dozen roses with the doorman in her apartment building lobby. She carried them up to her apartment before reading the note.

*These roses, although lovely and elegant, pale in comparison with your beauty. I did not intend to offend you. Forgive me?*

*Gray Eyes.*

She smiled. How was she supposed to stay angry with him if he kept this up? He had nice eyes and a nice dick. She shrugged. So maybe she wouldn't be angry with him.

# Chapter Four

**ဢ**

"So? How did it go?"

Serge Dumont turned from the window of the small store-front shop on Chestnut Street and looked at the tall, slender woman sitting behind the round table that held the crystal ball. He frowned. "In a word—lousy. I don't know, Katie."

She smiled and crossed the room to touch his cheek. "Don't look so worried, Serge. Whether she's ready to admit it to herself or not, she wants you. You're more than capable of fulfilling her fantasy. You *are* her fantasy."

"Only part of her fantasy," he said gloomily.

"Trust me, Serge. Once you fuck her, she won't want anyone else...except, of course, Mikhel. But that's to be expected. So what are you doing standing around here moping? Go out and get her."

He shook his head. "Getting her is going to be a lot harder than I thought. She lectured me on what she called my lack of finesse, called me a college boy, and told me not to rely on my looks and the size of my cock to get women in bed. Then she told me to go to hell."

Katie arched a finely plucked eyebrow. "She's a discerning wench, isn't she?"

He glowered at her. "She is not a wench. Are you saying she's right? That I rely on my looks and dick size to attract women?"

"Yes, I am. And before you start letting your nostrils flare like a bull, hear me out." She stepped back and looked him up and down. "You have everything women want in a man—

you're a big, well-built, handsome man with a very big dick. Why shouldn't you flaunt your many assets?"

She tossed her long dark ringlets of curls and touched a hand to her breasts. "I use all my womanly wiles to get what I want—lots of cock. What's more, I get paid very handsomely for doing what I love best—fucking."

Serge felt his jaw clench compulsively, but he bit back his inclination to frown. As Katie and their mother were so fond of reminding him, Mikhel, and their father, Katie had a right to live her life as she liked.

Watching his face, she nodded. "That's right, Serge, leave it alone. We were talking about you and your Derri."

"That's the problem, Katie, she's not *my* Derri!" he snarled angrily.

She made little effort to hide her smile of amusement.

He frowned. "What's so amusing?"

"Oh, come on, Serge. You have to admit that being turned down is a totally new experience for you."

"It's an unpleasant one," he told her darkly.

"It'll give you that much more incentive," she said, wiping the smile from her face.

For the first time in his life, Serge was unsure of his ability to attract and hold the woman of his choice. "I don't know if I can change her mind," he admitted. "At least not without force."

She shrugged. "So use force. That's what I intend to do if and when my bloodlust comes along but doesn't show any inclination to fall madly, passionately, and irrevocably in love with me."

He bit back his inclination to ask her to speculate on the likelihood of her meeting her life partner in her line of "work." He shook his head. "No. I don't want to do that with her."

She widened her gaze. "Since when have you taken no for an answer?"

"Since I met her."

"So you've met?"

"No, not exactly. Not yet—not formally, no." He told her about the incident on Chestnut Street.

"Okay. New plan. Mikhel is going to be spending a long weekend with her in The Poconos. Why don't you go instead or too?"

"And have her tell me to get lost again?"

"When did you first notice your skin thinning?"

Since the only woman he'd ever met who left him feeling breathless just looking at him had told him he probably didn't know how to fuck. To his surprise, he found he couldn't admit that to Katie. He shook his head. "You don't understand."

"What's not to understand?"

"She's different. I want her to welcome me."

"Welcome you? You've been spending too much time with Mikhel." She tapped his shoulder. "Trust me, show her the family jewels and she'll drop her drawers and part her legs in a flash, just like all the others before her."

The annoyance Katie's words caused surprised him. Less than five years apart in age, he and Katie had always been close and given to discussing their sex lives in graphic detail. Now he felt reluctant to have Katie think Derri was like all the other women he'd bedded and discarded over the years.

"She's not like that," he said coolly.

Katie arched both brows. "Isn't she?"

"No, she isn't."

"Newsflash, big brother. There's nothing straight women love more than cock. So give her some of yours already."

"Not against her will."

She smiled indulgently. "Don't give me that holier than thou look, Serge. I'm not suggesting you rape her."

"I know, but if I compel her into my arms against her will, it would be the same thing as raping her."

"Really? It didn't bother you when you and Chan were whoring all over Philly while pretending to attend college."

"Hey, Katie, we both got degrees in our chosen fields and graduated Magna Cum Laude. And that was nearly twenty years ago. I was too young and too stupid to know that using my abilities as a latent to entice women into bed was wrong."

He sighed and took a deep breath. "I'm sorry I ever did that and I wish I could go back and undo some of the things I did."

Her blue eyes softened and she touched his cheek. "Have you looked in the mirror lately? You are a hunk. If you ask me, you've never really coerced a woman into your bed against her will. You never needed too. Even if you weren't a latent, you'd still be a hunk. So don't sweat the past, Serge."

He smiled slightly and nodded, but there were things he'd done that he regretted. Things he'd never told anyone. Not even Chan or Mikhel. "You should have been a counselor, Katie, instead of a..." He realized what he was about to say and abruptly fell silent.

She grimaced. "Serge, I know you're one of my big brothers and you love me and feel protective, but this is my life. I need you to understand that I enjoy what I do. You and Mikhel enjoy protecting people and fucking every willing woman in sight. I enjoy reading palms and fucking selective men for money. There's no real difference. We all love to fuck. I just refuse to do it for free. Accept it."

"I have," he lied. "It's just that I-we worry about you."

"There's no need. You know that I am perfectly capable of taking care of myself. And another thing, Serge, don't think I didn't know that you, Mikhel, and even Dad have been lurking around when I work."

He sighed. "We told Dad you'd know, but Katie, you're his little girl."

"And you and Mikhel's little sister." She held up a hand. "I know all that, Serge, but I am far from helpless."

He nodded. "I know that, Katie, but—"

"I have yet to meet a man I couldn't handle." She squeezed his arm. "It's you I'm worried about." She shook her head, her blue eyes dark with worry. "I've never seen you like this, Serge."

"I've never felt like this."

"Are you...in love with her?"

"I've never been in love. I've never even kissed her. How can I be in love with her?"

"I wouldn't be so quick to dismiss the notion that you're not in love with her. You know Mikhel knew the moment he saw Erica. Even before he'd spoken to her. I think you're in love. Tell me what you feel, Serge."

He shook his head. "I feel like I have to have her. I can't stop thinking about her or wanting her." He shrugged and took a deep breath. "Maybe it is love. Oh, damn. Katie, what will I do if she won't have me?"

Katie's eyes glowed like blue fire. "Oh, she'll have you all right, or she'll answer to me!"

"No!" he said quickly. He knew some of the things of which Katie was capable. Women with vampire blood had a tendency to be more vicious than vampire men. He didn't want Derri on the receiving end of Katie's wrath.

He sighed. Mikhel must have felt this same sense of panic when she'd threatened to go after Erica after she'd left him.

"No," he said again. "I won't have her coerced, Katie."

"You have been spending too much time with Mikhel. Next you'll be telling me she's your bloodlust."

"I didn't say that. I'm just saying...never mind."

"No, Serge. Tell me."

He shook his head. "I can hear her thoughts, Katie."

"Why should that surprise you? We—"

"No, I don't mean I can pick up vague images or impressions. I can actually hear her thoughts and she can hear mine."

She stared at him. "Are you telling me she's your bloodlust?" She shook her head. "But that goes beyond bloodlust—unless both partners are full-bloods. What are you saying, Serge?"

"That she might be my life partner."

"How can you be so sure when you haven't even slept with her yet?"

"I don't know how I know. I just know." He shook his head again. "Maybe I have been spending too much time with Mik or maybe it's those talismans Chan gave me. Maybe Chan was right. Maybe the talismans do exert undue influence on their owners."

"No," she said decisively. "I can't see any evidence of that. What you feel are your own feelings, Serge." She frowned. "Of course if you two can share each other's thoughts, maybe the talismans are responsible for that aspect of your relationship, but the feelings you have, Serge, those are your own. So go for them and her."

He sighed. "We'll see. Now what do you know about the guy who's been stalking her?"

She went back to the table and gazed into the crystal ball. After several moments, she shook her head and looked at him. "I can't quite get a handle on him, Serge." She paused, frowning. "You know what that usually means."

He nodded. "A full-blood is involved."

"Serge, if a full-blood is involved, maybe you'd better leave this to Mikhel."

He shook his head, his eyes darkening. "No. I don't care who is involved. Full-bloods can die just like any one else. Whoever is threatening her is going to answer to me."

Sighing, she retraced her steps and put her hand on his arm. "To us, Serge. Whoever threatens you or Mikhel or the women in your life, has to face all the Dumonts."

He smiled, touching her cheek. "Not this time, Katie. You've already committed yourself to helping with Erica. Mother will have a cow if she finds out that you're now risking your life for another human."

She shrugged. "Mother will just have to get used to having cows because there is no way I am going to let you face a full-blood by yourself, Serge."

"I won't be by myself, Katie. Mikhel will stand with me."

"As will I." Her blues eyes swirled with dark lights. "Don't try to turn big brother on me, Serge. It didn't work when I decided to go into the Navy. Or when I decided how I wanted to live *my life* and it won't work now."

He swallowed the urge to frown. As Katie said, his disapproval of her lifestyle was old news. The Dumont males would have to accept that in the true tradition of the female vampire, Katie loved to fuck—just not for free.

She frowned at him and he knew she was sensing his thoughts. He put up a mind shield.

"I will stand with you and Mikhel, as I always have, Serge. Whoever threatens one of us, threatens us all. I will take my turn looking out for your Derri, just as I do for Mikhel's beloved Erica."

He reached out and engulfed her in a bear hug. "There's one big difference, Katie. Erica knows she belongs to Mik. Derri is going to fight me every step of the way."

She grinned up at him. "Which will make her surrender all the sweeter. I want to watch when you take her."

"No!" He released her and stepped back. "I don't think she would like that. And I want our first time together to be special...just the two of us." He frowned. "*If* there is a first time."

"There will be a first time, Serge and many more times after that. Still, you're right about it not being easy to win her. In any case, when she comes back, I'll give her this." She reached in her dress pocket and produced the talisman.

He hesitated. He knew his long-time friend, Chan Raven had found his life partner, Cassy Morgan, by means of the small charm in Katie's hand and another, larger one called the Ebony Venus, that Serge kept on his nightstand at home and carried with him when he traveled.

He watched Katie's face for any signs that having the talisman bothered her. Nearly eighteen years earlier, when Chan had spent the Christmas break from college at The Dodge House, the Dumont family Boston home, he'd slept with Katie, who'd fallen rather hard for him. Both he and Mikhel had come close to killing Chan when he decided he didn't want a relationship with a woman with vampire blood running through her veins—and this from a man who'd ingested enough vampire blood of his own so that he had strength near comparable to a human latent.

Katie met his gaze and shook her head, smiling slightly. "Don't worry, Serge. I got over Chandler a long time ago. Not that there was much to get over. It was a schoolgirl crush. I wish him well with his Cassy." She smiled. "In fact, I've actually met someone I think I might like."

He blinked in surprise. "Who? Who is he? What does he do? Why didn't you tell me? When do we get to meet—"

"Hey, hey." She held up a hand to silence him. "Not so fast. I want to take this slow. It's still so new and I'm not sure if this is going anywhere." She frowned. "You know I can't foresee anything to do with my own future."

"Who is he? Where did you meet him? Does he treat you properly? Because if he doesn't—"

"Serge! Hold on. I can handle my own love life." She lifted a finger and stabbed angrily at his shoulder. "And understand this Serge—I do not want you, Mikhel, or Dad trailing me to see who he is."

"At least tell me where you met him."

"At work."

"At work? Oh, come on, Katie. At *work?*"

"Yes, at work and don't give me that look, Serge."

"Why not? You can't really expect any of the men who would patronize a prostitute to be worthy of you."

She tossed her head. "The term I prefer is call girl, Serge and very, very high class at that. And I'll just bet you didn't ask Mikhel how he could expect his precious Erica to be worthy of him considering she was dressed as a hooker when he met her and she let him fuck the hell out of her the same night they met. Mother said when she watched them fuck, she couldn't get enough of his cock."

"Kattia, that is different," he said curtly, feeling the need to defend Mikhel's Erica. "She is his bloodlust."

"Yeah? Well, I'll just bet if your precious Derri lets you drill her the first time you're alone, you'll still think she's the salt of the God Damned earth!"

"Kattia, it's not necessary for you to trash Erica or Derri. It's unworthy of you."

She stared at him, her blue eyes angry and cool. Finally, she tossed her head again and averted her gaze. "Oh, I know and I didn't mean to trash either of them. They mean a lot to you and Mikhel, so they mean a lot to me. But Serge, you have got to stop judging me! When you do, you make me say things I shouldn't."

"I am not judging you!" he snapped, not quite appeased. He caught her narrowed gaze and nodded. "Okay. Okay, I was judging you. But I shouldn't have." He cupped her face between his palms. "I just want what's best for you. We all do."

"I know that," she hissed at him, jerking away from him. "But why can't any of the Dumont men trust me to decide what's best for me?"

"All right. All right. I'm sorry. I love you and want to protect you, so stake and behead me, why don't you?"

She laughed suddenly and linked her arms around his neck. "Oh, I do appreciate your concern, Serge, but I can and do take care of myself. In fact, I'll probably do a better job of picking my life partner than either you or Mikhel."

"Oh, Mikhel and his Erica are all right," he said softly. He had doubts that he and Derri would mesh as beautifully as Mikhel and his Erica had without some outside assistance. But he could and would cross that bridge when he came to it.

He looked down at Katie. "Does Mother know about this guy?"

She nodded, frowning. "Of course she knows. And before you start glowering at me and demand to know why I told her and not you, I didn't tell her. She just knew. Just as she knew Mikhel was having trouble getting Deoctra off him in Salem without him calling out for help."

She shrugged. "You know how nearly impossible it is to keep anything from her, but she's promised to let me reveal things in my own time. Okay?"

He nodded reluctantly. "Okay."

She smiled and kissed his cheek. "Good. Now." She closed her palm over the charm and let her eyes drift shut. "I can feel some of what Chan felt with his Cassy and it doesn't bother me. In fact, I'm glad he's so blissfully happy. You know he never deserved the beating you and Mikhel gave him. I was the one who got in bed with him and took him. I know you have some lingering resentment over that. Get over it."

"I have."

"No, you haven't. Not entirely."

"Okay, then I will."

"Good." She patted his arm. "And in the interim, I'll give this to Derri when she comes back."

"Not if?"

"When," she repeated.

Although he nodded, he didn't miss the fact that her voice lacked a certain amount of conviction. He had a feeling he was going to have make a choice between letting Derri go and relying on coercion to "win" her. In which case, would he really have won her?

* * * * *

Barefoot in a sheer, silk nightgown, with her breath escaping in painful gusts and her side aching from exertion, Derri fled along the dirt and grass path. She moved between the headstones, guided solely by the light from the stars. Several hundred feet back, she had run full speed into a headstone. The breath had left her lungs and the flashlight had flown from her hand as she was doubled over by the impact.

She had watched helplessly as her flashlight rolled down a small incline and disappeared from view. The sound of the pounding feet behind her and flapping wings above, drove her on.

A large stone mausoleum appeared out of the mist in front of her. Oh, God! What should she do? Through the open door, she could see that several candles lit the interior. She knew she had been driven to this place, which could only mean it was a trap. Behind her, her pursuer rushed along the path, a dark, ominous blur. He moved too fast for her to see him, but she could sense the menace emanating from him.

She didn't have much choice. It was either take her chances inside this crypt or let him catch her in the open with nothing between them. Heart thumping, she dashed into the tomb, and began pushing at the door.

It was heavy and tears of frustration and terror filled her eyes. "God, please help me!" She sobbed and shoved harder.

59

Slowly, the heavy door began to close. With half an inch before the heavy door finally shut, a dark shape whipped through the opening. Feeling a chill all through her body, she spun around. She faced her recurring nightmare—a tall, muscular man. As usual, his face was in shadows, but she could see his dark glowing eyes and his unusually sharpened and long incisors.

Oh, God! The vampire was back.

With a silent scream of horror caught in her throat, she was seized and tossed on to the top of the casket in the middle of the cold, musty mausoleum.

"I have come to give you what you want most of all, Derri. Open your legs and receive the sweet gift of my big, pussy-hungry cock, my luscious, licentious wench."

"Please," she begged. "Please let me go."

In response, the vampire ripped the sheer gown from her body, leaving her completely naked. After allowing his eyes to feast on her, he rose above her, exposing a large and impressive cock. He mounted her and she felt the big head searching for her opening.

"No! Please! Why are you doing this? Please! No!"

"You say no with your lips, but your pussy wants my big, thick cock." He rubbed the head of his dick against her clit and she shuddered with revulsion.

"No! Please!"

"I can smell you. I'm going to give you all the cock your frail human pussy can take."

"No! No! God, please, no! No!" She thrust her hands out and tried to shove him off her, but she couldn't budge him.

He laughed and batted her hands away with enough force to make them both sting and burn. "Get your cunt ready for a real cock. Here it comes."

"Get the hell away from her! Now!"

Suddenly, the vampire above her growled and snapped his head around just as he was snatched off of her. Derri struggled to her knees in time to see the frat boy, stark naked, with glowing eyes, and a foot long piece of wood in his right hand, confront the vampire. "Leave now or die!"

"Low breed! You dare confront me? A full-blood?"

"Not only do I dare confront you, but I will run this stake clear through your putrid and cowardly heart and cut off your goddamned head and your cock. Get the hell away from her. Stay away from her or die now! The choice is yours," he said, his voice full of contempt.

The vampire slowly advanced. "I will kill you quickly, low breed. Then I will fuck the human whore sore and senseless and kill her too."

The frat boy backed against the wall and crouched, his dark eyes glowing. "You will harm her over my dead body."

"That's the plan, low breed."

"You will find that this low breed is very hard to kill. Come get staked, full-blood," he taunted.

The vampire flew at the frat boy.

"No! Please, don't hurt him! Let him go!" Afraid she was about to see her frat boy torn to pieces before her eyes, Derri's screams shattered the tense, oppressive quiet of the night. "Please! Don't hurt him!"

"Derri. Derri. It's okay. It's okay. Shhh. It was just a dream. I have you now. You're safe."

A sense of calm settled over Derri. Her sobs subsided and she fought her way out of the terrors of the nightmare and into blessed consciousness. She opened her eyes and looked around. She was confused for several moments until she realized she was in the dimly lit master bedroom at The Retreat.

The frat boy was holding her body close to his. Okay, she slept in the nude, but why was he naked?

Her lips parted and she glanced up into a pair of dark, gray whirling eyes. "I...I don't understand," she whispered. "What are you doing here?"

"I'm here to protect you," he told her softly, caressing her cheek and shoulders, "with my life if necessary."

The lingering sense of alarm evaporated.

He drew back from her, allowing his gaze to rest on her breasts. "You had a bad dream, but it's all right now. You can go back to sleep. I'll stay here and guard you while you sleep." As he spoke, he pressed her back against the pillows and pulled the covers up over her breasts.

She sucked in a breath, waiting for him to steal a cheap thrill by caressing her breasts. She ignored her disappointment when he didn't. "You planning to stop my nightmares, college boy?" she demanded.

"No, but I can share them with you. Make sure you know you're not alone, even when you're in the midst of a nightmare."

"How are you planning to do that?"

He stroked her cheek. "When we're close, I can hear your thoughts and you can hear mine, Derri. I know what was about to happen in that crypt."

"How? How can you know?"

"I felt your terror. You need have no further fear of him. In order to hurt you, he'd have to kill me first and I am not so easy to kill."

She grabbed his hand. "Don't be so damned arrogant. He's a vampire."

He squeezed her hand. "I'm too close to being one myself to be afraid of him. I will not let him hurt you or haunt your dreams anymore. I'm going to protect you, Derri. I promise."

That's when she realized that she was still dreaming.

Her gaze moved over his body. In the dim light, she saw his cock and wet her lips. God almighty, he was huge. Her cunt pulsed as she looked at him.

She forced her gaze from the thick, hard cock protruding from the dark mass of hair on his groin. "This is a dream."

"No. It's not."

It had to be. Mikhel was in the room just beyond the bathroom. Surely, if she had really cried out, he would have heard her and come to see if she were all right. Since this was a dream, she didn't need to hide her desires. She could sleep with this man and pretend he was the sexy Mikhel Dumont.

She pushed the sheet he'd pulled up to her chest down, exposing her whole body to his gaze. She smiled when she heard his breathing quicken. "When we met, you said something about liking a woman with a hot, yielding pussy."

"Don't hold that against me," he said quickly. "I didn't mean that."

"Oh yes you did," she contradicted. "Remember, I can hear your thoughts."

His hesitation surprised her. "Why so shy, college boy?" she taunted. "I thought you said you wanted to fuck me."

"I do. Oh, I do."

"Then what's stopping you?" She reached out a hand and closed her fingers around his hot flesh. "Don't tell me this big, thick thing doesn't work?"

"It works just fine," he grated.

"You know how to use it?"

"I've never had any complaints before!"

"Really? I'll be the judge of how this works," she told him softly. "That is if you're in the mood for some hot, hungry pussy, Gray Eyes."

# Chapter Five

ജ

It took all of Serge's self control not to hop on the bed, mount her, and fuck her senseless. He knew that she thought she was dreaming. She didn't really want this, at least not with him. He finally met a woman he wanted enough to consider the possibility of giving up other women and she wanted his brother. He felt a streak of jealousy and a resentment he'd never felt for Mikhel before.

With her still holding his cock, he eased onto the bed beside her. He tipped up her chin and brushed his mouth lightly against hers. Her lips were sweet and soft against his. He licked at them, teasing them apart. Making a soft, incoherent sound, he sought her tongue. God, she was so sweet.

Her body felt warm and yielding and yet firm. Damn she had a beautiful body and such sweet, kissable lips. Deepening the kiss, he eased her onto her back and slipped his body on top of hers. His cock threatened to explode prematurely when she parted her thighs and rubbed against him.

"Take me, Mikhel," she whispered, running her hands down his back.

For the first time in his adult life, Serge lost his erection. Snarling angrily, he pulled away from her. He felt a ball of rage knot in the pit of his stomach as he sprang to his feet and stood near the bed, staring down at her. He knew his eyes were glowing and he probably looked like a lunatic. He felt like a lunatic.

She stared at him wide eyed. "What's wrong?"

"What's wrong? You called me Mikhel! That's what's wrong!"

She sat up. Despite his anger, he couldn't keep his gaze off her breasts. God, they were beautiful—big and firm with wide aureoles and hard nipples that stood at attention, begging to be sucked. Her whole body was gorgeous. Every, dark inch of her—long legs, big ass, and dark hair covered mound included.

Damn, but there was nothing half as beautiful or as alluring as a naked, aroused black woman.

She was absolutely breath taking. He wanted to fuck her like he'd never wanted to fuck another woman. How the hell could she want Mikhel, who was crazy in love with his Erica?

"This is a dream. You can be anyone you want to be, college boy." She extended her arms. "Come fuck that big dick of yours into my pussy."

"I'll take you all right! I'll fuck thoughts of Mikhel right out of your head." He rejoined her on the bed, urged her onto her back and mounted her. To his chagrin, he couldn't get his cock hard. He kept thinking that she didn't really want him and his dick refused to cooperate.

After several frustrating minutes, he fell away from her, onto his back. Now she'd really think he was some damned college boy. He took several deep breaths and waited for her to taunt him for his inability to perform.

Instead, he felt her soft hands touch his shoulder. "Hey, it's all right," she assured him, curled her body against his side, and lay her head on his shoulder.

He half turned and put his arms around her. "I'm sorry," he muttered, his face burning with unaccustomed embarrassment.

"Shhh." Her warm lips brushed against his chest. "Shhh. It's all right."

Her hands reached for and surrounded his cock and he sucked in a breath. "I'm sorry, but...I can't."

"Shhh," she said again and gently began to pump his cock. "Just relax, gray eyes, and enjoy this."

He closed his eyes and felt the pressure slowly building in his balls. As soon as he was sufficiently hard, he would mount her and give her a long, slow fuck that would chase all thoughts of Mikhel out of her head.

Her lips, moist and hot, touched his in a teasing, feather light kiss that sent a shiver of desire all through him. She rubbed her breasts against his chest, causing him to suck in a deep breath. "I like your lips," she whispered.

"You do?"

"Oh, yes. They taste sweeter than anything I've ever tasted," she told him.

"They do?" he asked amazed.

"Hmm." She climbed on top of him and nibbled at his mouth, pressing her mound against his crotch. "Very sweet. Your big body's rather nice too." She stroked her hands down the sides of his legs, setting off a series of smothering fires in him. "Very nice. I think I'll commandeer it for the night, college boy."

"I'm not—"

Her lips against his stilled his protest. She settled between his thighs and kissed him again. "Shhh. You talk too much at the wrong time. Lips these sweet were made for kissing, not talking."

He parted his lips and she deepened the kiss and aggressively snaked her tongue in his mouth, in search of his. He shuddered and clutched her to him, cupping his hands over her shapely behind.

*I love you. I love you,* he moaned, sending the frantic words along the bond they shared.

Her primal response left him devoid of words. They kissed and caressed each other with a growing urgency. Finally, she lifted her head and looked down at him, her dark eyes warm with unmistakable passion.

"You are one sweet piece of meat," she teased. "And I am hungry. I want some cock." She fondled him and he found breathing difficult. "First, I think I'd like to make love to you. Would you like that, Gray Eyes?"

He'd made love to more women then he could keep track of. An equal amount had made love with him or allowed him to make love to them, but none had ever made love to *him*.

"Oh, God, yes."

Still gently kneading his cock, she began to kiss her way across his chest. He shuddered and moaned softly when her teeth closed around his nipple. She bit and sucked at one small knob, making his cock jerk uncontrollably before moving onto the other one.

"You like that?" she asked confidently.

"Yes! I like anything you want to do to me."

"More coming, Gray Eyes. Let's see how big that cock of yours can get." She gave each nipple a final sweet suck before she began kissing her way down his torso. When she positioned herself between his legs, his cock was so hard it felt like it was ready to burst. Then her mouth touched the top of his dick and he couldn't breathe. He'd had more than his share of blowjobs, but none that gave him this incredible level of pleasure that bordered on pain.

She kissed her way down the length of his dick. She cupped his balls in her hands and licked her way up the other side of his cock. At the top, she took a deep breath, then slowly closed her lips over the head of him. Sweet Lord! Her lips felt like liquid fire. The sweetness of feeling her mouth and tongue caressing his cock was too much. He tried to hold back.

*Wait. Slow down*, he pleaded. *I can't hold on. I'm going to come if you don't slow down.*

She fondled his balls and continued slurping hungrily at his dick. He shuddered, groaned in dismay, and gushed in her mouth.

Instead of jerking back and spitting out his seed, she sank her short nailed fingers into his thighs, settled against him and swallowed quickly and steadily, until his cock was dry. Then she kissed the head of his quickly deflating dick before she slowly slid her body up his. When she kissed him, he tasted his cum on her lips.

"Oh, damn! I am so sorry!" he groaned.

"You're sorry?" To his surprise, she sounded surprised. "Why? Sucking your big dick was…hot. I thoroughly enjoyed it. I don't swallow on the rare occasions I suck cock, but your cum tasted…different from any I've ever inadvertently tasted."

That would be the traces of blood latents sometimes secreted when they came. He'd learned early that the amount of blood he secreted during sex was directly related to his level of satisfaction—the more he enjoyed himself the more blood he passed in his semen. He'd really come hard with her so she had probably ingested a considerable amount of his blood. Not that he was about to tell her that.

She pressed a light kiss against his mouth. "I could easily become addicted to slurping on your big hot sausage and swallowing your cock cream."

He sucked in his breath. He'd never had a woman talk this way to him. Damn, he liked it. "What about you?" he asked. "I haven't done anything to satisfy you."

"You think not? Here. Feel." She captured his right hand and guided it between her legs.

He gently inserted several fingers into her. Her flesh felt warm and creamy. "It feels as if you…did you come?"

"No, but I feel as sated as if I had." Her low, sultry laughter stirred his cock. "Your cum must contain a secret ingredient. Whatever it is, I like it, college boy." She nuzzled his neck. "I like your cock. I like your cum. I like you. A lot."

"But I haven't done anything for you," he protested. "Let me eat your pussy."

"You can definitely eat my pussy as much as you like another time. Right now I just want to sleep without fear," she told him, settling her breasts against his chest. "Just hold me until I go to sleep. I don't want to have another nightmare."

"If you do, I'll be here to intervene and stop it," he promised. "Sleep with no fear, Derri. I'll be here."

She kissed his lips. "What's your name, college boy?" she asked softly, stroking her hands down the sides of his legs.

Her hands on his body stirred emotions he'd never felt. "Serge," he whispered, his voice unsteady.

"Serge," she repeated. "Nice name, nice cock, nice body." She peppered his mouth with sweet, quick kisses. "Nice everything. Serge, you owe me a fuck."

"Oh, God, I'm sorry I can't give it to you now."

"Not to worry, college boy." Her warm fingers closed around his cock. "I know it'll be worth the wait and I'm too tired to be fucked properly anyway." She laughed and kissed his chest. "I shouldn't be tired like this in a dream, but I am. Give me a kiss, big dick, to tide me over."

His annoyance at her repeated reference to the size of his cock surprised him. He'd always taken pride in the fact that the size of his cock had always surprised and pleased his lovers. Still, he shielded his thoughts from her and obediently and eagerly parted his lips, threaded his fingers in her short hair, and urgently kissed her. Again, he tasted himself in her kiss and decided he didn't like it. Small wonder women didn't want to swallow that crap, but Derri had. His Derri was different from any other woman he'd ever met.

*Don't you forget that, college boy and who says I'm yours?*

*You're mine, Derri Morgan. You're my woman.*

*Serge's woman? In your dreams, frat boy.*

*And in yours,* he told her and took her lips in a soft, sweet kiss. *Can I call you Derri?*

*You keep giving me these sweet kisses and let me suck your cock again and you can call me anything you like, college boy — including your woman.*

69

*You are mine.*

*The thought holds some appeal, college boy,* she admitted. *We'll discuss it again after we have that fuck you owe me.*

*I will make this up to you. I promise.*

*Hmm.* She gave his balls a gentle squeeze. *I'm counting on that, my big dicked, gray-eyed, handsome college boy.*

*I love you,* he told her again.

*Hmm. You're sweet, college boy. I'm looking forward to getting acquainted with your cock. I'm sure I'll love that.*

*There's more to me than my cock,* he told her coolly, deciding he didn't like this dirty talk after all. He frowned. Was this how women felt when he talked about wanting to fuck their pussies with no regard for their feelings?

*Sure there is,* she said, making no effort to conceal the condescension in her voice.

Long after she slept against his chest, he lay awake, shaken by his inability to maintain his erection. He was holding the most beautiful woman he'd ever met in his arms and what did he do? He lost his erection and then he came in her mouth without giving her any satisfaction whatsoever. Even a teenage boy out for his first piece of pussy would have made a better showing than he had.

* * * * *

"It's not a big deal. It happens to every man sooner or later."

Serge, pacing in front of the big bay window of The Poconos Mountains cabin, turned to face Mikhel. The other man lounged naked in one of the chairs before the fire in the big, two-story high living room. "It doesn't happen to me, Mikhel! I've never met a willing woman I couldn't completely satisfy."

"Don't think so much of your sexual prowess, Serge," Mikhel warned. "You are part human. You live long enough, it'll happen."

"Has it ever happened to you?"

"Yes, it has."

He took a deep breath and glared down at his cock. Like Mikhel, he was nude. Unlike Mikhel, who was semi-hard, his cock was flaccid. "With Erica?"

"No," Mikhel admitted. "But I can imagine that if Erica ever called out another man's name as we were about to make love, I'd be distressed too." Mikhel grinned. "Especially if the man in question had a bigger cock and was my little brother."

"This is not funny, Mikhel! I'd trade my cock for a smaller one in a minute if she'd just think of me instead of you."

"Don't worry about it, Serge. These things have a way of straightening themselves out."

He glanced up towards the staircase. Derri still slept, but it was nearly dawn. Soon she would wake—wanting Mikhel.

"She doesn't want me. She wants you," he said bleakly.

"She thinks she wants me because I'm older. Serge, you look like you're about twenty years old. She's nearly thirty-three. Naturally, she's going to think she's too old for you. It's up to you to change her mind."

He raked a hand through his hair. "She doesn't want me!"

"She's your woman for the taking, Serge. She'll just need a little time to realize that. She has a lot on her shoulders right now. She recently broke up with her long time lover, she's been handed the biggest case of her career, and she's scared. That's a lot to handle. Give her time, Serge."

He sighed. "So. I guess you'll get to sleep with her before I do."

He watched Mikhel and saw his cock twitch at the thought. Damn, just as he thought. Mik wanted to sleep with his Derri. Worse, he was probably going to get her into bed before Serge had a chance to make love to her.

Mikhel glanced up towards the wide staircase. "She's…very sweet," he said.

He blanched. He suddenly knew how Chan had felt when he'd asked for an hour or so with his Cassy. A raw sense of jealousy, possessiveness and need ate at him, making him long to deck Mikhel.

"When you make love to her, don't get too used to it. She's mine."

Mikhel shook his head. "I could tell you the same thing about Erica."

"I haven't touched her yet, but you can damn well bet I will," he said bitterly.

Mikhel's eyes glowed and he streaked across the room and grabbed him by the throat. "You had better not use coercion and you had better not hurt her."

He shoved Mikhel's hand away. "I know the deal. Just make sure you do."

Mikhel shook his head. "Serge, this is getting us nowhere. You're overreacting. For God's sakes, you said she gave you an incredible blowjob. And she swallowed all of your seed. That's something Erica hasn't done for me. And I know she loves me. So how the hell can you believe Derri doesn't want you? Any woman who'd sucked that dick of yours wants you. So stop your damned whining and concentrate on winning her."

"You know, Mikhel, I'd give anything to knock you on your ass," he said angrily.

Mikhel shrugged and spread his arms wide. "Think you can? Come try it, little brother," he taunted.

Once when he was fifteen and Mikhel thirty-five, Mikhel had stopped him from taking the virginity of a fifteen-year-old human girl. In a rage, he'd gone at Mikhel with incisors bared, eyes blazing. After easily warding off his best efforts, Mikhel had decked him, busting his lips and bruising him. When he'd bounded to his feet, Mikhel had slapped him around until their father had intervened.

Mikhel was physically bigger and as a half-blood, possessed physical strength superior to his. Still he'd learned a few things since the last time he'd taken Mikhel on. Besides, he was mad as hell that his woman wanted Mikhel instead of him.

He bared his incisors and leapt at Mikhel, fully expecting to be cuffed against the side of his head and knocked nearly senseless. Instead, Mikhel's reaction was sluggish and both the vicious right hook and the brutal follow through left he threw caught Mikhel on either side of his jaw. He watched in amazement as Mikhel went down.

He dropped his hands and fell to his knees beside Mikhel. "Damn! Mik, I'm sorry," he muttered. While he knew that, had he chose to, Mikhel could easily have evaded his blows, he also knew that they had hurt.

Mikhel shook his head and got to his feet. "Forget it, Serge. Every little brother needs to kick his big brother's ass occasionally. It's like chicken soup for the soul. Yes?" he said, sounding like their mother.

Laughing, Serge sprang to his feet and the two embraced.

Mikhel cuffed him none too gently against the side of his head and released him. "Serge, I think she's your bloodlust."

"What?"

Mikhel rubbed both sides of his jaw. "I felt that, Serge. Really felt it. Your punches have never packed that kind of power. You're getting stronger."

"I work out, Mik. You know that."

"You've been working out for years, Serge, but you've never packed a wallop like that. Don't get me wrong. I can still kick your whining ass around this room, but I think you're in bloodlust."

He wanted Derri Morgan more than any woman he'd ever met. He would willingly die to protect her. Hell, he'd give up all other women, except maybe Erica for her. He was in love with her. But in bloodlust with her? He shook his head. "I'm a latent, remember, Mik? We don't do bloodlust."

Mikhel shrugged. "You have the same blood running through your veins as I have. And since I met Erica, I am stronger than I've ever been before. Serge, I'm not so sure anymore than I am only a half-blood."

Serge stared at him. "You're serious."

"Yes. My...need for blood is increasing."

"What need?"

"That's what I mean, Serge. I now feel a *need* for blood."

"But, Mother said —"

"I know what Mother said, but I'm beginning to wonder."

"About what?"

"If she's told us everything. You know how protective she is. What if there are things...darker things than she's told us awaiting for us as vampires?"

"Are you saying Mother has lied —"

"Not lied, just withheld. Serge, haven't you ever thought it strange that in nearly four hundred years of living Mother never got pregnant until sixty-one years ago?"

"No. You know a fem can only get pregnant in bloodlust. And even being in bloodlust is no guarantee."

"Serge, Mother and Dad met about a hundred and seven years ago. That leaves nearly three hundred years unaccounted for. Don't you think she must have experienced bloodlust at least one other time?"

"What's your point, Mikhel?"

"That there are things about being a vampire we don't know. Have you ever noticed that we've never met anyone of vampire stock who wasn't a full-blood?"

He frowned. Mikhel was right. All the vampires in the gated community where they lived were full-bloods mated to other full-bloods. "What's that supposed to mean?"

"It means we're being shielded from something...probably very dark and very ugly. When you finally make love to your Derri, I think you're going to be in full-blown bloodlust. I just want you to be careful. Okay?"

"Careful? What do you think I'm going to do?"

"You're a hot head, Serge. Don't go out looking for the full-blood who's stalking her alone. Bloodlust can be as heady an experience as getting drunk, only you don't come down off the high. Even though you'll be much stronger and feel invincible, the full-blood will still be stronger and have more experience. Don't make the mistake of going after him alone."

"I won't—unless I have no choice."

Mikhel frowned. "Then make sure you have a choice. I mean that, Serge."

He shrugged. He'd avoid a premature confrontation with the full-blood if he could, but if he couldn't, well he didn't do running.

"Now what's this about Kattia and this man she's seeing? Who is he? What do we know about him?"

Serge walked across the room and threw himself into one of the chairs in front of the fire. "Nothing! She practically went for my jugular when I asked her to tell me something about him."

Dark eyes narrowing, Mikhel sank into the other chair. "Mother knows of course."

"Of course."

"How did she seem the last time you saw her?" Mikhel asked, surprising him.

"Mother? She seemed fine. Why?"

He shrugged. "I saw her briefly when I flew home the other day to spend the night with Erica. She seemed agitated."

"About Katie's lover?"

"I don't think so."

"Why else would she be upset?"

He frowned. "I don't know. She and I are going to have a talk. But if she wasn't upset about Katie's lover, this man must at least be a latent."

Serge nodded, then shook his head. "Even a latent wouldn't stand for Katie fucking anyone with whom he didn't share a blood tie."

Mikhel frowned. "Damn. You're right." He sighed. "Well, you know what this means?"

"Yes. We're going to have to check the guy out," he said, dreading Katie's reaction when she found out they'd spied on her. "She's not going to be happy when she finds out. And she will find out, Mikhel."

"Yes, I know. Suppose you let me handle Katie."

He frowned. "That's easy for you to say, Mik. You're the big brother she adores. I'm only the slightly older brother she still thinks she can take in a fistfight. She won't give you the level of grief she'll give me. She pretends to diss you behind your back, but she really thinks you're the greatest thing since a hard cock."

Mikhel grinned and shrugged. "Hey, there'd better be some fringe benefits for putting up with you two immature knuckleheads."

\* \* \* \* \*

Despite the series of nightmares she'd suffered through the night before, Derri woke feeling relatively well rested. She lay for a time curled under the blanket covering her nude body. Remembering the more pleasant of the nightmares, she smiled. Well being rescued by the frat boy hadn't really been a nightmare. That had been a pleasant and very realistic dream. She recalled the cock she had conjured up for him and shivered. No wonder she'd been brazen enough to ask him to sleep with her.

Okay, so he hadn't slept with her. But sucking his big, warm cock had been awesome. Talk about a sugar dick. She licked her lips, remembering the feel and taste of his cum shooting into her mouth—and her barely gagging. What a sweet dream.

That was the beauty of dreams—the freedom they allowed one to do or say anything, no manner how outrageous with little regard for the consequences. Recalling how greedily she had slurped at his cock, she grimaced. Definitely a dream. No way she'd ever attempt to tame or conquer a cock that size with her mouth. And just forget swallowing even a drop of his cum. On rare occasions, she gave a mean blowjob, but she did not swallow. Still, the dream had seemed so real. She glanced at the other side of the bed and narrowed her gaze. There was a definite indentation in the other pillow.

Her cries must have awakened Mikhel. He must have had to hold her to comfort her after the nightmare. In her confusion and terror, she had somehow turned him into the frat boy. When he had put his arms around her and held her, he'd chased away her fears.

Eager to see him, she got up and headed for the bathroom. In the shower, with the warm water cascading over her body, she closed her eyes and allowed her thoughts to wander. She was in the fortuneteller's palm, naked and on her side facing not Mikhel, but the handsome, gray-eyed frat boy. She looked down at his erection and knew it was intended for her alone. And she wanted it. She gasped as he tenderly pushed his cock into her waiting pussy.

Her whole body convulsing with heat and lust, she clung to him. "Serge," she moaned his name and pressed against his shoulders as he eased the last few inches of his dick into her.

He tipped her chin up and stared down at her. "Are you all right?"

For all his lack of finesse, her college boy was gentle and considerate. She nodded, gasping, "Oh, my God, Serge. I'm so full of you."

"And I of you. Now you're mine, Derri. My woman."

"Yes. Your woman, Serge," she moaned, as he slowly, carefully began to screw her. "Serge's woman."

Serge? Who the hell was Serge? Derri shook her head and opened her eyes, forcing the daydream from her thoughts. Serge was Chandler's friend. But she'd never met him, so why should she daydream about him? She frowned. Serge was also the name the frat boy had given himself in her dream. In her dream. It had been a dream. She had to keep her dreams separate from reality.

*Okay, Derri. This is getting way out of hand. You have to pull yourself together. Now. No more daydreams — none about Mikhel and certainly none about your frat boy.*

*And he's not your frat boy*, she scolded herself. *At best he's a dream. At worst, a damned stalker.*

But thoughts of Mikhel quickly returned to taunt her and she gave up the effort to vanquish them. Oh, what the hell. What woman could be faulted for daydreaming about that hunk? Especially when she knew he was definitely not a figment of her rather active imagination. And he probably had a nice dick. Maybe not as nice as the one she had conjured up for her frat boy, but a horny beggar couldn't be choosy.

# Chapter Six

ℰꙊ

Standing outside the bathroom door, hearing her thoughts, Serge's hand tightened about the small, exquisitely carved Ebony Venus he'd cherished since Chan had given it to him.

Through the special bond he shared with Derri, *he* had entered her nightmare and rescued her from the vampire about to rape her. And what did he get for it? Squat. She gave Mikhel the credit.

He glanced down at the statuette in his hand. The features and body mirrored those of Derri's. He had a good mind to follow the ritual and compel her to him. But hell. He didn't need any outside help. He was perfectly capable of seducing her using his natural abilities as a latent.

A sudden memory of how sweet and understanding she'd been when he couldn't perform assailed him. She'd gone out of her way to reassure him and then she'd made love to him, making light of his premature ejaculation. She deserved better than to have his will imposed on her.

Swearing softly, he turned and left her to her erotic fantasies of Mikhel.

He ran lightly down the steps to the living room where Mikhel, finally dressed, sprawled in a chair in front of the fire.

Mikhel looked up from the book he was reading. "Feeling better?"

"No! She's upstairs in the shower fantasizing about you." He swore violently and hurled the small statuette towards the raging fire.

Mikhel sighed and moved across the room in a blur of motion. He reached out and caught the small carving just before it entered the licking flames. He studied the statuette thoughtfully before placing it on the top of the mantle and turning to look at him.

Seeing the censure in Mikhel's gaze, he grimaced.

"I thought we'd settled this earlier, Serge."

Damn it to hell, sometimes Mikhel sounded more like a father than a big brother. "Well, we didn't."

"No?" Mikhel's lips tightened. "That's unfortunate, but do not think for one moment that I plan to let you knock me down again."

He attempted to swallow some of his rage. "You don't understand."

"I do understand, Serge. Trust me, you *are* overreacting. We both know that Erica lusts after you. Do you see me stalking around in a black rage whining about it and knocking you on your ass?"

"You have no reason to whine because you know what she feels for me is pure lust that in no way detracts her love for you. Hell, if it wasn't for the fact that you and I share vampire blood, she wouldn't even lust after me. Now that she's tasted Dumont blood, she lusts after both of us, but she loves you."

"I'd still *prefer* she didn't lust after you. If you can't see that, then you're an asinine fool! And have you thought the same could be said of your Derri?"

"How?"

"She hasn't sucked your blood, but there's healthy traces of Dumont blood in your seed and you said she swallowed all of it."

He nodded slowly recalling both his and Derri's pleasure as she'd sucked his cock. "It's not the same as ingesting it unfiltered and in larger quantities. If it was, she wouldn't be in the shower now, wondering how the hell she can get you to sleep with her!"

Mikhel blinked at him and his gaze turned towards the stairs before he met Serge's gaze again. "Is that what she's doing?"

"Yes, damn it! And don't bother telling me you're not interested. I can see your damned cock hardening at the thought."

Mikhel shrugged. "Fine, I won't deny that I find her extremely attractive. I wouldn't mind making love to her. There. I've admitted it. Satisfied?"

"Hell, no!"

"Well, too damn bad. It's time for a reality check, Serge. Our first order of business here is to protect Derri. Now you either learn to deal with this situation or you get the hell out of here."

He bared his incisors. "So you can spend the next few days in bed with her? Not bloody likely."

Mikhel swung away from the fire and rapidly closed the distance between them. "I know you're upset, but get a damn grip, Serge. Do you really think I'd do anything to hurt your chances with her?"

He met Mikhel's dark, angry gaze head on. Mikhel. This was Mikhel he was accusing of trying to stab him in the back. Damn he had it bad. If this was what bloodlust felt like, who the hell needed it? He sighed and shook his head. "No. No, Mik...I'm sorry." He raked a hand through his hair. "I just can't seem to think clearly. I feel so...inadequate."

Mikhel's gaze softened and he clasped a hand on his shoulder. "It'll be all right, Serge. If the two of you can hear each other's thoughts, there's a special bond between you. You were meant to be together."

"Try telling her that," he said gloomily.

Mikhel laughed, kissed his hair, and hugged him. "Chin up, little brother. I've never seen that Dumont charm of yours fail yet. Not to mention your very big dick." Mikhel moved away, his mood darkening. "Now, what can you tell me about the full-blood in her dreams?"

"Not much. I could only see what she could see and she couldn't see his face."

"But it was definitely a full-blood?"

"Yes, the bastard admitted it."

"He admitted it? To who?"

"Me."

"You?" Mikhel's dark brows rose. "Are you saying you actually talked to him?"

"Yes. He was outraged at being confronted by a low breed."

Mikhel grinned. "He lets Mother hear him call you that and he'll have to learn sign language after she rips his tongue out of his mouth."

He laughed, his mood lightening. "And you ain't just whistling Dixie, boy."

Mikhel's smile vanished. "Why would a full-blood want to haunt Derri's dreams? Did you ask him?"

"No. After I threatened to stake and decap him, he decided that discretion was the better part of valor."

Mikhel gave him a long look. "You backed down a full-blooded male? I'm impressed."

He shrugged. "What else could I do? She was terrified. He was going to rape her. There wasn't time to find out if you could enter her nightmare with me, so I faced him alone."

"Okay, Serge. Remember what I said. Backing him down in a nightmare and in reality aren't quite the same."

"It doesn't matter, Mik. I'm going to kill him."

"If only your Derri knew what you'd risked on her behalf."

He shook his head. "I don't want her to know. I don't want her to feel as if she owes me anything."

Mikhel nodded. "You begin to understand the lure of wanting one woman more than life itself."

He nodded. "But unlike you and your Erica, I don't think—"

"Serge. Give her a little time. It'll work out," Mikhel assured him. "In the meantime, we have to find out who the full-blood is and what he wants from Derri. We need to find out soon. "

He nodded. Full-bloods had been known to enter dreams and cause fatal heart attacks. "And when we find out who's responsible, he's going to die."

Mikhel sighed and nodded. "Agreed, but with the prospect of our killing two full-bloods, Mother is not going to be happy."

"It can't be helped," he said coolly. "Whoever is stalking Derri has to die and Deoctra has to go too."

Mikhel gave him a curious look. "Mother told me you fucked her—in the ass yet. So, how was it?"

He shrugged. At the time, it had been a real turn on to know he'd balled a full-blooded fem in the ass who liked to think Mikhel belonged to her. "All right."

"Just all right? Mother said you seemed to enjoy it. She said Deoctra screamed like an alley cat in heat."

"It was just a fuck, Mik, nothing special. Hell, I don't even like asses particularly."

"Is that why you used a condom?"

He sighed. Was there any portion of that fuck their mother hadn't shared with Mikhel? "No. I used one because if Derri ever found out, she would probably not want to sleep with me if she knew I'd had unprotected anal sex."

"And this condom? It just fell out of the air?"

"I had it in my wallet. You know human women expect a man to have one in his wallet, even if he doesn't use it."

"So you didn't really enjoy balling Deoctra?"

"I fucked her to get her off your Erica."

"I know. I just want to make sure you won't have any problems killing her now that you've balled her."

"Why should I? She means nothing to me. If she threatens Erica, she threatens you. She has to die. Mother will understand. You know what happened to the last full-blood who dared to try and entice Dad away from Mother."

Mikhel nodded. "She had it coming."

"You know Mikhel, Mother would never tell me and Katie exactly what she did to her. I mean we heard the screams, but…what happened?"

"Mother beat her, staked her, decapitated her, and then cubed her body. It was not a pretty sight." He shook his head. "She learned the hard way that there are two things you don't do—mess with Palea Dumont's children or try to steal her husband."

Serge shrugged. "What did she think? That Mother would just allow her to come in and take Dad from her? She got what was coming to her and so will these two."

They both heard Derri's footsteps on the steps and Serge experienced a sickening sense of dread. "She doesn't know me. I'd better go."

"No," Mikhel said. "It's time she met you, Serge."

He shook his head and began backing away. "No. Not yet."

"Yes, Serge. Now." Mikhel raised his voice. "Derri, come meet my brother, Serge."

He'd never felt more like a clumsy teen about to be introduced to the school's most beautiful girl. She was going to cut him to shreds and spit him out like so much fodder.

His heart thumped like a tightly wrapped drum as he listened to her footsteps on the stairs. When she appeared at the bottom of the steps, she looked liked a vision of beauty dressed in the sleek, form hugging body suit that clung to her breasts and spread enticingly down her long, lovely legs.

Her makeup was so subtle it was almost invisible. He watched her full lips part in surprise as she met his gaze. "You!" She charged across the room and stabbed a finger against his shoulder. "What are *you* doing here?"

Feeling like a grouchy teenager, he backed away and cast a beseeching gaze in Mikhel's direction. "Mik?"

"Good morning, Derri. This is my brother, Serge," Mikhel said, sounding amused. "Have you two met?"

Serge released a deep breath when she turned to face Mikhel. "If you want to call being groped by him on the street meeting, then yes, we've met."

"Ah." Mikhel nodded. "Well, our Serge here is a little on the touchy feely side, but he is very good at what he does."

"Yeah? And what would that be? Groping strange women on the street?"

"Ah, actually I meant security. He's here to help provide security for you."

She glanced in his direction and Serge felt an urge to slink off into the sunset. "And just how long have you been here?" she asked, her voice low and dangerous.

He knew where the conversation was headed. Short of turning and running like a coward, there wasn't much he could do to derail it. "I arrived late last night."

"Really?" She turned to Mikhel. "Would you excuse us?"

Mikhel inclined his head slightly. "Sure thing." Ignoring the pleading look he cast at him, Mikhel grabbed his jacket. "I'll take a walk. If you want me, holler. I have excellent hearing."

Serge watched him head for the door, longing to ask him not to leave him alone with Derri. He could sense the rage she barely held in check, waiting to explode.

She waited several moments after the door closed behind Mikhel before she stalked across the room and stared up at him. "Explain your damn self."

He shrugged, trying to project an air of nonchalance. "What would you like me to explain?"

"Last night. It *was* a dream. Wasn't it?"

Her anger was almost palpable. He gave her a weary look. Any moment now she was going to haul off and slap the hell out of him. Of course he could always lie, but just as he knew what she was feeling, she'd probably know what he felt. Besides, he didn't want to lie to her.

"It depends on what part you're talking about."

"All of it."

"Can you be a little more specific?" he asked, playing for time.

Her beautiful dark brown eyes narrowed. "The nightmare. In the crypt."

"Yes. That was a dream."

"Then how the hell were you in it? And how the hell do you know what I'm talking about?"

He took an involuntary step back. "You know that we can…hear, feel each other's thoughts. We did it that day on Chestnut Street. I was in the room next to yours and I heard your screams, so I came to you."

She cast him an angry, hostile look before turning to pace in front of the fire.

The fire. The mantelpiece. Oh, shit! She would see the Ebony Venus there and think he'd tried to use it to influence her. He released a quick breath when he saw it wasn't there. Mikhel must have palmed it before he left.

"And just where was Mikhel?" she asked suddenly. "Why didn't he hear my screams?"

Watching her, Serge felt his cock harden. God, she was so beautiful. "He'd gone outside to do a perimeter check."

86

"If I screamed why didn't he hear me and come to check on me? He just told me how excellent his hearing is."

Sometimes, Mikhel talked too damned much. "You didn't scream out loud."

She stopped pacing and turned to stare at him. "What? Then how did you hear me?"

"I don't know. I just did. Derri, you must know there's something special between us."

"I don't know any such thing and I did not give you permission to call me Derri."

"Actually, you did."

"When?"

"Last night when you told me I could call you my woman."

She blanched. "You mean that part wasn't a dream? Are you telling me that I…" she stopped and took a deep breath. "Exactly when did the dream end?"

Now was the time for a good strategic lie. "It ended shortly after I pulled the vampire off of you," he admitted.

She stared at him. "Are you telling me you were really in my bedroom, naked as the day you were born and I…surely not everything after that was real."

He knew she was recalling how she'd talked dirty to him and sucked his cock and then swallowed his seed. He found her distress at the realization that it had really happened, painful. "Yes, it was."

She ran across the room. When she reached him, she raised her right hand and slapped him across his lips. "Bastard! You sick bastard! What right did you have to come into my room naked and…and make me do disgusting things to you?"

The last person to hit him had ended up in the hospital. He didn't do being hit. He stared down at her, trying to prepare himself to contain his rage. But there was no rage—at least not with her. What he felt was self flagellation that he had let her suck his cock when he'd known full well that she'd thought she was dreaming.

"I'm sorry," he told her and prepared to be slapped again.

Instead, she swung away from him and paced in front of the fire in silence for several moments. Finally, she turned to face him. "You understand this, college boy, everything I said…I thought it was a dream."

He nodded, feeling an emptiness he'd never felt before. "I know," he said bleakly.

"But you knew it wasn't and yet you let me say and do all those things…why?"

He stared at her, knowing climbing into that bed with her had been the biggest mistake of his life. She was never going to forgive him or believe he loved her.

"Love?" Her eyes narrowed. "Don't you talk to be about love," she said angrily, just as if he'd spoken his thoughts aloud. "A man does not behave that way with a woman he loves, damn you! Or should I say a boy?"

He blushed and swallowed quickly. It was coming. She was going to taunt him for losing his erection.

"No. No, I'm not," she said, looking surprised. "But that doesn't excuse what you let happen. How do you expect me to ever trust you? I feel almost like you raped me, damn it!"

His stomach roiled. "Oh, God. Please don't feel that way."

"How do you expect me to feel?"

"I…I never meant to do anything to hurt you in any way."

"Then why the hell did you behave that way? I'd already told you that was not the way to my bed!"

"I did try to tell you it wasn't a dream," he said weakly.

"Oh. So now it's my fault! You know, college boy, I had the right idea when I told you to go to hell."

He shrugged helplessly, extending his hands, palms up. "What can I say? If I could relive last night and do things differently, I would. Believe me. I would if I could. I just lost my head."

"You let me suck your damned cock!" She stared at him and suddenly shuddered. "Oh, my God! There was blood in your semen!"

Her horrified reaction was similar to that of one of his earliest lovers when, at her request, he'd pulled out of her and come on her body. She'd looked down, saw the blood mixed in with his semen and had started screaming, thinking she'd somehow hurt him during sex.

After that experience, he'd been careful to insure that he came inside his lovers so they were unaware that there was blood mixed with his seed. Now, Derri's horror and anger dismayed him.

"I…I…"

"Damn you!" She grabbed her jacket and ran towards the door.

"Derri, wait! Please!" He ran after her.

She spun around and slapped him again—several times. "Get the hell away from me!"

He retreated. "Derri, please. Let me try to explain."

"What's to explain, college boy? You took advantage of me when I was most vulnerable."

"It wasn't like that."

"Wasn't it? Didn't you know that I thought I was dreaming?"

"I…yes," he admitted.

"Then what the hell do you think requires an explanation? Do me a favor and stay away from me and out of my head, college boy!" She pulled on her jacket and stormed from the cabin.

"Damn it! Damn it to hell!" He raked both hands through his hair. He'd made one big, ugly mess. What the hell was he supposed to do now? How could he make this up to her? He dropped his hands and squared his shoulders. He didn't quite know how he'd make it up to her, but he did know he wouldn't accomplish anything standing there feeling sorry for himself.

Grabbing his jacket and a single rose from one of the dozen sitting on an end table, he left the cabin.

# Chapter Seven

## ॐ

Outside the cabin, Derri walked briskly along the back trail, taking several deep breaths and brushing angry tears away from her cheeks. Damn him. What gave him the right to invade her thoughts and her dreams? And make her say and do outrageous things to him? *And stop your nightmare rape?* An irritating voice demanded. *And face it, Derri, it wasn't all his fault. He did try to tell you the dream was over, but you were hell bent on fucking him. When that didn't happen, you were determined to suck his cock.*

Heat rose up her neck and flooded her face as she recalled the sheer joy she'd felt as she'd swallowed his seed, his blood-laced cum. Oh, God! How could she have done such a thing? How could she have enjoyed such a thing? She had ingested bodily fluids of a man she didn't even know. Worst yet she had loved it and wanted to do it again. This is what came of indulging in fantasies.

She looked around, spotted her favorite tree, and made her way over to it. She sat down under the branches with her back against the trunk. So, what was she supposed to do now? She shook her head. She was overreacting. What was done was done. What could she do now except…a vague memory from the night before intruded on her consciousness then danced away before she could fully grasp it.

"I need you to forgive me."

She let out a startled squeak and looked up. Serge Dumont stood less than two feet from her. "What do you want?" she asked wearily.

He was silent for several moments, just staring at her. She felt him brushing against her mind and knew he was trying to feel her thoughts. She made no effort to block his intrusion. Hell, she'd sucked his cock and swallowed his blood-laced cum. What thoughts did she have worth hiding from him? Damn her lack of self-control. She'd needlessly exposed herself to a host of sexually transmitted diseases at best. At worse…she shivered.

"You don't need to worry on that score," he said suddenly. "I am physically healthy."

"So you say."

He shook his head. "It's the truth."

"Fine. There's still a small thing called pregnancy."

Watching his face, she saw his gray eyes flick with an expression gone so fast that she couldn't decide what emotion had triggered the reaction. "You don't have to worry about that either."

"And why not, college boy?" She allowed her gaze to move up and down his body. He was wearing black again. Black jeans, black pull over shirt, a short, black leather jacket, and a black ball cap with the slogan North Philly Diamonds Basketball. He looked sexy as hell in black. "Surely a big strapping boy like you isn't going to tell me he's…sterile."

"No! Well…it's hard to explain. Derri, you can feel my thoughts, so you know I regret last night. I'm sorry. Forgive me. Please."

She could feel his sorrow. More she could feel something that felt very much like…love. At least that's what he thought it was. Well, that was something she was not interested in from or with him. His lust and his big cock? Those she wanted. A man in love got awfully possessive and wanted a long-term commitment. As did she. Just not yet and definitely not with him.

He approached the tree and kneeled at her side. "Why not with me?"

She shook her head. "Look, I told you, stay out of my head."

"How can I?"

"I don't know and I don't care how. Just do it."

He brought his right hand from behind his back and offered her a single, red rose. "Forgive me?"

Despite her mood, she smiled as she took it. "Where did you get this?"

"I brought two dozen up with me. Didn't you notice the vases on the side tables in the living room?"

"No. If you remember, I had other things on my mind—like bawling you out." She paused. "What did the card say?"

He shrugged. "Simply that I love you."

"Enough with the love already, college boy."

"Derri. Please."

She looked at his face and noticed a slight imprint of what was clearly her hand on his right cheek. "Oh, damn!" She lay the rose down and touched his arm. "I'm sorry! I...I had no right to hit you."

"It's okay," he told her. "I had it coming."

"No, it's not okay. I can't stand women who think they have a god-given right to smack a man with impunity."

"Impunity? Whoa!" He grinned at her. "Haven't heard that word since they made me read Poe in high school."

She laughed. "You know, college boy, you're rather sweet."

"That's what you said last night."

She nodded. "I know." She touched his cheek. "I'm sorry I hit you."

"I'm not. Not if it'll help you forgive me."

She looked away from him. "There's not really that much to forgive. I wanted to do it and I did."

"I wanted it too," he said softly.

"That's not a hell of a consolation, college boy."

"Why do we need to regret last night if we both wanted it to happen?"

"Because last night shouldn't have happened. Lately all kinds of crazy things have been happening to me and they've been hitting so fast. It's a little frightening."

"I know, but you don't need to feel alone."

"And why is that, college boy?"

"Because you're not alone. I'm here now, but I am not a college boy."

She turned back to him. "What are you? Last night, in the nightmare when I told you the man stalking me was a vampire, you said...well, you know what you said about yourself. Was it true?"

She watched his face and reached out as he tried to shield his thoughts from her. *Don't,* she told him. *You won't stay out of my head, it's only fair I know what's in yours.*

"I...yes...sort of."

She bounded to her feet and moved away from him. "Sort of? How can you be sort of a vampire?"

"Okay. I'm more vampire than human."

"How can that be? How can you stand there and tell me you're a vampire?" She looked around. "It's daylight, for God's sakes. If you're a vampire, how can you be out in daylight?"

He rose to his feet. "You've been watching too many movies, Derri. Neither day nor sunlight bothers me and I eat, drink, and sleep, just like any other man—and not in a coffin either."

"Really? And do you also drink blood? Is that a myth too, college boy?"

"I don't need blood to live, if that's what you're asking." He closed the distance between them and stared down at her. "If you're asking if I'd like to drink your blood, then yes. I would. It would in no way hurt you. I would never, ever hurt you. I need you to believe that."

She sucked in a breath and retreated towards the tree. She should be afraid of this man, but somehow she wasn't. "I know," she nodded. "So, if you're a vampire, then Mikhel…"

"Yes. He's one too, but he wouldn't hurt you either."

She laughed and sank down against the tree. "Oh, God, I've entrusted my safely to a couple of blood sucking vampires."

He retraced his steps and kneeled next to her. "Search my thoughts and you will know that neither Mikhel nor I would do anything to hurt you. We're here to protect you."

"Right. That's what the firm is paying you for."

He blinked at her. "You think this is about money?"

"Isn't everything, college boy?"

"No!" He exploded to his feet and stared down at her. "For your information, Ms. Morgan, I come from a very, very wealthy family. I don't work for money. Neither does Mikhel. We do what we do because we enjoy it. Is that clear?"

The angry, steel gray eyes boring down into hers held the glint of sincerity. "Yes," she said softly. What was it about him that made her goad him? She shook her head as he dropped back down beside her. "How can you be a vampire?"

To her surprise, he smiled suddenly, with no trace of anger. "The usual way. My mother is a full-blooded vampire, but my father is what is called a human latent, so I'm not a full-blood or even a half-blood like Mikhel."

"What's a human latent?"

"After years of…being married to my mother, Dad's developed strength far superior to any normal human male, but not quite comparable to a vampire latent, which is what I am."

She shuddered, considering how that strength had been developed. Oh, damn. This had to be a dream, a bad one. She put a hand against her forehead. "The blood I ingested last night, is that going to hurt me?"

"No. You can't get pregnant or catch any nasty little STD. We don't contract STD's and it's very hard for a vampire to get his lover pregnant. I guess that's God's way of keeping us in check. Not that you could get pregnant from oral sex."

She dropped her hand. "I know that, but damn you! You were going to sleep with me last night without a condom until…"

"Until you called me Mikhel," he reminded her coldly.

She shrugged, then stared at him. "Ah, did you just mention God? Do you believe in God?"

"What do you take me for? Of course I believe in God."

"This is getting asinine. I've never heard of a vampire who believed in God."

"Ah huh. And just how many vampires do you know personally?"

Her lips twitched with suppressed laughter. "Point taken."

"I'll have you know, my whole family believes in God."

"Even your mother?"

"Especially my mother. You know, unlike her children, she was not born a vampire."

Vampires who believed in God. What next? Werewolves unaffected by moonlight? "Tell, me, just how young are you, college boy?"

"I am forty years old and I graduated from college eighteen years ago. Bear that in mind the next time you call me college boy."

She shook her head and wrapped her arms around her up drawn legs. "Well, you look like a college boy. What do you want from me?" she asked.

"Nothing, except…I love you. I know you find that hard to believe, but it's true."

She turned her head and looked into his eyes. "You know your eyes change colors or at least shades of the same color. They range the spectrum from light to dark gray and everything in between. As for loving me, you don't know me, college boy."

"It's different for us, Derri. We know when we're in love almost immediately." He touched her cheek. "And I *am* in love with you."

"And I'm in lust with you and your big dick."

He surprised her by exploding to his feet and moving away from her. "Enough with the big dick crap," he said angrily. "I am more than just my dick. I'm a man with feelings, Derri."

She sprang to her feet and walked over to him. "I don't know how to break this to you, college boy, but my sole interest in you is your big dick."

"What? You stripped my ass bare of skin and kicked me to the damned curb when I talked about the size of your as...behind, but it's all right for you to keep harping on the size of my cock? What kind of double standard crap is that?"

"It's not the same thing," she said lamely.

"It's the exact same thing. How can you deny it?"

She held up both hands palms out. "You know what? You don't want to talk about your...genitals? Fine. We have nothing else to say to each other."

"What? I object to being treated like some damned piece of meat and the conversation's over?"

"In a word—yes."

"Why?"

"I don't want love from you, just a big, thick, willing dick. You interested in being a donor, college boy?"

"The name's Serge and no, I am not interested in being your big dick donor!"

Derri felt her cheeks rapidly heating. He'd called her bluff. "Fine. You don't have the market on big dicks."

His eyes darkened, his lips parted, and she saw the first physical evidence that he was indeed a vampire, his incisors. "Don't push me too far, Derri," he said in a low, barely audible voice. As she watched, his dark eyes began to glow.

She sucked in a breath. While not quite afraid of him, the abrupt realization struck her that this man she'd slapped and taunted was in fact much more than a man. She sensed an air of menace and power in him that was both disconcerting and yet strangely exhilarating.

She wrapped her arms around her body. "Are you threatening me, Serge?"

"No!" But his incisors were still bared and his eyes still glowed.

"That's what it sounds and feels like. Is this a vampire's idea of love?"

"I am not a vampire! I am a latent and I need you to stop taunting me."

"Or what? What will you do to me, Serge, if I don't?"

He immediately retracted his incisors and his eyes no longer glowed. "Nothing. I told you I would never hurt you. You know that. You can feel it."

"I felt the threat and the menace you just generated, Serge."

"Why the hell must you taunt me? You know how I feel."

"I know how you *think* you feel," she contradicted.

He leveled an angry finger at her. "Listen, you. I am older than you, both in chronological years and in experience. I had my first woman when I was thirteen and I haven't stopped bedding them since. So don't you presume to tell me how I feel!"

"Had a lot of women have you, college boy? I wonder how many you were able to satisfy."

She watched the blood flood his face. He stared at her with a hurt look in his gray eyes. He took a deep, gasping breath, then he turned, she saw a lightening fast blur, and she was alone.

If she'd had any lingering doubt that he was just want he'd said he was, his little disappearing act would have convinced her. She stumbled back to the tree and sank down against the trunk.

*Damn it, Derri. That was so uncalled for. You didn't need to hit him below the belt like that just because he wouldn't play house with you.* She gave an angry shake of her head and closed her eyes. *Serge. I'm sorry. Come back.*

She was sitting there forty minutes later, still hoping he'd come back when she heard the approach of footsteps. She had to swallow disappoint when she saw the man on the path in front of her. "Mikhel."

His dark eyes flicked over her with no sign of warmth. "You shouldn't be out here by yourself. Are you ready to come back to the cabin?"

She nodded. He extended a hand. She clasped it and he pulled her none too gently to her feet. They walked back through the surrounding woods in a chilly silence. With the cabin in sight, her foot caught in a tree root protruding from the ground. She stumbled and lost her balance. Mikhel, beside her, allowed her to nearly go down before he reached out a hand to steady her.

She shook his hand off her arm and ran the rest of the way to the cabin. He was right behind her. She closed the door in his face. She barely had time to clear the frame before he shoved the door open and stormed in, his eyes narrowed, his lips thinned.

He looked angry and dangerous. A shiver danced down her spine. Where the hell was Serge? She couldn't feel him. He must still be in the woods licking the needless wounds she'd inflicted. *Okay, Derri, don't freak. He's angry, but he's not going to hurt you.* "You want to talk about it?" she asked, somehow managing to keep her voice steady.

"Why did you have to crush him like that?"

So, the all grown college boy had gone running to his big brother, who now looked as if he'd like to wring her neck. Lovely. She licked her lips, wrapped her arms around her body, and kept telling herself he wouldn't hurt her. "Crush him? I simply told him—"

"I know what you told him," he said, his voice cold. "Did it please you to treat him that way and then crush him?"

Okay, this was getting scary. She forced herself to meet his dark eyes, which were now glowing. Any minute now, he'd bare his incisors. "Are you planning to hurt me?"

"No!" His snarled response only served to increase her fear.

She considered backing towards the door, but decided against it. She'd seen how fast Serge could move and he was a latent. Mikhel was a half-blood. There was no way she could escape or stop him if he wanted to hurt her.

"You're scaring me," she admitted, her eyes welling with tears.

He slowly advanced and glared down at her. "And that should worry me why?"

"I...I don't think Serge wants you to frighten me," she whispered and the tears spilled down her cheeks.

"No." His eyes returned to normal and the air of hostility vanished. "No. You're right. When he finds out I have, I'll have to end up knocking him on his ass. Erica wouldn't like it either. I'm sorry."

With tears streaming down her cheeks, she stumbled across the room and sank into one of the chairs in front of the fire. She turned her face against the back and sobbed.

She was too afraid to protest when he suddenly lifted her to her feet. He sank down in the chair and cradled her in his arms, his lips against her forehead. He held her, stroking her shoulders and letting her sob until the tears subsided to helpless sniffles. Then he cupped her face in one big hand.

"Listen to me. I was never going to hurt you. Never. Not only because I've promised to protect you, but also because of how Serge feels about you. I'm sorry I frightened you. It was unworthy and I apologize."

She pulled away from him and he allowed her to get to her feet. She moved quickly away from the chair as he rose. "I want to go home. Now. Please."

He sighed. "You're afraid of me."

"Yes! But that's what you intended, isn't it?"

"Yes, it is." His admission surprised her. "But as I said, I was never going to hurt you or allow anyone else to hurt you."

"Why should you want to frighten me?"

"Why should you want to crush my little brother?" he demanded angrily, his nostrils flaring and his eyes narrowing. "You tell me why that was necessary."

"I didn't crush him!" she snapped back, anger superceding her lingering fear of him.

"Didn't you? A human male in love is a vulnerable, pitiful creature. But a vampire in love is even more fragile."

"A vampire in love? He doesn't even know me. He's seen me three times. He's in lust with me."

"Don't presume to judge things about which you know nothing," he told her with an arrogance she wouldn't have expected from him. "*You* may be in lust. He's in love. We are not your feeble human males who need months and sometimes years to decide whether or not what we feel for a woman is love. We know almost immediately. Even if you're not in love with him, you should have treated him with the consideration you'd want had your roles been reversed."

She sighed. "You're absolutely right." She pressed her lips together. "I need to apologize." She looked around. "Where is he?"

"Gone."

"Gone where?"

"Home."

"Home?" She blinked at him. "To Boston?"

"Although we all have apartments in other places, that's where our parents are and that's where we live."

"Oh. Well, when he is due back?"

"He sponsors an inner city basketball league in Philly so he'll be back for the opening games after the first of the year."

She recalled the logo on his ball cap and leather jacket. The first of the year seemed a lifetime away. "Oh. I...oh." Damn. She'd blown it. He was gone and he wasn't coming back for weeks. *Way to go, Derri.*

# Chapter Eight

**∞**

After landing one of the Dumont family jets at the small hanger where they were kept outside of Boston, Serge climbed into one of the two SUV's inside the hanger and drove home. A feeling of calm settled over him as he drove along the quiet, private roads of the gated community his father had designed thirty years earlier. At the end of Dumont Drive, he encountered another fence, this one cyclone. He activated the release switch and drove through the gates of The Dodge House. He parked in front of the long, open square shaped ranch home. The lights in the main house were out and it was quiet in the compound. As he alighted from his vehicle, Princess, a huge white German Shepherd, padded silently to his side. The other dogs, also Shepherds, at a soft command from him, retreated back to patrol along the perimeter of the twelve-foot high electrical fence surrounding Dodge House and the two smaller guest houses in back.

"Hey, beautiful," he said, kneeling to embrace the animal and to allow her to lick at his face. "I missed you too." Allowing her one final lick, he rose, and headed for the house.

He opened the front door and stepped inside. He sighed. He was home where comfort and assurance were easily obtainable in his mother's arms. However, it was his father he wanted to talk to. He tossed his ball cap and his leather jacket onto one of the leather sofas in the large living room and made his way down the main hall towards his parents' bedroom.

The door of the big master bedroom stood open, as it nearly always did. He stood in the doorway and looked in. The curtains of the low windows were open. His parents, nude and asleep on the big bed, were bathed in the soft light from the moon. His father, a big, muscular man, slept on his back.

His mother lay on top of him with her back pressed against his front. Even in sleep, his father's big hands cupped his mother's small breasts. His mother looked like a doll lying atop his father's body.

He sniffed the air. They had made love. As usual, they were still joined. He could see part of his father's cock buried deep in his mother's small behind. This was the way it should be with a man and his woman. This is what he wanted, but couldn't have with Derri—unless he used coercion.

He glided across the floor and lightly touched his father's shoulder. "Dad?"

His father stirred, moaned softly, and pushed up into his mother's behind. His mother responded by pushing down. Great. Any minute now they'd start making love in their sleep. As children he and Katie used to wake in the middle of the night to come watch what their mother called night fucks. Sometimes his parents had a quickie and came, all without fully waking.

He touched his father again. "Dad?"

His father's eyes fluttered open and he looked up at him. "Serge? What's wrong?" he asked quietly.

"Dad, I need to talk to you."

"Now?" His father groaned, as in her sleep, his mother started rocking on his cock.

"I know it's late and you'd rather do other things, but I need to talk to you."

"Of course, Sport." His father grabbed his mother's slender hips and lifted her small body away from his.

Serge watched, holding his breath as his father's long, thick cock slowly emerged from between his mother's small, shivering nether cheeks. It always amazed him how his mother could take his father's girth and length in both her vagina and behind with no apparent pain.

His father laid his mother on her back, kissed her cheek, and rolled off the bed. "Let's go into the living room," he whispered.

Serge bent and kissed his mother's cheek.

She smiled without opening her eyes. "My little Serge," she said warmly. "We didn't expect you. All is well, with you, my little one? Yes?"

"Yes, Mother," he lied and followed his father from the bedroom.

In the living room, his father turned and looked down at him. "Serge? What is it?"

Matt Dumont was just three inches shy of seven feet. Looking up at him, Serge felt like a little boy again. "Dad, I need advice. I've met this woman. She doesn't want me and I don't know what to do."

His father sat in one of the deep, earth colored chairs his mothered favored in her western motif style living room. He extended a hand. "Come. Tell me how I can help, Serge."

He went and sat at his father's feet, much like he did when he was a young boy. And just as then, he felt safe. Taking a deep breath, he told his father about Derri. "She wants to use me as a big cock," he finished bitterly. "As if I don't have feelings and needs that do not center around my cock."

"So she lusts after your cock?" His father stroked his fingers through his hair. "Why is it a bad thing to have the woman you love lust after your cock? I've found it to be a very rewarding life knowing your mother can't get enough of my cock."

He leaned back against his father's leg. "But Mother loves you and worships the ground you walk on. She says having you fall in love with her was her salvation."

"Your mother and I had some very dark times, especially during her feast of indulgence," he said in a quiet voice.

Noting the tenseness in his father's tones, he half turned to look up at him. "Her feast of what?"

Matt Dumont shook his head. "That's not something your mother wants you or your siblings to know about."

He recalled that Mikhel had implied their mother was holding something from them. "Why not? What is it?"

"It was a very dark and scary time for us both. It's not something we like to talk about or remember. Suffice it to say, Serge, that love doesn't always run smoothly."

He frowned. It seemed Mikhel was right. They'd both need to talk to their mother about this feast of indulgence. "I know, but being in love makes all the difference. Derri is determined to view me solely as a damned sex object."

"What do you plan to do about it?" his father asked, his voice curious.

He looked up into his father's dark blue eyes. "What can I do? Mikhel was right. You can't force a woman you really care about into your bed against her will."

"No. You can't, but there's nothing to say that you can't romance her there."

"I've tried. It didn't work."

"Try again, Serge. You are a handsome, charming boy. Women, especially human women, like to be wooed and romanced. Sometimes they like to play hard to get. They like to have their men jump through hoops to win their affections. You can do it."

"No, Dad. I can't."

"Yes, you can. In the meantime, Serge, give her what she wants. She wants cock? Give her all she can handle. You know, your mother always says the way to win a woman's heart is to keep her pussy stuffed with a stiff dick. Yes?"

He laughed, then sobered quickly as he imagined Derri's reaction to such a axiom. "Dad, if she suspected I felt that way or even laughed when it was said in my presence, she'd pin my ears back and kick my bare ass to the curb."

"So? I'll bet your bare ass looks good on the curb."

They laughed and his father ruffled his hair.

He had a sudden thought and shuddered. "I told you she wanted Mikhel. I left them alone. Dad, you don't think Mikhel is—"

"No, Serge, I don't. He's your big brother. Do not underestimate his love and devotion to you and Katie. He will not touch her before you've made love to her."

He nodded. "I know that. It's just that I've never felt like this before."

"You've never been in love before. It can be very scary, because you're afraid of getting hurt, but it can also be the most rewarding experience of your life."

"Mikhel says it's bloodlust, Dad."

He saw a look that might have been alarm flick over his father's face. "Dad? What's wrong? It doesn't bother you that Derri is black...does it?"

His father's eyes narrowed and his lips compressed. "No, Serge! You know better than that."

He sighed in relief and nodded. "Then what's wrong? The look I just saw on your face..."

"Nothing's wrong, Serge. Do you think she's your bloodlust?"

He looked up at his father again. "I don't know. I just know I need her like I've never needed any other woman."

"So what are you going to do about it?"

He stood up and squared his shoulders. "The only thing I can—put on my best pair of running shoes and go jump through some hoops."

"That's the Dumont spirit."

He was at the door in the hall, heading for the front door when his father followed him. "Oh, Serge. I forgot to mention Diane called twice in the last week."

He turned with his hand on the door. "Diane Belmont?" He pictured the pretty blonde he'd been dating just before he first saw and fell for Derri. Even if he hadn't seen Derri, he would have broken off the relationship with Diane because she had become too needy. He didn't do possessive.

"Yes. She said she was in town and wanted to see you. She left a number." His father called it out.

He nodded, but didn't bother to write it down. "Thanks, Dad. Good-night."

His father joined him at the door. "Drive and fly safely, Serge."

They hugged. "I will."

* * * * *

Derri woke in the middle of the night, sweating and afraid. She sat up and looked around. She was still at The Retreat. She must have had a nightmare. She couldn't remember it, but her heart thumped and she trembled with fright. She glanced fearfully around the room. She was alone — at least there was no one in the room she could see.

Oh, why had she run Serge away? If he were there, he would have come to comfort her. Mikhel was in the next room, but she didn't dare call him. He'd probably come, but she could do without the attitude he would no doubt bring with him. Although he had apologized for frightening her, she knew he still resented what he considered her ill treatment of Serge.

Still trembling, she slowly lay back down. She reached over and clutched the other pillow against her chest. *Serge. Where are you, college boy? I didn't really want you to go away.* When she was still awake half an hour later, she got up, pulled an oversized nightshirt over her bare body, and got out her laptop. She worked on the jury questionnaire for the Smith-Barley trial for over an hour before she began to feel tired. She put her laptop away, tossed the nightshirt onto the foot of the bed and drifted into an uneasy slumber.

* * * * *

Serge smiled down at the pretty, blue-eyed blond who looked up from the reception desk as he walked into the plush office of Syndicated Newspapers Inc. "Good morning. I'd like to see Mr. Mariono."

"And your name?"

"Serge Dumont."

"Do you have an appointment, Mr. Dumont?"

"No."

"Then I'm afraid Mr. Mariono will be unable to see you." She glanced down at an open appointment book in front of her. "He has a full schedule today. Perhaps you can call and make an appointment, Mr. Dumont."

He widened his smile and leaned across the desk to stare into the woman's eyes. "Perhaps you'll tell him I'm here."

Her lips parted and her eyes took on a glazed look. She pushed her chair back and stood up without further protest. Serge moved around the desk and followed her down a long, carpeted hall with large, oak doors lining both sides. She stopped at the end of the corridor and opened the door.

Serge moved to one side so that the door shielded him from the view of the room's occupant. Still, he could see a middle-aged man with salt and pepper hair turn from the window behind the desk and look at the woman. "Yes, Karen? What is it?"

"There's a Mr. Serge Dumont here to see you, sir."

"Dumont? Did you say Dumont? Tell him I'm busy."

Serge eased the woman out of the doorway, stepped into the office, and closed the door. Only then did he notice the other two men sitting on a leather sofa along one wall. Damn. He should have seen them *before* he entered the office. He was getting sloppy, but no manners.

"I'm sure you can spare me a few minutes of your valuable time, Mr. Mariono."

He watched the other man's face tighten and noted the almost infinitesimal inclination of his head. He spun around and grabbed the two men charging towards him by their throats. He lifted them off their feet and applied sufficient pressure to their Adam's apples to discourage any attempt to reach the guns protruding from their shoulder hostlers.

Still holding them several inches off the ground, he turned back to face Ralph Mariono. "I'll say this once. Call your dogs off Derri Morgan or face the consequences."

The other man's eyes narrowed. "You have no idea who you're trying to push around. There are forces…" He glanced at the two men struggling in Serge's grip and broke off. "I know people you do not want to tangle with, Dumont. Stay out of this and maybe you and your brother won't get hurt."

"I know what forces you're using, Mariono!" he snapped angrily. He tossed the two men in his grasp into a tangled heap on the floor and flashed across the floor to grip Ralph Mariono by the throat. "I come from the same stock, so they don't frighten me. This is your only damned warning. Call off your dogs or I will kill them." He tightened his grip and the other man began to gasp for air. "And then I will come back to settle accounts with you."

He tossed the man onto the floor at his feet. At the door, he turned to look at the three men struggling to their feet. "Don't bother calling the police. That will just piss me off. And you don't want to piss me off." He whipped out a small steel sword from a scabbard on his back under his leather jacket and twirled it around with lightening speed. "Don't make me come back here." He turned his attention to the two bodyguards who were on their feet and trying to decide if they should go for their guns.

He twirled the sword again. "I can and will slice both your arms off before either of you can clear your guns out of your holsters. Trust me, you don't want to fuck with me."

Both men averted their gazes and dropped their hands to their sides. Serge leveled the sword and pointed it at Ralph Mariono. "Call them off or else."

There was no fear in the other man's eyes, only hatred and determination. And knowledge. He knew what Serge was and wasn't afraid. The man was a human latent or a vampire lackey. He was probably going to have to die. "You've been warned," he said, sheathed his sword, and left the office.

* * * * *

A knock on her bedroom door woke Derri. Struggling up from layers of restless sleep, she sat up, rubbing her eyes. "Yes?"

To her surprise, the door opened and Mikhel entered carrying a breakfast tray.

She gave a small squeak of surprise and scrambled to snatch the sheet tangled at her feet up to cover her bare body.

"Mikhel! Damn it! You might have knocked!"

A dark brow arched. "I did knock," he said and continued across the room to the bed. He set the tray on the nightstand to her right and turned to look at her. "It's nearly twelve o'clock. Where you planning to sleep all day?"

"Mikhel! Do you mind? I'm naked here."

He sat on the side of the bed and grinned, his dark eyes surveying what he could see of her body. She realized the side of her breast was visible and adjusted the cover.

"So I noticed," he said, clearly amused. "Very nice too. Like to sleep in the nude, do you?"

"That's none of your business," she said wearily. "What do you want?"

"To apologize for yesterday." He cupped a hand over one cheek and bent to kiss the other one. "We vampires are an ornery lot, but I never want you to fear me again." He drew his head back, but kept his hand on her cheek. "If Serge treated Erica the way I treated you last night, I'd deck him. Whatever happens between you and Serge, what happened yesterday between me and you, will not happen again."

She stared in his eyes and sighed. "Serge told you about my fantasies, didn't he?"

"We're very close and have few secrets from each other."

"Well, I think you should know that after your raging bull act yesterday, any fantasies I'd been harboring about you were blown clear out of the water, guy."

He laughed and to her surprise, kissed her again, very close to the corner of her mouth this time. "I'll have to see what I can do to rekindle them," he whispered and lightly brushed a big hand against her breasts before cupping as much of them as one hand would hold. "Serge was right, your breasts are exquisite."

Heart thumping, she jerked away from him.

They stared at each other in silence for several moments before he dropped his hand and rose. "I'll see you when you come downstairs."

She nodded. "Okay."

His gaze met hers. "Unless, of course, you'd like me to stay here with you."

"No! Please. Go."

He grinned at her. "All right. I'll wait for you downstairs."

She couldn't decide if his parting shot had been a threat or a proposition. Damn him. Now he decided he wanted to play jungle fever with her? After he left the room, she pulled the oversized nightshirt at the foot of the bed over her head. No more sleeping in the nude around him, she decided, settling against her pillows. She set the tray across her lap and dug into the eggs, link sausages, and toast. She found the coffee a little too strong for her taste. She set it aside and drank the orange juice.

After she ate, she headed for the bathroom. In the shower, her thoughts turned to Serge. Where was he? Was he still angry with her? Would she see him again? The thought that she might not was an unpleasant and unwelcome one. Refusing to allow her thoughts of him to turn lustful, she alighted from the shower and went back to the master bedroom. With her thoughts still on him, she pulled a red, clingy one-piece pantsuit over her bare body. Staring at her reflection in the mirror, she sighed. "Too bad you're not here to see this, college boy—especially since it's for you."

Mikhel was in the living room reading when she went down with the tray. He tossed the book onto the end table and met her at the bottom of the stairs. He took the tray from her. "Feeling better?"

"Much," she said, aware of the appreciative gleam in his dark eyes as he looked at her. She looked at him through narrowed lids. "I hope you're not going to turn into a wolf, Mikhel."

He laughed and left out a long, deep whistle. "I'm already a wolf."

She shook her head. "Mikhel."

He set the tray aside and touched her cheek, his gaze on her breasts. "What do you expect from a vampire? We're a horny lot with huge sex drives, Derri. We enjoy making love. And you are a pretty woman with a very lovely body."

While she still found the thought of sleeping with him exciting on a distant, but primal level, she couldn't vanish thoughts of Serge from her mind. Then there was this Erica Mikhel had talked so much about on the long drive to the mountains. She didn't sleep with other women's men.

He surprised her by linking an arm around her waist and pulling her body against his. She gasped. He stared down at

Marilyn Lee

her, his dark eyes glowing with unmistakable desire. "Are you sure you wouldn't like a taste of Dumont cock? Human women seem to enjoy it."

She felt his cock harden against her and had to swallow several times before she could speak. Damn these Dumont males were hard to resist. She pushed at his shoulders. "Mikhel! You're not serious. Are you?"

His arm tightened around her waist and he bent his head to brush his warm lips against the side of her neck. For a moment she thought he was going to bite her and she shivered with fear. "Mikhel, don't!"

He shuddered, slowly rubbed a very impressive feeling cock against her, and then suddenly released her. Before she could release a relieved breath, he was standing across the room, taking slow, deep breathes. "I'm very serious, but I can't touch you before Serge makes love to you. I would like to take you to bed."

She took a deep breath. Seemed the Dumont males weren't much on finesse. They both seemed to think all they had to do to get a woman in bed was to rub their big cocks against her. She grimaced. They might just be right. "I think I'll go for a walk." She stared at him through a narrowed gaze. "And you should take a shower. A very long cold one."

He laughed. "It won't change anything. I'll still want you and that lovely body of yours when I come out."

"You're as bad as Serge. Do you Dumonts think of anything besides sex?"

"Not when we're alone with a beautiful, sexy woman." He arched a dark brow at her. "Why don't you admit you'd like to go to bed with me too?"

Heat burned her cheeks. "I'm not admitting anything. Now I think I'm going for that walk."

"There are men guarding the perimeter, but I'd just as soon you didn't go far."

"I won't, just to the spot where you found me yesterday."

114

"Okay. If you need me, holler. I'll hear you."

"In the shower with all that cold water pouring over you?" she asked, arching a brow in her turn.

He smiled. "It's my job to keep you safe. I'll hear you and when necessary, I can move very fast."

"You can't...fly or anything. Can you?"

"Like a bat?" He laughed. "No. I don't turn into bats and I don't fly, but I can move very fast when I need to. I'll be there if you need me."

"Thank you."

"Friends again?"

She nodded. "Yes."

"Good." He whipped across the room and tipped up her chin. He stared down into her eyes. "People should always be friends before they become lovers."

She stared at him, the breath catching in her throat. "Lovers? Mikhel, I do not sleep with other women's men."

He pressed a thumb against the corner of her mouth. "You have a lot to learn about us, Derri. One of these days, you and I will be lovers."

He sounded so confident that she was momentarily left speechless. "What...what about Serge?"

The question seemed to surprise him. "He'll be your lover too."

"What? Have you lost your mind? I'm not going to sleep with both of you."

"Of course you will." He bent and kissed her on the side of her neck, sending a bolt of desire down to her toes. One big hand fondled her breasts, causing her breath to release in a series of hisses.

When he lifted his head, she backed away from him and grabbed her jacket. "I'm...going for that walk."

He nodded, his eyes dark. "Don't be afraid of me, Derri. I won't ever hurt you. Nor would I ever force you into my bed. When we become lovers, it will be because we both want it."

"Stop dreaming, Mikhel."

His smile, slow and intimate, made her heart thump in her chest. Damn the man but he was so sexy. "Stop looking at me like that," she ordered. "I am not sleeping with you."

He nodded. "Not until after you've slept with Serge. After that...I'm looking forward to getting to know you...in the biblical sense, Derri."

She swallowed slowly, ashamed that the thought of sleeping with Mikhel was making her wet. "You'd better give up whatever drugs you're using," she told him coolly.

Widening his smile, he sensuously ran the tip of his tongue along his lips. "The only thing I'm high on is being alone with you, sweet Derri."

Oh, God! If he kept talking like that and looking at her as if he'd like to rip her clothes off her body and eat her whole...she turned and hurried from the cabin with the sound of his confident laughter echoing in her ears.

# Chapter Nine

ಬಿ

Walking quickly away from the cabin, she shook her head. The man was mad if he thought she was going to sleep with him and Serge. Granted, the thought of having two handsome, virile lovers at the same time was rather exciting. But only while she was on her quest for sexual experimentation before settling down. Even then, she did not intend to do brothers. Half an hour later, she sank down onto the ground under her favorite tree. She felt the coldness of the ground through her sheer pant bottom and shuddered. What the hell was she thinking, wearing this stupid hooker get up? It had probably helped give Mikhel ideas. Well, he could just forget them. Her pussy was set on being drilled by the younger of the Dumont brothers.

"Hi."

At the sound of Serge's voice, Derri bounded to her feet, her heart beat rapidly increasing. "Serge! What...Mikhel said you weren't coming back."

As usual, he wore all black. Damn he looked good in black. He stood staring at her, his right hand behind his back. He shrugged. "I couldn't stay away. Please tell me you're glad to see me."

"I am," she admitted, feeling almost breathless with delight.

He closed the distance between them and brought his hand from behind his back to reveal a medium sized box of expensive chocolates. "Hello."

She smiled. "These are my favorite. Hello, college boy." She took the box and placed it in the bow of one of the branches. "I hope you're not still angry with me."

"No. I'm just happy to see you. I love you."

She caressed his cheek. "Is there any lust attached to that love, gray eyes?"

"Yes. An ocean full."

She took a long, deep breath. "You want to do something about it?"

"Which part?"

She placed her hand on his chest and felt his heart beat. "The lust part."

"Yes. Yes, I would. What about you?"

She grimaced. "I think you know the answer to that. I want to fuck you or make love to you. Which would you prefer?"

"I aim to please, ma'am," he said, grinning. "Which would you like?"

"I don't care which we do, as long as I get to feel your cock inside me. That's what I want…what I've wanted from the moment we met. Plain and simple, I want you."

"I want to make you happy and give you whatever you want, whenever you want it."

"That would be you…now."

Just looking into his gray eyes and remembering their early morning love session two days before made her wet. This was crazy, but she'd already gone beyond the pale so what did she have to lose?

She opened her jacket and unzipped the bottom of the cat suit. She heard his breathing quicken as his gray gaze noted the fact that her pubic hair was revealed. *That's right, college boy. I'm not wearing anything under this suit.*

His hand trembled as he unzipped his jeans. With his hand in the opening, he paused and looked around. "Are you sure you want to do this here? Now?"

"Yes."

"It's a little cold."

"We'll make our own heat, college boy."

Still he hesitated. "We could go back to the cabin."

"Mikhel is there and I want to be able to moan as loud as I like without worrying that he'll hear us."

"I have my SUV. We could go get a room somewhere. I don't want you to say later that I didn't do this right."

She felt her frustration level increasing. "What's the matter, college boy?" She bit back the urge to ask if his dick was still incapacitated. She noted the look on his face and could have kicked herself for forgetting that he would know what she was thinking. She shook her head. "Don't look at me like that. I didn't mean that."

"The hell you didn't."

She felt the moisture between her legs increasing. "Okay. I meant it, but just for a moment. Wanting you is making me crazy. Make me eat my words. Right here. Right now." She put her hands on his shoulders and pushed him against the trunk of the tree.

She reached her hand in his jeans and was delighted to encounter his bare flesh. She gently closed her fingers around him and eased his dick through the opening in his jeans. No. That wasn't enough. She gently pushed his erection back in his jeans, undid the top button and eased his pants down his strong muscular thighs. She wanted to be able to cup his behind in her hands and feel his pubic hair against hers.

With his jeans down around his ankles, she stood back and looked at him. He was absolutely beautiful. His skin was dark, his body lean, and firm. She slowly licked her lips. It had not been a dream. He had a very big, very nice cock. With a trembling hand, she unzipped her top and allowed her breasts to spill out of the bodice, uncaring that the cold morning air immediately hardened her nipples.

"You wore this for Mikhel," he said suddenly, sounding angry.

"Really? Sure about that are you?" She reached out and closed her eager fingers over his hot flesh. "This isn't Mikhel's dick I'm holding in my hand," she told him. Without waiting for his response, she pushed him back against the tree trunk again. "And it isn't Mikhel I want. It's you. So, are we going to fuck or are we going to talk?"

"We're going to fuck," he told her.

"No," she said, shaking her head. She felt his sudden panic and smiled to reassure him. "Not to worry, my gray-eyed college boy. I only meant instead of our fucking each other, I am going to fuck you."

"Oh, God, I'd love that."

She leaned up and pressed her parted lips against his mouth. As they kissed, he bent his knees, bringing his groin inline with hers, and she aimed his cock at her cunt.

His hands on her hips stilled them. "Wait a minute. Are you sure you're ready? If you're not, this can be unpleasant for you."

She looked down at his girth and size and knew he was right. This was going to hurt, but damn if she wasn't going to have him. "I'm ready," she told him. Her breathing quickening, she rubbed the thick head of his leaking shaft along the length of her outer lips before she slowly began to impale herself on his cock. The first few inches of dick sliding into her pussy was an absolute delight.

She moaned, shuddered, and dropped her head against his shoulder. "Oh, damn!"

He gripped her hips again and stilled her forward motion. "Am I hurting you?"

"Oh…not yet, but I'm sure you will before this is over. Oh." She pushed forward and bit her lip as he released her hips and more of his sweet cock plowed into her cunt. "Hmm. Oh."

She felt his intense pleasure at the partial coupling and lifted her head to look up at him. "We've barely started and this is good already, isn't it?"

He nodded mutely. She closed her eyes and immersed herself in his feelings, experiencing their first fuck from his perspective. Through their unique link, she saw him look down and delight in their contrasting skin tones. He took pleasure in watching his big shaft slowly disappear into her moist, heated, stretched passage.

She opened her eyes and unbuttoned his shirt. She brushed her lips across the fine hair on his chest, loving the feel of it tickling her nose. She rotated her hips and pressed steadily forward until she felt the last wonderful thick, hot inches slide into her pussy.

When they were groin to groin, pubic hair meshing, she cupped his face in her hands and stretched up to kiss him. "Oh, God, I'm so full of your delicious cock. Oh, damn, you are so sweet, college boy," she told him and slowly began to fuck her pussy along his dick. "Oh, damn, your big cock feels *sooo* good."

She kissed him again. "I'm going to fuck you now, gray eyes."

He seemed to have lost his ability to speak. Still, she could feel the tremendous joy and pleasure radiating from his cock to his own senses.

His body tensed against hers and she felt his cock pulse. He was fighting to control his desire to fuck her hard and furious. Her plan to have him do just that was quickly tossed aside. It was going to take a lot of practice before she could handle him pounding in her.

"Slow and easy does it, gray eyes," she told him, grinding her thrusting hips from side to side so she could feel every last inch of him. "That's a lethal weapon you're wielding." As it was she'd never had a cock that was this thick and long, and so incredibly hard. "Your cock is a horny woman's delight," she told him.

He didn't speak, just cupped his hands over her behind and pulled her body against his. It was a tight squeeze and he pushed slowly, gently into her. As her desire increased, the going was easier, although she still felt some discomfort. Moaning, he pushed his hips forward as she shoved hers against his. Her cunt swallowed his entire length.

Holding her body against his, he began to move with more speed into her body. Rotating his own hips, he thrust forward against her. At the same time she felt a distinct prick against the side of her neck as his incisors pierced her skin. He was about to drink her blood.

Even while excited at the thought of having his teeth and his cock buried in her body at the same time, she also felt an undeniable ping of fear. "No," she moaned. "No. Please no, Serge."

She was touched that he immediately withdrew his incisors from her flesh and gently kissed the small wounds. "I'm sorry," he whispered. "I didn't mean to hurt or frighten you."

She stroked her hands over his tight buns and pressed her lips against his neck. "You didn't hurt me. I'm just not ready for that, gray eyes."

"You're not angry?"

"Angry?" She nipped at his neck and ground her hips against his. She shuddered. Oh, God, that felt good. "I guarantee that anger is the last thing I'm feeling now, college boy. Can't you tell that?"

He laughed softly as he thrust forward again. Along with a surge of pain as he penetrated untouched depths, she experienced a sexual jolt like none she'd never felt before shake her entire body.

"Oh, God! Oh, God, almighty!" she moaned. Uncaring of the pain and desperate to feel that incredible jolt of pleasure again, she impaled herself on his full length. Digging her nails into his forearms, she withdrew slightly and shoved herself against him—again and again until, sobbing with pain and pleasure, her universe exploded and she burst into a million very happy pieces.

Cupping the back of her head in his hand, he snaked his tongue into her mouth, and now that she'd come, he thrust into her pussy with more vigor. Feeling limp, but still horny, she clung to him, experiencing their love making from his viewpoint. His passion built quickly. Biting her lip to keep from crying out with pain, she closed her eyes and held on, knowing he was seconds away from his release. He groaned deep in his throat and shuddered as he came.

His seed, quickly filling her cunt, soothed the battered flesh. She moaned softly, still impaled on him and dropped her head against his shoulder.

"Derri? Are you all right?" he asked, stroking her hair and shoulders.

"Oh, God! I have never, ever felt anything like that before. I don't know if I'll ever be all right again. That was…wow."

"So then you liked it?" he teased.

She laughed weakly and lifted her head to look up at him. "Maybe just a little, gray eyes."

His eyes darkened as he noted her wet cheeks. "Oh, shit! I've hurt you. I'm sorry."

He began to withdraw his still hard cock from her. She sucked in a series of sharp breaths and bit her lip. Although he removed his cock gently and her pussy was well lubed with their combined juices, his withdrawal still hurt. When the big head cleared the clinging lips of her pussy, she blew out a deep breath and several tears trickled down her cheeks.

"Oh, shit!" He groaned and gathered her in his arms. He buried his lips in her hair, near her ear. "I'm so sorry. I didn't realize I was hurting you."

She pressed her cheek against his shoulder and clung to him. "It's all right."

"All right?" He drew back and stared down at her. "You're crying."

She shook her head. "Not to worry, gray eyes. These aren't sad tears. That did hurt like hell, but, I wouldn't undo it for a million bucks. There was a staggering amount of sexual pleasure and joy intermingled with the pain." She stroked a hand over his troubled brow. "What's more, as soon as my pussy recovers, I plan to repeat the offense. Often."

She tried, but couldn't coax a smile from him. He frowned. "You're sure?"

She reached down a hand to cup his still hard cock. "Oh, I'm very sure, gray eyes. But right now, I need to soak."

He buttoned and zipped them both up, then he lifted her in his arms.

"Serge, what are you doing?"

"We're going back to the cabin so you can get in the Jacuzzi."

"I can walk."

He bent his head and brushed his lips against hers, sending a delicious tingle all through her. "Why walk when I can carry you?"

He really was sweet. She touched his face. "I appreciate the gesture, but I'm not exactly a lightweight and it's at least a mile back to the cabin."

He grinned at her. "Not to worry. I promise not to drop your big behind on the ground."

"Hey, watch it, buster," she warned, feigning annoyance. "I'll have you know I work out to keep in shape."

He leered at her. "It's working. You're in perfect shape."

"That's better," she said and linked her arms around his neck. "You're very sweet, Serge." She sighed. "If things were different, I could have fallen hard for you."

His lips compressed into a tight line. "What things? I love you. You know that, even if you won't admit it. What's more, you know in your heart you could love me too. I can make you happy, Derri. I'll do everything in my power to fulfill all your fantasies."

She pushed gently against his shoulders. "Please put me down, Serge."

When he complied, she put several inches between them before she spoke. "I told you that I'm not looking to fall in love with you. I—"

He held up a hand to silence her. "Please don't tell me again that I'm just a piece of meat to you. I can't bear to hear that from you. Not now."

"I wasn't going to say that because you're not. But Serge, I have plans for my future."

"Plans that don't include me?"

"That depends."

"On what?"

"On whether or not you can accept my terms. You are such a sweet man and a wonderful lover. If you're willing to be my lover until I'm ready to get married, I would really love that."

"What? Who the hell are you marrying? Some human bozo who can't fulfill your fantasies?"

"Serge, don't make the mistake of thinking you own me or are owed some explanation just because we fucked. My life is still mine to do with as I like. Accept that and we can be lovers."

His eyes darkened. "And if I want something much more permanent?"

She moved closer and touched his cheek. "Please, Serge. Something is better than nothing. Isn't it? Isn't being together for a short time better than saying goodbye now for good?"

His dark eyes glowed and he bared his incisors. "You expect me to share you with another man?"

"There is no other man at the moment, but there will be eventually."

"And just what is to prevent me from ripping his heart out of his body and decapitating him?" he snarled angrily. "Who the hell is going to stop me?"

She shivered at the violence and fury she saw in his eyes and heard in his voice. She knew he was deadly serious, which probably meant that her "sweet" Serge had killed before.

"Yes, Derri, I have," he told her. "What else would you expect from a latent vampire? I don't do competition."

"So you kill your competition?" She jabbed a finger at his shoulder. "Withdraw those damned fangs and stop your eyes from glowing. I am not afraid of you, Serge."

"You have no need to be. But any man who's foolish enough to think he's going to take you from me, had better be very afraid for the rest of his very short life. Because I will kill him."

"Is this a vampire's idea of after play?" she demanded. "No wonder your people are the scourge of the earth. After lovemaking, a woman likes to be kissed, talked to, and held — not told by her current lover that he plans to brutally off her next one."

To her surprise, he retracted his incisors, threw back his head and laughed. Then he enclosed her in a bear hug. "Derri, Derri. You are mine."

She clung to him, shivering with thoughts of the many sexual pleasures to come with this big dicked man as her lover. "For a time, Serge." She looked up at him. "Can you accept me on my terms?"

"I'll have to," he told her bleakly. "I love you."

She stretched up to kiss him. "Don't sound so forlorn, gray eyes. There's no one else on the horizon. At the moment, I am really looking forward to getting to know you." She reached down and placed her hand over his cock. "And him of course. I'm curious. Does he have a name?"

He sighed softly. "Woman, do you think of anything besides sex?"

"Not just sex, sex with you, gray eyes. Not with Mikhel or some other nameless man. For the moment, you have my complete and total attention, interest, and desire."

"I plan to keep it, Derri."

She shook her head. "Serge, don't cling. Please."

"I can get lust from almost any woman I meet. I want and need more than that from you."

"Let's just take it slow. One step at a time. Okay?"

"Okay." He pressed a quick, hard kiss against her mouth, and lifted her off her feet. "But be warned, I intend to do everything in my power to change your mind about you and me, including my abilities as a latent vampire."

She linked her arms around his neck. "That's the spirit. You go right ahead and give it the old latent vampire college try," she teased him softly. "And I will lie in your arms night after night and thoroughly enjoy all your efforts to persuade me we're meant to be together."

"We are meant to be together. Why else do you think we can hear each other's thoughts?"

She shook her head. "I have no idea. Nothing like this has ever happened to me. I don't know what's going on between us. I just know that I like you. A lot."

"I love you."

She smiled. She was beginning to like the sound of his earnest declaration. "So, you never said, does your cock have a name?"

"Yes—Serge."

"Yeah? Well, I like you both." She rubbed her nose against his. "We're going to be together for Christmas. What would you like, gray eyes?"

"You—naked and horny as hell."

She grinned and they shared a long, passionate kiss. "Hmm," she murmured when they came up for air. "With or without a bow?"

"Without a bow or a single stitch of clothes."

"What do you know? That's just how I want you for Christmas."

"You'll come to Boston to spend Christmas at home with my family?"

Her smiled wavered. That was too much like a commitment. "I don't know about that. I mean…no offense, but you're a bunch of vampires."

"Yes, but we have excellent table manners." He grinned. "We don't drink blood without permission. Come? Please. I promise you'll be safe."

"Serge…"

"Please, Derri. Come?"

"I…ah…I'll think about it. Can we leave it like that for now?"

He nodded. "Okay."

# Chapter Ten

છ

"Good." She smiled at him, reaching out to allow him to feel some of the warmth she felt for him. She wanted him to know that it wasn't just about sex for her.

He responded by dropping a shield from a place in his thoughts he'd kept hidden from her.

"That's right. Let me in, gray eyes," she encouraged. "Don't keep secrets from me."

Her smile vanished as her senses were overwhelmed with a graphic impression of a big room filled with numerous beds, occupied by writhing twosomes and threesomes. Women were gasping and shuddering as they were drilled in every orifice. Naked men with full and impressive erections roamed the perimeters, looking for an unoccupied female opening to dive into. Over looking the big, moonlit room, in a huge chair at one end of the glass-ceiling room, sat a stunning, nude pair. The couple were both facing the action in the room, although they seemed to be lost in each other. The handsome middle-aged man had gray hair and blue eyes. His tiny partner looked nearly young enough to be his granddaughter. He held her several inches above his lap. His expression became one of ecstasy as he vigorously thrust what looked like a horse dong up into the female's pussy.

The woman shuddered and moaned, tossing her head from side to side, her dark hair cascading around her beautiful face which contorted with lust and pleasure. Her dark eyes glowed, her incisors were bared, and her small breasts shook. The big man's thrusts became more frantic and powerful until both he and the woman cried out in unison. Seconds later, the man lowered the woman onto his lap, his cock buried deep in her still shuddering body. They remained that way for a time, then the woman lifted herself off the man.

Derri gasped. She'd never seen anything like the man's cock. Not only was it extremely long with a huge, angry looking dark pink head, but it was thicker than any cock she'd ever seen.

As she watched, the woman turned to face the man. Clinging to his powerful shoulders, she buried her incisors in his neck and began to feed on him. He shuddered and closed his eyes, a look of absolute bliss on his face. He held the woman's small, delicate cheeks in his hands as she drank his blood.

Derri's breath came in deep, almost aching gasps. She'd never seen anything so beautiful and sensual. While undeniably erotic, she could almost feel the love and devotion the couple clearly felt for each other.

After what seemed an eternity, with his eyes still closed, the man suddenly shoved his hips upwards and his huge dick began to disappear into the tiny body of his lover.

Although the countless others in the room were still wildly fucking each other, Derri couldn't remove her gaze from the couple in the chair. A steady milky stream began to trickle down the part of the man's cock that was still visible and Derri realized that one or both of the couple had come again. Watching, Derri felt her pussy creaming. God, what a turn on.

Finally, the woman lifted her face from the male's neck and slumped against him, her small body trembling.

He wrapped his arms around her and pressed his lips against the top of her head.

When her tremors subsided, the woman turned her body and keeping herself on the man's cock, she lay with her back against the man's body, a serene, satisfied smile on her face. Her dark eyes turned to the numerous mating acts taking place before the throne like chair where she and her lover sat, sated and satisfied.

Across the room, a woman lay on a bed, sandwiched between two men who stroked into her pussy and her rear end with hard, rhythmic thrusts. Not far away, another couple occupied another bed. On this one, a tall, muscular man, with skin the color of sunlight sprinkled cinnamon, long dark dreadlocks pulled back with a band, and startling blue eyes, kneeled on his knees behind a rather full-figured blond. The blonde's ample buns quivered uncontrollably as she thrust herself wildly back at his groin. He pushed into her with a quick, rhythmic series of strokes that triggered wild reactions as they each fought to reach their peak. Suddenly the man grabbed the woman's full hips, held his lover still, and drilled his cock into her with a speed and force that must have given them both incredible pleasure. It certainly turned Derri's cunt into a quivering mass of need.

The woman cried out and fell forward against the bed, moaning and whimpering with obvious satisfaction. The man tossed back his head and let out a lusty roar. As he came, he thrust himself deep into the woman's quivering body for what seemed an eternity. Finally, Derri saw a trickle of the man's seed run down the woman's thigh. The man laid his big body over the woman's back and sank his incisors into the side of her neck. He fed on her for what seemed a long time before he kissed the back of her neck and withdrew from her. He rose gracefully to his feet.

Derri sucked in a breath. God almighty but he was packing quite a wallop. For size and girth, his still erect cock rivaled Serge's. The woman collapsed onto the bed, sprawling her full-figured body out spread eagle. There was a wide, satisfied smile on her face.

Palming his rather impressive erection, the man looked around, clearly in search of more sex.

Derri's gaze was drawn across the room to a tall, dark woman with blue eyes and curly, dark hair, sandwiched between two men. All three people were on their feet. The woman faced the shorter of the two men, one long leg held across his body as he drilled his cock into her already dripping cunt. Another man, taller and well-built, held the woman's hips and pushed his cock into her rear end. Although she shuddered with the impact of the pummeling cocks, her gaze was riveted to the tall, dark man with the cinnamon skin. There was a look of clear desire in her eyes as she looked at his cock. Derri realized in stunned surprise that the woman being twin drilled was the fortuneteller.

The object of the fortuneteller's attention, settled his blue gaze on the first threesome. He quickly approached the bed where the trio lay thrusting and moaning. He paused near the woman's face. "Is there room for one more?"

Derri shivered just hearing the man's deep, sexy, compelling voice. Talk about tall, dark, handsome, and well-hung. And velvet voiced. This man could have anything he wanted from any woman he wanted it from.

The woman looked up and saw him. Her gaze went to the cock in his hand. Her eyes lit and she slowly parted her lips in a clear, unequivocal invitation. Muscles rippling along his big, extremely well-built body, the man moved closer.

Oh, God! Derri's heart thumped and even more moisture filled her already wet channel. She was about to see a foursome. She gasped, holding her breath. Lord help her, but she envied the woman about to receive that luscious looking weapon between her eager lips. This was the sexiest thing she'd never seen. The woman wiggled her tongue and smiled encouragingly up at the man. Derri licked her lips and waited, then cried out in protest as Serge put up a shield and the vision vanished.

She stared up him. "My God. What was that?"

"How much did you see?" he asked, sounding weary.

"A lot and all of it requiring an explanation, college boy."

"When you say a lot, what do you mean?"

"I mean I saw an orgy. Serge there was this room full of people making out like rabbits and…"

She frowned up at him. "Why am I explaining it to you? You know what I saw."

"When you say an orgy…what do you mean?"

"Don't play games with me, college boy. You *know* what I mean. You allowed me to see it."

"Did it…shock you?"

It wasn't shock that had her all wet again and longing for Serge's cock in her. "No." Titillated? Oh, yeah. "Now what was that?"

He hesitated before shrugging. "That was our last Family Fuck Fest."

She blinked at him. "Your family what?"

He sighed. "It's a long story."

"It's a long walk to the cabin. Tell me, who was the couple in the chair?"

"My parents."

"Your parents? Are you telling me that your parents…make out in front of other people?"

"You're making it sound like something they need to be ashamed of," he said coolly. "It's not. It's part of our culture, Derri. We're not ashamed of who we are or what we do to and with those we love."

"Love?" She shook her head. She'd seen lots of incredible, lustful rutting, but no lovemaking.

"Yes, Derri, love."

She thought of the couple in the chair. Those two had managed to convey an obvious tenderness and affection for each other—all without saying a word. Okay, so maybe they'd been making love, but everyone else she'd seen had just been fucking. Period.

"Your parents are a striking looking couple."

He grinned, his mood lightening. "Now you know the source of my good looks and boyish charm," he said.

She caressed his cheek. "You are very good looking, college boy and very charming."

"God, I'm glad you think so."

"Your father is very good looking too. And Serge, his cock..."

"Impressive, isn't it?" he said with no trace of envy in his voice. "My mother says a woman hasn't lived until she's been fucked by a man with a real cock like my father's."

Derri shuddered. "Really? Well, if it's all the same to her, your cock is plenty big and thick and good enough for me, college boy."

He rewarded her with a long, sweet kiss. "One of these days, you and I are going to be like my parents, Derri — still wildly in love after many years of marriage."

His use of the *M* word sent a shiver through her — part pleasure, part dismay. He wanted to marry her already? "Maybe," she murmured.

"They're still in love even after all this time."

"How much time?"

"They've been married for a hundred and seven years."

"What? How long did you say?"

"A hundred and seven years."

"How old is your father? I thought you said he wasn't a vampire."

"He's not, but he is a human latent. His aging process has been slowed so much that it's nearly stopped."

"How? I don't understand."

She felt the shield go up again. "There are...benefits to loving one with vampire blood. You need never grow old, Derri."

She shook her head. "Serge, put me down."

He lowered her to her feet. "Don't look at me like that, Derri. It can and does happen without your having to die."

"How?"

He shook his head. "You're not ready to know how yet."

She tried to probe his mind but she couldn't get past the shield he'd erected. She stared at him through narrowed lids. He was wrong if he thought he could keep anything hidden from her for long. When they made love, he exposed himself. She'd find out then.

She extended a hand. Correctly interpreting her mood, he swept her back into his arms.

She smiled. A woman could get used to a man who could pick her up and carry her with no apparent effort.

"Serge, who was the man with the dreads and the blue eyes?"

She felt a surge of anxiety from him. "Why? Are you interested in him?"

"I don't know him," she pointed out. "Besides, at the moment, I'm interested in you and you alone. Still, he's so...well...he is rather breathtaking. It's not everyday you see a man with such a beautiful skin tone and such blue-blue eyes...and so many other...manly traits."

"What the hell has he got that I haven't?"

"Did I say he had anything that you didn't also have in abundance? Serge, don't go postal on me, okay?"

"I am not sharing you with him!"

She blinked at him. "Who said anything about wanting him?"

"Derri. I can feel your interest in him."

"What's his name, Serge?"

"Alex."

"Does Alex have a last name?" she prodded.

"Madison," he said reluctantly.

"Family?"

"No."

"Family friend?"

He hesitated. "I suppose."

"Oh, Serge. Surely you know whether or not he's a family friend."

"Mikhel and my mother are quite fond of him. Why? I don't know."

"What about his family?"

"I don't know anything about him or his family or even if he has one."

That surprised her. "Nothing? How long have you known him?"

"He showed up one day when Mikhel was five and he's been coming and going in and out of our lives to suit himself every since."

"So he was a friend of your mothers?"

"No. She didn't know him."

"Serge, if he's been coming and going for over fifty-five years, surely you must know something about him."

"No. He doesn't like to talk about himself or his past."

"Vampire?" Stupid question. She'd seen him rising from the woman's body with blood on his face.

"Yes. Exactly what is your interest in him?"

"Come on, college boy, even you have to admit, he's quite an eyeful."

"Fine. He's an eyeful. Where does that leave me while you have your eye on him?"

She touched his cheek. "Right where you are now—the only male I'm interested in. I like my vamps with dark, smothering eyes and lethal size cocks."

"Our cocks are the same size," he said, clearly not appeased.

"Really? How do you know?"

She watched as his face flushed. "I...when I was younger, I measured."

She laughed. "Oh, college boy, you are a piece of work." She touched his cheek. "A sweet piece of work. And even if his cock is the same size as yours, he's not you."

He smiled at her.

She laid her head against his shoulder. Although the stranger was the most stunning man she'd ever seen, she was content with Serge. One lusty vamp in hand was definitely better than several in the bush—especially when the one in hand was handsome, exciting Serge Dumont.

"Well, as long as you don't start lusting after him," he said, somewhat mollified.

"When I have you lusting after me? Not a chance." She smiled up at him. "I don't think you realize how...very good your cock feels."

"If it feels half an good to you as your pus...vagina feels to me, then I know what you mean."

"It feels incredibly good and you know what, college boy? I think I'm going to like you talking dirty to me after all. Don't say vagina. Say pussy or cunt. That's what you want to say and it's what I want to hear from those sweet lips of yours. Makes me feel sexy to hear you talking about how good my pussy is."

"You'd better stop talking like that, or I'm going to need some more pussy. Right now."

She laughed and leaned up to brush her lips against his in a teasing kiss. "I didn't see either you or Mikhel. Were you there?"

"Ah,...yes."

"Ah huh. And who were you with?"

"Me? Ah,...no one important. No one you know."

"Did you enjoy yourself?"

"Enjoy? Well…ah…it's Family Fuck. It's not really a question of enjoying ones self, it's just…"

"What are you trying to hide from me now, college boy?"

"Hide? Nothing. I just don't want to talk about other women. For me now, Derri, there are no other women."

Even as he spoke she received a vague impression of him, naked and fully aroused on his knees on a bed behind a small, slender blond, thrusting almost violently into her while Mikhel eased his cock more gently in and out of the woman's mouth. Another of him and Mikhel lying on the bed with the same woman replaced that impression. In this one, the woman lay on her side, facing Serge who thrust into her pussy, while Mikhel, also on his side, thrust into her rear end.

Derri felt so much moisture between her legs that she shivered in the cold air. While she experienced an undeniable turn on watching Serge and Mikhel with one woman, she was also aware of a surge of annoyance that was strangely akin to jealousy.

She sucked in a breath and stared up at him. "You looked like you were enjoying yourself to me, college boy."

He shook his head, but remained silent.

"Is that what you two like? To double team a woman?"

"Derri."

"Is that what you think I'm going to let you and Mikhel do to me?"

"No! No! That was Family Fuck. Anything can and does happen then, but that doesn't mean that's what we do all the time. It's not like you think, Derri. You can't really think I want to share you with anyone…even Mikhel."

"Tell me, does Alex or some other vampire join you and Mikhel at these Family Fuck Fests? Do you always share your women?"

"No! Not always."

"But sometimes?"

"Yes! You obviously saw that we do...sometimes. If you come for the holidays, I promise no one else will touch you. You are mine and I don't plan on having every horny vamp in our community take a shot at you."

She shivered with revulsion at the very thought. "I should hope not, but—"

"Can't we just drop this subject?"

"All right—for now, but don't think for a moment we won't revisit this subject. Start walking and talking, college boy and don't leave anything out. I want to know what you expect me to get myself into by taking up with you. And while you're walking and talking, if you want to stop for an occasional caress and kiss, I won't complain, gray eyes."

# Chapter Eleven

တ

Just before they arrived at the cabin, Derri insisted on being put down. Although loath to let her out of his arms, Serge complied. He was surprised, but pleased, when she linked her fingers with his. He hoped that meant what he'd told her of his family and what she'd seen hadn't scared her off.

At the door of the cabin, she leaned up and pressed her sweet lips against his mouth in a quick, but explosive kiss that quickly stirred his passions. "Scared off? Not yet. I have plans for you tonight, college boy."

His breathing quickened as he looked down at her. "What plans?"

She outlined his parted lips with the tip of a finger. "Let's just say I hope you had a good night's sleep last night because you won't be getting much tonight."

Grinning, he opened the cabin door and stepped back. She brushed suggestively against him as she entered. He followed her and saw that Mikhel was no longer alone in the big living room. Alex, dressed in one of the fashionable suits and matching hats he was so fond of, was also there.

Damn. Alex was the last person he wanted to see. He cast a quick glance at Derri, expecting to find her staring at Alex, but after the first startled glance, she turned to look at him. He moved to stand behind her, not quite touching her, but close enough to make it clear to Alex that she belonged to him.

He watched through narrowed eyes as Alex swept off his hat. Those long, dark dreadlocks that women seemed to find so damned sexy fell onto his shoulders. Alex gave Derri a long, assessing look before he smiled. "Serge, introduce us," he kept his gaze on Derri as he spoke.

Serge fought off the sense of resentment he sometimes felt in Alex's company. The other vampire was so damned good looking and suave, other male vamps had a tendency to snatch up their current woman and head for the nearest exit on the rare occasions when Alex disdained to associate with his own kind. It wasn't so much that Alex overtly set out to take other vamps women. He never even seemed to make any real effort to lure another vamp's woman away. He just showed up, smiled, and spoke. Another thing about him women seemed to find so damned sexy was his voice. He always had more than his fair share of women at Family Fuck Fest. Small wonder none of the other vampire families in their communities ever invited Alex to their Fuck Fests.

Risking Derri's wrath by a show of possession, Serge slipped both arms around her waist and pressed close against her back. "This is Derri Morgan. Derri, this is Alex Madison."

Alex turned a slow smile on her. "Ms. Morgan. Aleksei Lacey Madison at your service ma'am." Alex crossed the room.

He narrowed his gaze. If he dared try that tired old southern crap on Derri...

Alex lifted her right hand to his mouth and kissed the back of it.

Serge sensed the stir of excitement in Derri and gritted his teeth. He resisted the urge to pull Derri away and deck Alex.

Alex looked into Derri's eyes, still smiling. "I must tell you, it is an absolute pleasure to meet you."

"Same here," she said and Serge was pleased not to hear or feel any further pleasure in her, although he was aware that she was intrigued to meet Alex after having seen him in his memories.

"What brings you here, Alex?" he asked coldly.

Mikhel, who hadn't spoken before, answered. "I asked him to come."

"Why?" He could feel Derri's surprise and knew she thought him ungracious. *You don't understand, Derri. I'll explain it to you later.*

*You'd better.*

"While you were gone I got an irate call from Ralph Mariono."

Derri stirred and turned to glance briefly up at him, a question in her dark eyes. *Serge? Just how much are you withholding from me?*

*I'll tell you about it, later,* he promised. He turned his gaze to Mikhel and shrugged. "So?"

Mikhel's gaze flicked slightly. "I think things will happen soon."

"And you think we can't handle it?" he asked, annoyed that Mikhel might not think him capable of protecting the woman he loved.

"I know you and I can handle it—together. However, I have to leave."

"Why? What's wrong?"

"I don't know. Mother called and said I should come home immediately."

He felt Mikhel's unease. "Is everything okay with Erica?"

"Physically? Yes, but mother says there's a problem I need to come home and deal with. Aleksei will stand with you while I'm gone."

He felt Derri's confusion and fear. He gave her a gentle squeeze and brushed his lips against the back of her neck. "Don't worry, Derri. I will not allow anyone to hurt you."

She turned to look at him. "I know that," she said softly. She pulled against his arms and he reluctantly released her. She walked over to Mikhel, whose dark eyes were hooded. "I hope everything will be all right with your Erica."

Serge watched as Mikhel smiled and engulfed her in a brief embrace. He felt her surprise when, as she started to pull

142

away, Mikhel jerked her back against him, bent his head and claimed her lips in a long, hungry kiss that forced her mouth open and gave him access to her tongue.

Through her shock, Serge could sense her becoming aroused by the feel of Mikhel's cock hardening against her. Although she shoved against Mikhel's shoulders, he continued to devour her lips.

Sensing her resistance dwindling, Serge lost his temper. When Mikhel slid his hand down to her behind and ground his hips against her, he exploded. "Mikhel! Have you lost your mind?" He rushed across the room to grab Mikhel by the back of his neck. "Damn you, let her go!"

He felt the long, last suck Mikhel gave her tongue before he lifted his head and finally released her. Mikhel knocked his hand aside and spun around to face him. "Back off, Serge."

"Back off?" He stared at Mikhel, who stared back, his eyes glowing, his incisors bared. About to bare his own incisors, he noted, for the first time, the fine line of moisture above Mikhel's lip. "What the hell is wrong with you?"

Derri clutched his arm and tried to tug him away from Mikhel. He felt her fear for him. "Let it go, Serge. Please. It's okay. It was just a kiss."

But he knew something was definitely wrong. He'd worry about what was wrong with Mikhel after he calmed Derri's fear for him. He turned to her with a forced smile. "It's all right, Derri."

"You're sure?"

He nodded, although he wasn't sure. He'd never seen Mikhel so confrontational—at least not with him. "Yes. Don't worry."

She leaned up and kissed him on the corner of his mouth. *It didn't mean anything to me, college boy. Not really. It was just a physical response.*

His smile this time was genuine. He gave her a brief hug and kiss. *When I join you upstairs, I'll give you something that does mean something to you.*

*That's what I'm counting on, gray eyes.* "I think I'll head upstairs. Good-bye Mikhel."

He tensed as he waited for Mikhel's response. If he tried to kiss her again…but he simply nodded. "I…I didn't intend…good-bye, Derri."

When she turned to look at Alex, Serge was aware of her pulse quickening. "It was nice to meet you."

Alex bowed his head. "I assure you, the pleasure was all mine," he said.

Casting his eyes ceiling ward, Serge bit his lip and held onto his tongue. Alex had come to help, not steal his woman. Still, as soon as Derri disappeared up the stairs, he looked at Alex through a narrowed gaze. "Let's understand each other Alex, she is mine and I intend to keep her."

Alex smiled slightly, raising a brow. "Then you have nothing to worry about, Serge, have you?"

He flashed across the room intent on grabbing the other man by the throat, but Mikhel moved quickly, intercepting him before he was halfway to his target, pushing him back. "Serge, get a grip on your emotions or you won't be any good to her as a protector."

He threw up his hands, backing away, his eyes glowing. "You're telling me to get a grip? That's rich. What the hell was that with Derri?"

Mikhel shrugged, looking weary. "I…I don't know. I'm sorry. Apologize to her for me, will you?"

He swallowed his rage with difficulty. "Are you all right, Mik?"

"Yes, I'm just feeling a little…strange."

"Strange how?"

"Don't worry about things of which you know very little or nothing, pup," Alex said suddenly.

Mikhel swung around and leveled a finger at him. "You're not going to be much help if you're going to goad him, Aleksei."

"Goad him? I've barely said two words to the young pup."

Serge took a deep breath and told himself he would not allow Alex to goad him into a fight he knew he couldn't win. Alex had an annoying habit of calling everyone younger than himself a pup when he wanted to be insulting. For the life of him, he couldn't understand how or why Mikhel valued the other vamp's friendship or why their mother always seemed so pleased to see him when he arrived without notice or an invitation.

"Aleksei, if this is the way you're going to behave," Mikhel began coolly.

Alex's face tightened suddenly and his blue eyes darkened, all traces of amusement vanishing from his face. "A slight lapse," he said, shrugging. "It won't happen again. I am here to take care of business. You go do what you need to do, Mikey and I will stand with the pup here."

Mikhel wasn't big on nicknames. He barely tolerated being called Mik by Serge and sometimes Katie. But only Alex could get away with calling him Mikey. Still, Serge saw Mikhel's gaze narrow and for a moment, he looked as if he'd fly at Alex.

He tensed. Although Mikhel was strong, there was no way he could prevail over Alex. Even if he and Mikhel double-teamed Alex, there was very little likelihood of their succeeding. The thought of Derri watching he and Mikhel get their asses kicked, held little appeal. Still, there was no question but that he would back up Mikhel.

To his relief, Alex defused the situation by suddenly engulfing Mikhel in a bear hug and kissing his hair. "It'll be all right, Mikey. What lies ahead of you will not be easy, but you will be all right," he promised. "I am here to help in anyway I can."

Watching, Serge was struck by how much like a big brother Alex suddenly seemed. Just for a moment, he envied the obvious affection between the other two. As long as he could remember, Mikhel had always been there for him. Now when Mikhel needed someone to be there for him, he wanted to be that someone. Instead, there was Alex, the prefect, quintessential vampire offering the comfort and assurance Mikhel had always offered him.

Alex released Mikhel and turned to face him, a small mocking smile on his face. "Feeling a little left out? Not to worry. Mikhel is still your big, indestructible brother. If you want a hug, pup, I have one with your name on it," he offered.

Serge felt his face flushing. Sometimes he almost hated the overconfident bastard. "You stay away from Derri. That's all I need from you."

"Not a problem. Oh, I'll admit that your Derri seems to have a lot of fire and passion. I can always tell that about a woman—just by looking at her. But you need not worry," he said with that underlying I'm-superior-to-youness in his voice that Serge hated.

"After all, she's a rather pretty woman, isn't she?"

Serge stared at him. He had a way of making pretty said like a dirty word. "As a matter of fact, she's very pretty...beautiful, in fact."

"Yes, well, no one's perfect. Not to down her because she certainly has her charms, but she is a little on the skinny side too. No offense."

Derri, with her curvaceous, voluptuous body and large breasts was a far cry from being skinny, but it suited Serge just fine to have Alex view her as skinny. "She suits me," he said curtly.

146

"Fine. Then we won't have any problems protecting her together?"

He slowly shook his head. In a fight, Alex was accurate, vicious, and deadly. If a full-blood was coming after Derri, it would be as well to have a back up who took no prisoners first and felt very little need to ask questions—ever. "No," he said.

Mikhel's dark gaze moved swiftly between the two of them before he nodded. "Good. I'll be leaving shortly, so let's discuss our plans."

\* \* \* \* \*

Derri undressed and slid into the Jacuzzi tub in the master bedroom. Closing her eyes, she allowed her thoughts to turn toward Serge. Allowed? She grimaced and admitted it wasn't really a conscious choice. Although she had no intentions of getting serious with him, it was kind of heady to have such a handsome, mysterious man so madly and vocally in love with her. And he was very sweet, not to mention a fantastic lover.

She thought of Mikhel and frowned. It was just as well he was going home to his Erica. Obviously, he needed to be laid rather badly. He'd been scary there for a few moments. Imagine kissing her like that in front of Serge. She shook her head and let her thoughts drift back to Serge. She smiled.

She had started to doze when she heard the bathroom door open. She looked up. Serge, naked and aroused, came into the room. He carried a tray with a bottle of wine and a vase of roses. He put the roses at the end of the Jacuzzi and kneeling, put the tray on the side of the tub.

"How are you feeling?" he asked.

She looked at him, noted his erect cock, and shivered. "Fine." She frowned. "How is Mikhel?"

He shook his head. "I don't know. I've never seen him like that." He sighed, his eyes darkening. "I think he might be…sick."

"I thought you said you guys didn't get sick."

"We don't…at least not…physically sick."

"Then what does that leave?"

"I don't know," he admitted.

"You're worried about him."

He nodded. "Mikhel has always seemed so…big, strong, and in perfect control. I don't know what's happening to him. But he's going home. Mother will know what to do and Erica will be there to give him all the comfort he needs or wants." He half filled the glass and offered it to her. "I'm hoping you'll do the same for me."

Smiling, she took it and sipped its contents. "What are we celebrating, gray eyes?"

"Love."

"Love?" She leaned forward and kissed him lightly. "Heady stuff that love."

"Very heady." He inclined his head toward the glass. "Do you like it?"

She nodded, took another few sips, and put it back on the tray. "Roses, champagne, sweet kisses, and incredible sex. A woman could get used to this very easily." She closed her eyes again and lay back against the cushioned pillow behind her neck and shoulders.

"Good."

Several moments of silence ensued during which she was aware that they were both content to just be in each other's company. Talking didn't seem necessary. Still…*This is nice.*

*Very nice,* he agreed. *But I know something nicer still.*

Before she could decide if she were up to making love again so soon, she felt his big hands lifting one of her feet out of the water. She knew what he wanted and did her best to shield her thoughts from him. If he wanted to get a little freaky, she'd just have to pretend she found it arousing.

The feel of his warm lips kissing and nibbling at her toes, felt...nice. Hmm. Maybe she wasn't going to have to pretend after all. His lips brushed against the sole of her foot and her heartbeat increased. Hell, that was more than nice. He kissed his way up her leg, planting a moist, heated kiss just behind her knee before he gently lowered her left foot and raised her right one.

By the time he'd kissed a slow, eager path up her leg to that spot behind her right knee, her cunt had began to ache. God, she wanted him. Breathing deeply, she opened her eyes. He stood at the end of the Jacuzzi tub, eyes glowing, cock fully and gloriously erect.

"The water's perfect. Why don't you join me?" she suggested.

"I thought you'd never ask." He moved so quickly, that she'd barely had time to take a deep breath before he'd lifted her, slid his body into the tub, and settled her against his hard warmth.

She could feel his cock, hard and hot against her behind as he cupped his hands over her breasts and brushed his lips against her neck. That was nice, but she wanted more. She wiggled her rear end against him. "How about giving a girl a little cock to tide her over until tonight, college boy?"

His hands tightened on her breasts, almost hurting her. "Are you sure?"

"I'm very sure."

He lifted her with one hand against the small of her back, lined his cock with her entrance, and slowly pushed into her. She closed her eyes and moaned as his hard warmth leisurely, but steadily filled every inch of her moist pussy. Hot damn, he felt so good inside her.

He cupped one hand over her breasts, which left one hand free to stroke and caress her clit as he began to move deep inside her. Oh, God! His cock was so damn good. Moaning, and already close to coming, she turned her head, blindly seeking his mouth. He lowered his head, allowing their lips to meet in a long, greedy kiss. She could feel him fighting against his natural inclination to repeatedly shove his cock up into her.

His consideration for her feelings and needs, even while making love, touched her. It made her more determined to make sure he was thoroughly satisfied before she thought of her own pleasure. She wiggled her behind and thrust down against him. He pushed back, still gently, and they kept it up until they found the prefect rhythm. When they had, they settled down to enjoy a slow, scrumptious fuck.

She tried to hold back until he came, but she'd never had a man who could stay so hard so long. She couldn't control her need for him or her desire.

*It's all right,* he assured her. *Let yourself go. Let it happen, sweetheart. Come for me. I love it when you come all over my cock.*

The words, combined with the awesome physical sensations radiating through her were too much. She moaned, dug her short nails into the sides of his legs and happily surrendered to the series of endless, delectable shivers that shook her body, obliterating everything except the sweet delight exploding between them.

When she calmed down, Serge, still hard and buried deep inside her, held her, kissing her along the side of her neck. "Are you all right?"

She turned her face against his shoulder. "I've never been better, college boy. If you keep this up, I'm going to be hard pressed to leave you."

"That's the idea, sweetheart," he whispered, licking at her neck.

She laid for a moment, breathing in the faint smell of cologne remaining on his skin, her heart thumping with the enormity of what she was contemplating. Then, her decision made, she thrust her satisfied pussy against his cock until he shuddered and began moving in her again.

She felt his climax building in him. She sucked in a breath. Now was the perfect time to take the plunge she suddenly knew she couldn't resist—didn't want to resist. *Serge,* she said his name softly and tilted her neck.

She felt the rush of emotion filling him as he realized what she was offering him. When he began to come, his incisors pierced the soft skin of her neck. His joy, as the first drops of her blood filled his mouth, was overshadowed by her own joy at the knowledge that while he was filling her with his seed, she was filling him with her blood. Her pussy convulsed and shuddered around his cock, as yet another orgasm hit her. Moving together as one, they came, clinging to each other.

Even after they'd both stopped coming, he continued to drink her blood. Feeling the blood rushing out of her body and into his mouth, she experienced a feeling of ecstasy. Finally, he withdrew his incisors from her neck, licked and kissed the two small wounds, and collapsed back against the padded rim of the tub, his breathing deep and almost painful.

Still impaled on him, she felt weak yet strangely powerful. She reached a hand between their legs to cup his balls. He made a small sound of protest and slowly withdrew his cock from her body.

Free to move, she turned so that her breasts now brushed his chest. She looked up at him. His eyes still glowed and his incisors were visible. She saw her blood on his teeth and lips.

"Got a little carried away there, didn't you, college boy? I need some of my own blood in my veins to live, you know."

She watched him flush. "I'm sorry. I know I took more than I should have, but Derri, your blood is like none I've ever tasted. It's hot, sweet, and completely intoxicating. I feel drunk."

"And I feel nearly drained," she complained, without any real heat.

"I'm sorry. Did I frighten you?"

"No," she admitted. "I knew you wouldn't hurt me."

"I'd rather die than hurt you," he said.

Somehow, the words, which she'd have considered a ridiculous line from any other man, struck a chord in her. She stretched up and kissed him, tasting her blood on his lips. "I think I'll keep you for awhile," she teased, stroking his sides.

"What about Mikhel?"

"What about him?" she asked.

"You're not looking for a chance to sleep with him?"

"Why should I waste time worrying about another woman's man, when I have you?"

His eyes gleamed with satisfaction.

Watching him, she frowned. Did she have him? She suddenly realized that she'd never actually asked him if there was another woman in his life. "There isn't any Erica in your life? Is there?"

"No. You're the only woman in my life."

"Ah huh. Look, you can't really expect me to believe that with your sexual appetite you don't have a woman or several women in your life."

"I do expect you to believe it because it's true," he told her coolly. "I admit I was seeing someone a couple of months ago, but once I saw you, that was over."

She laid her cheek against his shoulder. "And she was okay with that?"

"She had no choice but to be okay with it. When it's over, it's over."

The underlying ruthless in that statement gave her pause and strengthened her resolve not to let her heart become involved with him. She was not about to be on the receiving end of one of his Dear Derri, it's over speeches.

"It won't be that way between us," he said heatedly. "When are you going to realize that I'm in love with you?"

She kissed his shoulder. "I can't be the first woman you've imagined yourself in love with, college boy."

He lifted her chin and glared down at her. "It's not my imagination. You know that. You can feel it whether or not you're ready to admit it. And yes you are the first and the only woman I've ever been in love with."

She stared up into his dark, glowering gaze. "I just don't want to be tossed aside when you're finished with me."

"I'm never going to be finished with you, so you need have no fear of being tossed aside for any other woman. You are my woman—forever."

She certainly couldn't deny the fact that she was his woman for the moment—and very happy to be so. Forever was another story. Still it was sounding less and less outrageous. Not that she was ready to admit that to him. This was all still too new and rather frightening. Nevertheless, there was an undeniable thrill attached to being the one true love of a handsome, horny vampire.

Maneuvering her body so that his semi-hard cock lay between her thighs, brushing against her damp mound, she kissed him. His lips eagerly met hers and she sighed and lost herself in his kisses. She'd worry about the implications of taking on a vampire lover later. For now, she just wanted to enjoy being with a man she found more fascinating than any man she'd ever met. A man moreover, who she knew for a certain loved her with an all-consuming passion. Hell, she wasn't sure what more a woman could possibly ask from life.

She gave herself a mental shake. *Don't get crazy, Derri. This is sex. Sex with a capital S, but still just sex.*

*It's way more than sex,* he countered, stroking a hand down her shoulders and back. *And you know it. Admit it. Learn to deal with it.*

*In your dreams, college boy,* she said, settling herself against his shoulder.

"Hey, don't go to sleep," he said. "This tub is getting a little uncomfortable. Let's dry off and go to bed."

"In the middle of the day?" She thought of the tall, dark, handsome vampire on the floor below. She knew without being told that he was a full-blood. For all she knew he'd heard every sigh, moan, and groan they'd exchanged while they made love. Instead of embarrassing her, the thought provided an unexpected thrill. It might be worth going to Boston with Serge just to see one of the Dumonts' Family Fuck Fest up close and personal.

"I'm starving," she said suddenly. "Let's go downstairs and get something to eat."

He lifted her out of the tub, sat her on her feet, and got out himself. She stood with her eyes closed, a smile on her face as he slowly rubbed the towel along her body.

When it was her turn to dry him off, she started at his chest and worked her way down his hard abs. She stopped at the top of the dark triangle of hair on his groin, went down on her knees, and dried his feet. The breath caught in her throat and her heart began to thump as she moved up his leg and encountered his cock, which was fully erect again.

She bit her lip, remembering the feel and taste of his cock and seed in her mouth. Still kneeling, she raised her head and met his dark gaze. As they stared at each other, his eyes began to glow and he bared his incisors. She felt the surge of lust that shot through him. Felt it and matched it.

She placed the folded towel under her knees, gripped his thighs, leaned forward, and kissed the tip of his cock. He shuddered as she slowly closed her eager lips over him. Hmm. Oh, that was nice. His cock was delicious both in her pussy and her mouth.

He sucked in a breath and gently urged his hips forward sending several more inches into her mouth. She closed her eyes, leaned closer, swallowing even more of him and eagerly began to suck the sweet, hot dick filling her mouth. Oh, damn, but that was nice.

Although she made a conscious effort to suck slowly, hoping to prolong the pleasure they both felt, he quickly reached the point of orgasm. He moaned softly, closed his hands in her hair, and came in several hot torrents.

Swallowing quickly and greedily, she kept her mouth over his dick. Knowing she was ingesting his blood along with his seed gave her an extra charge. Cupping his balls in her hand, she continued sucking until he'd pumped the last few drops of his seed down her throat.

Only then did she rise, lick her lips, and smile at him. "Did you like that college boy?"

He wrapped his arms around her and buried his face against her neck, his whole body shaking. "Oh, damn, I love you."

She laughed and rubbed her body against him. "You have the most sumptuous cock and come. I could develop quite a taste for both."

He lifted his head to look at her. "Yeah? Well, feel free to suck and taste them anytime you like."

She laughed again. "Delicious though they are, I'm still hungry."

"Okay. Let's go out to eat. There's a nice restaurant thirty miles up the road where we can eat and dance. I want to dance with you."

She nodded. "I think I'd like that, college boy."

He shook his head. "You know, Derri, I think I'm losing it."

"Why?

"Because gray eyes and college boy are actually beginning to sound like endearments," he told her.

"What makes you think they're not?" she demanded in a soft suggestive voice.

"Don't tease, Derri. You know how I feel. It's not fair to tease."

"Don't whine, my gray eyed college boy. It's unbecoming in a big, handsome vampire." She gave his cock a gentle squeeze. "Besides, who says I'm teasing?"

She eased from his embrace and walked away. "Let's get dressed and go eat," she called over her shoulder.

She felt his confusion as he followed her. Good. Judging by some of the impressions she'd received as they'd made love, he hadn't always been kind or particularly considerate to his women. It would do him good to see how being treated in an insensitive manner by a lover felt.

# Chapter Twelve

As they followed the waiter to their table in the restaurant an hour and a half later, Derri was very aware that nearly every female head in the room was turned in Serge's direction. She saw envy in more than one pair of eyes. What effect was so much feminine admiration having on him?

"None," he told her as they were seated and handed menus. "My days of womanizing are over. As the saying goes, I only have eyes for you."

"Yeah, well, stay out of my head, college boy," she snapped.

He grinned at her. "Admit it, sweetheart, you kind of like that we share more than just great sex. We share each other's thoughts and feelings."

She sure liked having him call her sweetheart. "Stay out of my head," she said quickly, hoping he hadn't picked up on that last thought.

"You knew I wanted you to suck my cock and you did."

"Serge! Keep your voice down," she said, feeling her cheeks burn at the thought that the other diners might have heard what he'd said.

"And I knew you wanted to swallow more than just my seed, so I made a conscious effort to expel more blood than usual when I came in your sweet mouth," he said softly.

She glared at him, fully aware that he was enjoying her discomfort. "Keep it up, college boy and you'll be sleeping alone tonight," she threatened.

He leaned forward, captured both her hands in his, lifted them to his mouth, and planted a warm kiss in the palm of each hand.

Mollified despite herself, she smiled at him. "Oh, you are smooth and sweet, college boy."

The waiter approached and they both ordered iced tea. They sipped in silence while they studied the menu. After their orders were placed, she sat back against her chair, staring at him.

He wore almost all black again—a custom made black suit and shirt. His silk tie was black with small gray dots, the color of his eyes, placed at strategic intervals. Damn, but he was one handsome hunk.

"Tell me about the women in your life, Serge."

He sighed. "Which ones?"

"All of them."

"There's been a lot, Derri."

"Too many to remember?"

His cheeks reddened and she knew he had forgotten some of the women he'd bedded.

"Don't look at me like that, Derri. I was young and horny and women threw themselves at me. It's not all my fault. And I never lied to any of them. They all knew I had no real interest in them beyond sex."

She held up a hand, deciding she didn't want to hear any of the sordid details. "Stop. You're sounding more and more like a first class heel, Serge."

"I never said I wasn't, but please don't hold my past against me. I didn't know you were out there waiting for me."

"I wasn't waiting for you," she said, aware that the feeling very akin to jealousy was forming in her gut again. "I told you what I want out of this relationship. That hasn't changed."

He shook his head and looked away from her. "Well, I want more—a lot more." He turned his gaze back to hers. "And I usually get what I want, Derri. I think you should know that."

"And I think you should know that I control my own life and my own destiny, Serge. I know you must have some connection with that medium on Chestnut Street in Philly."

He glanced quickly away and she knew he was trying to shield his thoughts from her. After a moment, he sighed, and brought his gaze back to hers. "She's my sister."

Well, that explained what she'd been doing at the Dumont Family Fuck Off. "Your sister is a fortune teller and a...you know what?"

He nodded. "Yes, well, she's a latent."

"She has the..." she broke off and stared at him. "Oh, God, you're Chandler Raven's friend."

"Yes," he admitted.

"He gave you the talismans...both of them."

"Yes."

She took a deep breath and leveled a finger at him. "I am warning you, Serge, don't you dare try to use them on me. If I'm foolish enough to fall for a womanizing vamp, I'll do it on my own. You promise me, Serge—now or stay the hell away from me."

"I haven't followed the ritual, Derri and I promise I'll try not to."

Derri knew there were rituals attached to both of the talisman. She knew the golden figurine, which her friend Cassy had owned, had required the female possessor to stroke the tiny male buttocks until the cock was exposed. The possessor was then supposed to place the small shaft inside herself to release the power of the talisman—something Cassy had never done. Nor would she.

The Ebony Venus required the male in possession of it to stoke the bigger statuette until an opening appeared in the vaginal area. The thought of Serge trying to get his huge shaft in the resulting opening was laughable. Still. "You'll try? What's with this try crap?"

"I love you," he said through his teeth. "And if I have to sell my damned soul to keep you, I will. You think I can let you go now that I know what it's like?"

"What what's like?"

"Bloodlust," he said simply, projecting a series of images and feelings at her that overwhelmed her senses. Feelings of love, lust, bliss, the sheer joy at being with her, an insatiable need for her company, her happiness, and her body, flowed over her like a heavenly wave.

She gasped and bit her lip, speechless at the magnitude of the feelings, needs, and sensations she'd just experienced through him.

"You are the one woman...the only woman who is my perfect mate...the only woman who spawns a lust, desire, need, and love, not just for blood, but for sex with you only. You are my bloodlust and I need to be yours."

"Oh...Serge..." she whispered his name.

"How can you expect me to give that up without a fight?" he asked in a voice that pleaded for her understanding.

She sighed and shook her head. "Serge, I want to fall for you or not on my own. I don't want to be coerced."

He took a deep breath. "It may be a little late. When I touched the talisman Cassy had, I felt a distinct and unmistakable electrical charge. I'm betting you felt one too when you held it."

"I did. So you're telling me I have no choice?"

"No. I'm telling you you're my bloodlust. Our both having held the talisman is what created the extra bond between us. It's why we can hear each other's thoughts – but only because we were meant to be together anyway."

She wanted to dismiss his assertion as nonsense, but she wasn't so sure anymore. There had to be a reason they could get into each other's heads.

Their meals arrived. She had a large salad with low calorie dressing while he'd chosen a huge stake so rare that just looking at it nearly turned her stomach. "Oh, that's practically raw, Serge!"

He grinned at her. "It's delicious. Would you like to try some?"

"No!"

"Don't knock it until you've tried it."

"I hope you don't eat all your food raw," she said, shuddering.

He raised a brow. "I have sharp teeth," he told her, his eyes dancing with amusement.

She laughed. "Oh, you are so cute, college boy."

"Why thank you, sweetheart. You're pretty cute yourself."

She rolled her eyes and ate in silence.

After finishing their dessert, they went to the lounge to dance. He held her close with both arms wrapped around her body. *I love you.*

She lifted her head from his shoulder and smiled up at him. At that moment, feeling the full depth of his need for her, she almost felt as if she loved him too.

*That's enough for now.* He bent his head and brushed a soft, tender kiss against her parted lips.

Still smiling, she pressed her cheek against his shoulder. She felt warm, safe, and happy—happier than she'd ever remembered feeling.

"It's that way for me too, sweetheart," he whispered.

Later that night, lying naked in his arms in bed, she found sleep elusive. She knew she was close to the point when she'd find giving him up impossible. Yet, how could she have a real relationship with a vampire? What future did falling for him hold?

He brushed his lips against the back of her neck and tightened his arms around her. "What's wrong?"

"Nothing."

"You want to try again?"

She sighed and turned in his arms so that she lay with her face against his shoulder. "Tell me about your childhood and your family, Serge."

"What do you want to know?"

"Everything. How does a vampire raise her children?"

"Pretty much like any other mother. We had house rules we had to follow. We had an allowance, granted it was more generous than most kids receive, but then my parents have a lot of money."

"How much is a lot?"

"A lot. My mother had lots of money before she married my father and my father was a renowned architect who commanded huge fees before he retired. So we've always had money."

"What about your mother?"

"What about her?"

"She's what you call a full-blood?"

"Yes, but don't get the wrong idea about her. She's not some vicious killer."

"But she's killed before?"

"She's nearly four hundred years old," he said, sounding defensive. "She's done what she had to in order to survive. No more, no less."

"And does she have to have blood to live?"

She felt his reluctance to answer the question. There was almost a resentment that she had asked it emanating from him.

"Yes," he finally admitted. "But none of the rest of us do." He stroked a hand over her shoulders. "Please don't hold that against her. She didn't choose to become a vampire. Once it was forced on her, she had as much right to live as anyone else. She's a loving mother and wife and she loves us with all her heart and we love her."

She could feel his love and affection for his mother. "I'm not judging her, Serge, but if she has to go around killing other people to survive—"

"Who said anything about her killing people to survive? As far as I know she hasn't killed anyone for a very long time."

"Then how does she survive?"

"It's a long story, Derri."

"The night is young and I'm listening."

"It's not something I want to talk about."

"Why not?"

"You wouldn't understand...not yet. Please, sweetheart, leave it for now?"

The sweetheart left her wanting to melt. "All right. I'll reserve my judgment until we meet."

"Good. You'll like her."

She rubbed her cheek against his shoulder. She wasn't so sure about that, but she'd play it by ear.

"So, will you come to Boston for Christmas?"

"We'll see, Serge. Now tell me about the North Philly Diamonds."

She immediately sensed a spirit of excitement coming from him. "They're a basketball team of young guys from North Philly ranging in age from 13-17. And Derri, a couple of the guys have real potential. I know they're going to make it to the pros and I'll be able to say I knew them when."

"And you sponsor them?'

He shrugged. "It's not a big deal. They have so little and we have so much. I like basketball, I like Philly, and it's something I enjoy doing."

"Serge, that's so sweet."

"What?" he asked, surprise in his voice.

"You're providing scholarships for several of them who don't have enough skill to earn sports scholarships."

"Who told you that?"

He sounded defensive and annoyed. Clearly he didn't want her to know. "No one told me. This reading thoughts and feelings work both ways you know."

"It's not a big deal, Derri. All they need is a chance…and to know that someone believes in them."

"And you do."

"Yes, I do." He paused. "Would you like to…come to a couple of games and meet them?"

"Ah…yes, sure." She smiled. It seemed her college boy had the proverbial heart of gold. She admired men who were involved in community service projects, as Serge so clearly was. That he wanted no accolades, endeared him her all the more. "You're sweet and there's more to you than meets the eye. I want to get to know you, Serge. All of you."

"We're not just talking about my cock. Are we?"

"No! I said all of you, didn't I?"

"Yes." He tightened his arms around her and she could feel his excitement. "I'll be good to you, sweetheart. I promise."

"I think I know that." She settled against his shoulder. "Serge, you never told me what your degree was in."

"Social work," he said after a long pause. "Go ahead…laugh. I'm used to it."

"That explains it," she said smiling.

"Explains what?"

She stretched up to pepper his lips with kisses. "Why you're such a loving, caring vamp," she said snuggling against him again.

"So tell me why you're in security instead of social work."

She felt the turmoil in him. "I worked as a social worker briefly when I graduated from college."

"What happened?"

He sighed and took a deep breath. "There was this father with two young kids. We received a report of abuse. I investigated and was able to substantiate the allegations of abuse. I suggested immediately removing the children from the house. My supervisor intervened and said my solution to the physical abuse was overkill. He insisted that it was important to keep the family together. So we arranged counseling and intensive supervision. I didn't agree but I was overruled. After the fourth counseling session, the bastard went home and beat both kids to death."

Her eyes filled with tears as she felt his pain and rage. "Oh, Serge. That must have been awful." She stroked his chest. "And you got frustrated and left the field?"

"I would have stayed, but after I beat the hell out of my supervisor, I was asked to resign or face prosecution."

She brushed her lips against his chest. "I'm sorry," she said softly.

"Why?"

"I know you still miss it."

"Sometimes I do," he admitted, "But I still do what I can."

"You're very sweet, college boy."

She drifted to sleep to the sound of his whispered love words in her head.

\* \* \* \* \*

Derri woke first the next morning and lay watching Serge asleep. She reached out a hand and touched his cheek. He sighed softly and smiled. She smiled too. He felt like such a part of her life. Yet, five days earlier, she hadn't even known he existed. Now, she couldn't imagine what her life was going to be like once it was over between them.

How would she ever be content with an ordinary, normal man after having been loved by Serge Dumont, latent vampire? She sucked in a deep breath. The answer was simple—she wouldn't. Not only did they share an incredible physical desire for each other, but they shared a common need to spend part of their lives and financial resources in community service projects. In nearly every way that mattered, he felt like a perfect match for her. So where did that leave her and her plans for the future?

She slipped from the bed, being careful not to pull the cover from Serge's nude body. She moved across the carpeted floor to the balcony. The view before her was breathtaking. She saw evidence of the remnants of frost on the trees and grass. If it weren't so cold, it would be a perfect day for a picnic with her tall, dark, and handsome gray-eyed college boy.

She caught the suggestion of movement from the corner of one eye and turned her head. On ground level, Alex stood to one side of the cabin with a perfect view of her nude body. He was dressed in a dark gray suit with a matching hat that provided a perfect frame for his handsome face. With his long dreads hanging down onto his shoulders, he was stunning and so completely…sensual.

Despite herself, Derri felt her heart thump and moisture pool between her legs. God, almighty, but he was almost hot enough to make a woman forget the man she loved. The man she loved? Realizing the implication of her thoughts, she backed quickly away from the window and scampered back to bed. She needed her man.

She slipped under the cover and pressed her body close to Serge's. She reached down and gently closed her fingers around his semi-erect shaft. He stirred slightly and murmured softly in his sleep. Without waiting to see if he would awaken on his own, she pushed the cover back, straddled his body, and slowly began to lower herself onto his thickening shaft.

His eyes snapped opened and he stared up at her with a look of surprise on his face. "Derri? What are you doing?"

She took a deep breath and shoved her hips down, until she and Serge were groin to groin and he was buried deep inside her no longer aching passage. "After all the women you've had, college boy, one would think you'd know when you were being taking advantage of," she told him as she slowly began to thrust herself up and down on his cock.

Caught off guard and incredibly turned on by what she was doing to him, she knew what was about to happen. When he shuddered helplessly and then swore softly, she laid her body flat on top of his, as he ejaculated into her.

"Shit!" he groaned, stroking his hands down her back when he'd regained his breath. "I'm sorry, sweetheart."

She laughed and ground herself against him. "Hmm. Pussy too good for you, huh? Make you lose control and wanna holler?"

He laughed, but she could sense his disgust with himself.

"It's all right, college boy," she told him, still rotating her hips against his. "You're still hard and you're still inside me. Make it up to me."

Holding her close, he rolled them over until he was lying on top of her. He lifted his weight onto his extended arms and began thrusting into her. His hard, rapid strokes sent chills of pain and pleasure all through her. In a manner of moments, she was almost robbed of her ability to breathe. He showered her face, neck, and breasts with warm, hungry kisses as he probed the depths of her pussy with his hard, hot cock.

Oh, God. How could anything that hurt so much feel so good at the same time? He bent his head and closed his lips over her right breast and began sucking her. Her climax hit with bruising and almost frightening force, shattering any lingering doubts she had about her ability to give him up.

"That's the idea," he told her, lowering his weight onto her body. "You are mine. You're not supposed to be able to give me up."

Still trembling, she clung to him. "Hold me, college boy, and never let me go."

"Never." He rolled them over so that he lay flat on his back with her sprawled across his body.

"Derri, why can't you just accept that you are mine and I have no intentions of letting you go?"

"Serge, I'm a black woman who fully intends to marry a black man."

"Why?"

"Why? Because I'm black."

"So why does it follow that you have to marry a man you don't love just because he's black?"

"You don't understand, Serge."

He stroked her shoulders. "Okay. Explain it to me."

She shook her head. "Can't we just leave it for now?"

"Fine—for now."

"Serge, let's just enjoy each other and what we have now. Let the future take care of itself. Okay?"

"Okay…as long as our future is together."

Holding each other and exchanging tender kisses devoid of passion, they fell back to sleep.

# Chapter Thirteen

ഇ

When they woke again, they showered together, and dressed. Ignoring the knowing look in Alex's eyes, they left the cabin to have lunch out.

After lunch, they drove along the back roads of the Pocono Mountains for several hours. Sometimes they talked. She told him how she hated growing up an only child with no older siblings to look up to and no younger ones to look out for. "You're very fortunate to have a brother and a sister, college boy."

"Yes," he agreed, his voice warm. "I wouldn't trade either one of them for love or money."

Sometimes they enjoyed long periods of silence when they just basked in their feelings for each other. Derri, who had never imagined she could feel so strongly about a man she'd known for such a short time, felt a little overwhelmed by what was happening between her and Serge.

When they passed a strip mall, he stopped and bought her a dozen roses. "Serge, you don't have to keep buying me roses," she protested.

He stopped in the parking lot near his SUV and looked down at her. "You'd rather something else? Like jewelry? Maybe a ring?"

"A ring?"

"Yes. Nothing fancy...gold...maybe a diamond...just a little something you could wear on the third finger of your left hand. Would you like one of those, sweetheart?"

She licked her lips and shivered in the cold air. "Serge...it's way to soon for talk like that."

He bent his head and gently brushed his lips against her mouth. "Not for me it isn't. I knew the first time I saw you I'd want you forever."

She leaned into him and wrapped her arms around him. "It's cold out here."

He kissed her again and helped her inside the SUV before getting back in the driver's side.

She waited until he was back on the road before she spoke again. "When was that?"

"When I first saw you?"

"Yes."

"It was after your boss contacted Mikhel about security for you back in October. I shadowed you for several weeks to get an idea of your routine and to see if I could detect anyone else shadowing you."

"Several weeks? Come on, Serge."

"Several weeks. I was there when you went to the Fifth Street Soup Kitchen, the shelter on Ridge Avenue, and the Boone School for Girls. But the first time I saw you was at the spa. You had on those baggy sweats you're so fond of, but I knew you were packing all kinds of curves under them."

She shook her head. "Serge…how could I have missed you at the spa and all those other places? Granted I have a busy schedule and the spa is a big place, but you'd stand out anywhere you went. In a word you're…gorgeous."

"You think so?"

She smiled at his surprise. "I know so. I would not have *not* noticed you, college boy."

"I'm only noticed when I wish to be noticed, Derri."

"Ah…the vampire mystique," she drawled dramatically.

They laughed together and lapsed into another comfortable silence.

Over dinner at a dimly lit couples restaurant, he asked her about Karl. "Was he…good to you?"

She nodded, smiling slightly as she thought of the man who'd been her only lover for three years. "He was more than good to me. He always treated me with respect and he was a wonderful man."

"Then what went wrong? Weren't you sexually compatible?"

Incredibly, after all she and Serge had shared, she felt her cheeks burning. "We were very compatible. Not only is he kind, considerate, and funny, but he's a fantastic lover."

She felt Serge's unease and held up a hand. "Don't ask me to compare the two of you. As lovers, neither one of you leave anything to be desired, but I left him and I'm still deciding what to do about you."

He lifted her hands to his face and planted a warm kiss in each palm. "He was fortunate to have had you for three years."

She smiled, but shook her head. "I shared in that good fortune, Serge. Karl is a prize that any woman with good sense would be thrilled to death to have love her."

"He loved you and wanted to marry you."

She nodded.

"And you said no because?"

Her smile turned into a grin. "Don't hold your breath waiting for me to say I was waiting for you to come along, college boy," she teased.

"Okay." He gave her hands a gentle squeeze. "But we both know it's true, sweetheart."

She smiled and arched a brow. "Don't get cocky."

He leered at her. "You want to talk cock?"

They laughed together and lapsed into what was quickly becoming a comfortable silence. They danced until she was tired before returning to the cabin. Their love making that night was tender and sweet and Derri felt herself falling just a little bit in love with him. As she drifted off to sleep, she felt almost giddy with happiness.

She woke in the night, to find Serge between her legs, eating her pussy. Moaning softly, she wrapped her legs around him, shoving her hips up against his plundering tongue and fingers. When she began to gush, he buried his face even deeper between her legs and licked her so long that she had another climax.

That one was so intense, that she moaned and pushed at his shoulders. "Please, Serge. No more...no more. It's too good. No more. Please."

He rose over her, pressed his cock against her pussy, and pushed into her. She gasped and pressed against his shoulders. "Oh, God, Serge! Wait! Oh, God, I don't know how much more pleasure I can stand."

"Just a little more. I'll be quick and gentle," he promised and suggestively licked her neck while he thrust slowly, leisurely into her.

After a brief hesitation, she titled her head. She closed her eyes and shuddered with ecstasy as his incisors pierced her neck. Oh, damn, but a woman could easily become addicted to being fed off of by her vampire lover. He drank briefly, came quickly, and settled her limp body against his damp one.

"Now that's what I call a midnight snack," she murmured. "I'm satisfied for now, but tomorrow, I'm going to have to feed my other addiction."

"What other addiction?"

She smiled and projected an image of her down on her knees, clutching his thighs as she greedily swallowed the seed spewing from his ejaculating cock.

"Oh, shit," he protested. "You're gonna make me hard again."

She laughed and pressed her cheek against his shoulder. "You're almost always hard." As she fell asleep with him holding her close, she realized she was definitely going to have to reassess her game plan. There was no way she was going to let another woman have this sexy, loving vampire. He was hers.

"Completely," he promised.

When Serge was sure she was asleep, he eased off the bed, and picked up his cell phone. He left the room, closing the door behind him. In the hallway, he quickly punched out a familiar number.

"Hello."

Hearing his father's tense and worried voice, his shoulders slumped. "Dad. How is Mik?"

"He is not well, Serge."

"But he will be okay. Won't he?"

The ensuing silence felt like a huge weight on his shoulders. He closed his eyes and pressed his forehead against the wall. "Dad?"

"We hope so, Serge, but we can't be sure. He's...sick."

"I'll come home immediately."

"No. Serge...how are you feeling?"

He heard the anxiety in his father's voice and sucked in a breath. "Me? I'm fine."

"Are you sure?"

"I..." Granted he did feel...strange, but he attributed that to the fact that he felt high off of drinking Derri's blood and just being in love for the first time in his life. "I'm fine. I'll come home."

"No. Your mother and I will have our hands full with Mikhel. You stay there with Derri and Aleksei."

His stomach muscles tightened. "I don't need him, Dad. I'm going to send him packing. I can protect Derri by myself."

"No, Serge!" He spoke sharply. "Your mother and I trust him. You'll need him by your side...just in case."

"In case what?"

173

"In case you get sick too. You be careful, Serge."

He nodded. "I will. I'll call again tomorrow."

"Serge? We love you very much."

"I love you too, all of you. Tell Mik I said…"

"I will," his father said when he allowed his voice to trail off.

After he broke the connection, he stood in the hallway, his breathing coming in deep, almost painful gusts. The thought that Mikhel might somehow not make it, frightened him like nothing he'd ever encountered in his life.

He heard a noise and looked up. Alex came quietly from the back bedroom. He was still dressed, although he'd discarded his hat. "He will be all right, Serge," he said quietly.

He shook his head, resisting a sudden urge to strike out at the other vampire. "You don't know that."

"I know more about it than you do. Mikhel will be all right." Alex closed the distance between them and gave him a quick hug and a kiss. The need to lean against Alex, much as he would have done with Mikhel, surprised him. Before he could give in to the urge, Alex stepped away. "Now go to your woman for the comfort that only she can give you."

Feeling strangely better, he turned and went back into the bedroom. He climbed into bed. Derri had turned onto her stomach. Feeling a need for physical contact with her, he reached out and drew her against him. She murmured softly and burrowed into his arms.

"Serge? What's wrong?"

He pressed his lips around the top of her head. "Nothing. As long as I have you…everything is fine."

"Are you sure? I can feel…turmoil in you."

"Everything is fine," he lied.

\* \* \* \* \*

The ringing of his cell phone woke Serge a few hours later. Swearing softly, he eased away from Derri and reached over to snatch the phone up from the nightstand. As he did, he noted that it was only four a.m. His thoughts immediately turned to Mikhel. *God, please let him be all right.*

"What?" he asked in a low, terse voice.

"Serge? This is Diane."

"Who?" he asked curtly, although he'd recognized her voice.

"Oh, come on, Serge. You can't have forgotten me already. Not after all we shared."

He bit back the urge to remind her that they'd shared nothing but sex.

"What is it that you want?"

"I've been trying to reach you, Serge. Did your father tell you I've been trying to get in touch with you?"

Aware that Derri had stirred beside him and was now awake, he was careful to keep his anger out of his voice when he spoke. "Yes, he did. How did you get this number?"

"It wasn't easy."

"What can I do for you?" He spoke in a tone that made it clear he was not interested in doing anything for her.

"I heard you were in Philly and I was hoping...wondering if maybe we could see each other."

"No," he said shortly. "We can't."

"Serge, I know you don't want a commitment and I promise—"

"We have nothing to say to each other," he said coolly. "It's over. Good-bye."

He broke the connection, turned the phone off, and put it back on the nightstand.

"Girlfriend?"

"Ex," he said. "Very ex."

"If she's so ex, why is she calling you in the middle of the night? What did she want?"

"She said she wants to go out with me, but what she really wants is sex."

"Ah huh. And just how do you know she's not in love with you?"

"I know," he said coolly. "Derri, she's history. I don't want to talk about her."

"Why not?"

"Because there's nothing to talk about. It was over between us the moment I saw you. Besides, there wasn't much there but sex anyway. That's all there's ever been until you."

She turned and pressed her back against his chest. "Lucky me — at least until you tire of me."

He ground his teeth. Damn it to hell. He was not in the mood for any shit from her. "Derri, I am what I am. I can't change my past. How long are you going to beat me over the head with it?"

"Oh, stop whining, will you?" she snapped and pulled away from him. "You keep telling me you're not a college boy, but you keep acting like one. And you know what? It's getting a little old."

He felt his control over his temper slipping with alarming rapidity. Afraid that he might lash out at her in anger, he got up and headed for the door.

"Where are you going?"

Eyes glowing, he turned and glared over his shoulder at her. She sat up in the bed, straining her eyes to see in the dark. "Where ever the hell I like! How much of your pushing and taunting do you think I intend to take?"

"Oh, don't be so dramatic, college boy. Come back to bed and we'll talk about it like two adults."

"You go to hell!" he snapped and slammed out of the bedroom. He went into the bedroom two doors down the hall, locked the door, and threw himself across the bed. He lay in the dark, his incisors bared and his eyes glowing. Why the hell did she have to keep pushing and pushing? Damn her to hell. Damned if he was going to continue to allow her to treat him like some damned inexperienced college boy.

On a subconscious level, he was aware that he had overreacted, but he knew he couldn't go back to bed with her. The sudden, inexplicable rage he felt made it necessary for him to stay away from her.

It took a long time for him to calm down sufficiently to fall asleep. Just as he turned onto his stomach and buried his face in his pillow, there was a light tapping on the bedroom door. He knew it was Derri. He laid where he was—still and silent.

"Serge, I know you're not sleep," she whispered. " Open the door."

He didn't respond.

"Serge? Talk to me."

"When hell freezes over."

"Okay. You've made your point. All right? Now open the door. Please."

"Leave me the hell alone."

He felt her shocked surprised. There was a long silence before she spoke again. "Serge, come back to bed. Please? I don't want to be alone."

"I'm already in bed and I'm staying here. If you don't want to be alone, you'd better learn when to shut the hell up!"

"I...I..."

"Just leave me alone, Derri. In the morning, we'll have to have a talk."

"About what?"

"Maybe you're right...about what I'm actually feeling for you. I have no intentions of being in love alone or of allowing

177

you to use me as your damned whipping boy. Now leave me alone."

There was another prolonged silence before she spoke again. "What do you want me to say? I'm sorry? Fine, Serge, I'm sorry. You know that. Now please come back to bed?"

"All I want from you now is to be left the hell alone!"

He heard her suck in a breath before the sound of her running down the hall to her bedroom reached his ears. He could feel her confusion. Part of him yearned to comfort her — another, frightening part felt like shaking her until her teeth rattled. She needed to be taught a damned lesson. And if she kept pushing him, she would be sorry.

\* \* \* \* \*

Two and a half hours later, still unable to sleep, Derri got up and went to shower. With the water cascading over her head, she tried not to think of Serge. After a moment, she gave up the effort. She had missed him after he'd stormed out of the bedroom just hours earlier. Granted she had goaded him, but she hadn't expected him to react so explosively. She was never going to understand him. Just when she thought she had him wrapped around her finger, he turned vampire on her.

How was a woman supposed to know where she really stood with him? She smiled suddenly. His volatile temper would make for an exciting relationship. Eager to see him, but determined not to show it, after her shower, she dressed in a pair of baggy sweats. Her makeup consisted of foundation and lipstick only. Then, taking a deep, calming breath, she went down to the living room.

Alex, wearing a winter white suit, rose and swept off a matching hat as she entered the room. Wow. She didn't usually like dreads, but they definitely worked on Alex Lacey Madison. He was several degrees beyond hot. God he sizzled. The suit fit him like none she'd ever seen. She could see his muscular biceps, shoulders, chest, and molded thighs under the suit. Unlike Serge and Mikhel, who made little effort to hide their impressive cocks, Alex appeared to wear a cup.

He moved like a graceful, stalking predator. Emanating from him was an aura of sexuality that hit her with the force of a physical blast. If not for Serge, she knew he was a man she'd like to be taken to bed by. She couldn't feel Serge's presence, but she could feel Alex's "need" for sex. If she'd met him another time, she would gladly have offered herself as his willing sex slave. But now, all she could think of was Serge.

"Good morning, Derri."

"Good morning." She looked around. "Where's Serge?"

"He left."

"He...left?" She swallowed slowly, several times. "What do you mean...left?"

His blue eyes were piercing. "He packed his bag and left."

Oh, God. When would she learn? She'd goaded and taunted him again. And he'd left. This time he might not come back. She closed her eyes. Serge. Serge. Serge, please.

"Is he coming back?"

"I don't know. He's just a young pup, you know. He needs to be treated...kindly. He was fairly distraught when he left."

She heard the censure in his voice and shivered. Oh, God, not again. Was he going to turn on her as Mikhel had? To her relief, although his blue gaze had cooled, he evidenced no other signs of anger.

Her thoughts turned back to Serge. He'd left. Thinking about his abrupt departure, anger replaced her regret. He'd abandoned her to the tender mercies of this strange, full-blooded vampire. A vampire whose gaze kept straying to her neck. For all Serge knew, Alex might be on her the moment he left, draining her dry. Although professing to love her, Serge had drank more of her blood than he should have—twice. How did he know this vampire could be trusted not to hurt her?

"Alex, would you please take me home? I want to go home."

"Of course. I will be very happy to take you anywhere you want to go."

The sexual undertones were so obvious that she shivered. Damn Serge for putting her in this position. "I'll just go...pack." She turned and ran back upstairs. In her bedroom, she tossed her clothes into her suitcase. This was it. She'd had it. She was not going to forgive that infantile, college boy. The next time he showed up telling her how much he loved her and how he would die for her, she was going to slap him so hard he'd be wearing the imprint of her hand on his face for days.

After she finished packing, she looked around the room to make sure she wasn't leaving anything. She spotted Serge's cell phone on the nightstand. She hesitated only briefly before picking it up and putting it in her shoulder bag.

She let out a small gasp as she turned and found Alex standing in the doorway. He extended a hand. "Let me take that," he said.

She gave him her suitcase and silently followed him down to the living room. She waited by the front door while he checked to make sure the cabin was secure.

"Why did he leave?" she asked suddenly.

His blue eyes cooled considerably. "A latent pup in love is fragile. If you want him to stay around, maybe you should start acting like it."

She averted her gaze. There was no way she was going to Boston just so every vampire she met could scold her for treating Serge badly. Granted she had treated him badly— again, but damned if she wanted a bunch of pissed off vampires pointing that out to her.

"Of course, if you're interested in a more mature model," he began, his seductive voice dropping several notches.

She glared at him. What was up with these damned vampires? Why did they think every woman they met had the hots for them? She thought of the three male vampires she knew and acknowledged that they all probably had reason for their self-confidence. "I'm not!"

He smiled and shrugged. "If you change your mind —"

Thoughts of Serge's tenderness as they made love washed over her. She had no doubt that Alex was an exquisite lover, but she didn't need any more sexual expertise than Serge was capable of giving her. "Thanks, but I won't."

"Then treat him better the next time you see him," he said coolly.

She glanced up at him. "Then you think he'll be back?" She realized how needy she sounded and bit her lip. Damn. She had better not start feeling anything beyond desire for Serge.

"The pup's in love, what do you think?"

She shook her head. "I don't know what to think. One moment he's behaving as if he loves me, the next he acts as though he almost hates me." She knew she was exaggerating, but she was feeling particularly needy and vulnerable. And damn it, she wanted Serge back with her.

He sighed. "If you have any real feelings for him besides sexual —"

"I do!" she said, blushing.

"Then you're going to need to be patient and understanding. Things are going to be rough for you both."

"Rough how? Do you mean...the full blood who's stalking me?"

"No." He waved a hand in dismissal. "That bastard will be taken care of in short order. I mean Serge is sick."

"Sick? But he told me you guys don't get sick."

"Not the normal sicknesses, no. But there are consequences when a man with vampire blood falls for a human woman, as Mikhel and Serge have."

She remembered Mikhel's frightening behavior and swallowed quickly. "That's what's wrong with Mikhel?"

"Yes and it's also what's wrong with Serge. It's not easy to reconcile bloodlust with a person with no vampire blood. If you care for our little pup, you're going to have to be brave and patient. He'll need your understanding and forgiveness because he is almost certainly going to behave in what you'll no doubt consider an outrageous and unforgivable manner."

"You're frightening me, Alex."

He touched her cheek and a shock of desire sizzled through her. "That's not my intention. I just want you to know what's coming…what's already started."

She bit her lip. "He'll be all right. Won't he?"

"He's strong and unlike some less fortunate vamps, he has the support of a loving family."

He sounded almost bitter and she cast a quick look at him. Serge hadn't wanted to talk much about Alex, so she didn't know much about him. Nevertheless, she sensed an air of mystery and danger surrounding him that seemed to be absent in Serge and Mikhel.

He opened the door and she preceded him out.

The first indication she had that they might be in danger, was the low, ominous growl she heard from Alex. He dropped her suitcase and used his arm to sweep her behind him, against the door. Looking around his shoulder, she saw the other man, the vampire from her nightmare seeming to appear right before her startled gaze out of the fog.

"Full-blood," he said, his voice low and abrupt. "The human whore is mine. This is not your fight or your concern. Stand aside."

Alex's rich, full laughter rumbled from his deep chest. The confidence behind it lessened some of her mounting fear.

182

Alex was much stronger and more experienced than Serge. She knew that, still, she wanted Serge. *Where are you, college boy?*

*Here. To protect you with my life if need be, as I promised.*

She looked around. She could hear Serge's voice, but she couldn't see him. Then as suddenly as the other vampire had appeared, Serge was there, behind the man. The full-blood swung around and backhanded Serge. At least Derri thought he must have hit Serge. She didn't see the blow connect but one moment Serge stood behind the full-blood, the next, he was somersaulting in the air and landing on his feet.

The full-blood, his eyes red, his incisors bared, snarled and closed in on Serge.

Derri gripped Alex's bicep. "You have to help him," she begged. "Please don't let him kill Serge."

Alex pushed her gently back. "There's no need for me to interfere. Serge may be but a pup, but he's a very capable pup."

She hit a fist against his shoulder. "Why are you here if you're just going to stand by and let him hurt or kill Serge?" she cried and tried to move past him.

He again pushed her back, without taking his gaze from the other two. "If the need arises, I will intercede. Now be quiet and allow Serge to do what he needs to do," he ordered in a low, deep voice that sent a tingle of fear through her.

Heart pounding with a combination of fear and anxiety, she subsided, her gaze locked on the two combatants.

The two vampires began to exchange a flurry of blows that Derri could barely follow. Then, she screamed. The full-blood suddenly pinned Serge to the ground and began choking him.

She felt Alex tense and relaxed. He wouldn't let the other vampire hurt Serge. She knew he was about to intercede when Serge bought both hands clenched into fists up and delivered a series of hard, brutal blows to the front of the other man's arms. To Derri's great relief and surprise, the full-blood's hands opened around Serge's neck. Before Derri could decide what had happened, both vampires were on their feet again, facing each other.

A short but lethal looking sword seemed to jump into Serge's right hand.

Derri again gripped Alex's bicep, her heart thumping with a surge of fear. *Serge. No. Don't. Please.*

As the other vampire began to retreat, Serge lunged forward. The full-blood threw up a hand. With his left hand clenched into a fist, Serge knocked the arm aside. Derri watched in horror as Serge swung the sword with unbelievable speed in a wide, vicious arc towards the man's neck. For a time, it seemed as if the other vampire had somehow managed to evade Serge's swipe — until he crumbled to the ground and his head rolled off his body.

Derri stared, her lips parted in a silent, horrified scream.

His face contorted with rage and hate, Serge stalked over to the full-blood. He snatched a small piece of wood from the side of his right boot and drove it into the chest of what was clearly the corpse. He put his foot on the stake and shoved it completely into the body. Blood seeped out from the wound.

The sheer brutality shocked her. "Serge, no! Why?"

He glanced up at her, his eyes glowing, his incisors bared. "You would have preferred that I allowed him to live so he could continue to stalk you?" he snarled. "He intended to kill you, *after* he'd raped you. Or maybe I should have allowed him to kill me? Would you have preferred that?"

"No! You know that's not what I meant, but you didn't need to kill him! You enjoyed that!"

"And you have a problem with that?"

She stared at him, shaking her head. "I...what do you expect me to do? I'm an officer of the court! I have an obligation to report a murder."

He stalked over to her and pushing Alex aside, he glared down at her. "Oh, you do, do you? And I'd be doing what while you're calling the cops to report this supposed murder?"

She could feel the power, the anger, and the rage in him. For the first time, she was afraid of him. She shrank back against the door. She knew he could sense her fear of him. He seemed to enjoy it. "Serge, what are you doing?"

"Doing? Showing you the real me. What's the matter, Derri? Don't you want to call me college boy now and taunt me?"

His gaze moved to her neck and she shivered with fear. If he bit her now, she was afraid he might kill her. Her eyes filled with tears and she stared up at him, seeking reassurance from him. She felt none. *Serge?*

"Why the hell do I bother with you?" He stepped away from her and looked at Alex. "I'll leave her with you to do with as you like."

Alex nodded. "It's best that you go now. You're bordering on being out of control."

"And you'd have a problem with that?"

"No, you would because I am not Mikhel."

"Meaning what?"

"Meaning there's only so much crap I'm willing to take from you before I take that sword and make you eat it, pup."

He turned and glared at Alex. "What?"

"Oh, you heard me. Don't for one moment think that that sword means anything to me. You're sick and you need to be home with your momma. So go."

"Who the hell do you think you're talking to?"

"I'm talking to you, arrogant pup. Take your behind out of here before I kick it."

She felt Serge's rage spiraling out of control and bit her bottom lip hard. Oh, God! He was going to kill Alex too.

He turned his cold gray gaze on her. "What do you mean, too? I didn't kill that piece of trash. Whoever turned him into a vampire killed him a long time ago. I just put him out of his misery. But you think whatever the hell you like."

"Serge, please, I—"

"Save it, Derri. I no longer care what you think about anything."

She bit her lip, forcing herself not to cry as he disappeared as suddenly as he'd arrived.

She reached out blindly to Alex. He put his arms around her and she turned her face into his shoulder.

"Shhh. It's all right," he said softly. "He wasn't going to hurt you."

"Yes, he was."

"No. He wasn't, but I can see that you need comfort." He drew her body close to his and tightened his arms around her. She sucked in a breath and shivered as she felt his cock stir against her body.

She lifted her head and stared up into his blue eyes. Although she'd never felt more in need of comfort than she did at that moment, what she saw was a level of desire and lust the equal of which she'd never seen. It nearly took her breath away.

He stroked his hand over her shoulders. "What do you say?" He eased her back against the door and slowly rubbed his swollen cock against her. "Shall we go back inside and go to bed? I guarantee you'll enjoy it."

Despite herself, a wave of desire washed over her. She's never met a man as sensual as this vampire. He emoted sex appeal with his sky blue eyes and hard cock. Hell, he was probably a better lover than Serge and certainly more even tempered. Somehow, he reminded her of Serge. And after the way Serge had just behaved she owed him nothing.

Nevertheless, she couldn't help worrying about Serge. Where was he? Would he be all right? Still, to her confused shame, she found the feel of Alex's big body irresistible. She swallowed slowly.

"Do you…have a condom?"

He caressed her cheeks. "Didn't the pup tell you they're not necessary?"

"Serge said lots of things, including the fact that he loved me, but that didn't stop him from just trying to terrorize me."

"He's sick, Derri," he reminded her. "You mustn't hold anything he does against him."

Sure. Vampires were like all other men in one respect—they stuck together and tried to cover for each other. "Do you have a condom?"

He treated her to a slow, intimate smile that made her legs shake and moisture rush between her legs. "As a matter of fact, I do have one. Actually, I have several. Would you like to try them?"

Sucking in a deep breath, she lifted her head and looked up at him.

# Chapter Fourteen

೫

Erica lay alone in bed, crying softly. She wept for her lust for Serge, her almost constant fear of Deoctra, and the possibility that she might have to leave Mikhel. But how did one leave a vampire who didn't want to be left?

Then there was Mrs. Dumont to contend with. Having her as an enemy would be worst than having Deoctra as one.

Lost in despair, she was unaware that Mikhel had arrived with his usual near silence until he touched her cheek. "Erica? Why are you crying?"

"Damn it, Mikhel! I am sick and tired of you sneaking up on me!" she screamed, jerking away and scrambling to her knees. "Make some noise like a normal man. Oh, I forgot. You're not a normal man, are you? Hell, I'm not even sure you are a man at all! Tell me Mikhel, what exactly are vampires?"

She watched his gaze narrow. Without answering, he quickly shed his clothes. Despite her agitation and confusion, the sight of his nude, aroused body had the same effect on her it always did—her cunt began to ache for his cock.

He pushed her gently back onto the bed and kissed her pussy. She shivered and closed her eyes. She didn't want sex, but her body had other ideas. Especially, when he cupped her butt in his palms and slowly began to eat her. Her pussy was extremely sensitive and in just a matter of minutes, she was moaning and gushing into his mouth.

He spent several minutes licking at her cunt after she'd come before he slid his big body up hers, put his cock at her entrance, and pushed quickly, almost roughly into her. She welcomed his hard dick deep into her pussy. Although it had only been a few days since he'd flown from Philly to spend the night with her, it felt as if it had been an age since they'd made love.

She knew with the first few thrusts that he was going to fuck, rather than make love to her. She lifted her legs and crossed them over his body, urging him on. He lifted his weight onto his extended arms and began moving in her with a speed and fury she'd never experienced. In less than a minute, she experienced the most explosive orgasm she'd ever had. It was so intense, she nearly passed out.

As she lay under his pummeling body, limp and sated, he continued to pound in her. It began to hurt. She lifted her hands weakly, intending to push against his shoulders in protest. He brushed her hands aside, tilted her neck, and sank his incisors into her flesh.

He rotated his powerful hips and shoved his cock deep into her. As he fed on her, he began coming, filling her with his seed.

She felt as if she were floating on a cloud—carefree, weightless, and blissfully happy. Oh, Lord, there was no feeling in the world quite like this. She suddenly understood why women willingly allowed themselves to be killed by their vampire lovers. What a way to go. She lifted her hands and cupped his head against her, silently encouraging him to drink as much of her blood as he liked.

With a hard, painful thrust, he buried his cock as far into her pussy as it would go and finally lifted his head to look down at her. His eyes glowed, his incisors were bared, and her blood trickled down his chin. "Now, Erica, you will tell me what's going on," he commanded. "Now."

She licked her lips and took several deep breaths. She longed to ask him to remove his cock, but didn't quite dare. He was somehow different than he'd ever been before—more demanding. She shivered as she realized that he was doing what he'd promised her he'd never do—using his superior will to subjugate hers.

"I said now, Erica."

"I…I'm pregnant," she told him.

"I know that," he said impatiently, surprising her.

"You…you know? How? Your mother told you! She promised she wouldn't."

"And she didn't. She only told me I needed to come home to deal with you. I've known you were pregnant or going to be for a while. I did tell you in Salem that your chances of getting pregnant were high."

No longer aroused, she was dry and his cock, still hard and thick was becoming increasingly uncomfortable. She pushed against his shoulders. "Let me up."

"I'll let you up when it pleases me," he told her coolly. "It's time you understood who's in charge here, Erica. I'll give you a little clue…it ain't you."

She fell back against the bed. What was wrong with her? His attitude should annoy the hell out of her. Why was she so damned docile? "Get off of me, Mikhel."

"When I'm ready, not a moment before."

She stared up into his still glowing eyes. "Are you going to hurt me?"

"Never," he told her, his voice softening. "When were you going to tell me you were pregnant?"

She wanted to avert her gaze, but he wouldn't allow it. She knew she'd have to tell him the truth. "I wasn't going to tell you. I've decided…not to have the baby."

"Why?"

"I'm not really very maternal."

"Are you forgetting that you told me how disappointed you were when your ex-husband told you he didn't want any children?"

She had forgot. She bit her lip. She couldn't seem to think clearly. "This is not a good time for me. I have plans that don't include being a mother just now."

His eyes seemed to turn completely red and he radiated an aura of pure menace. He gripped her shoulders, hurting her. "I don't give a damn about your plans. Don't make the mistake of overestimating my feelings for you, Erica. There is no way that I will allow you to abort my child. You'd better understand that. If you try it, you won't like the consequences."

"Are you saying you'd hurt me?" she asked, her voice a small, frightened squeak.

He released her shoulders and eased his cock out of her. He rolled over onto his back and lay staring up at the ceiling. "I will not allow you to abort my child," he said in a flat voice.

Oh, God! Shivering, she turned onto her side, pulled the cover over her body and lay with tears streaming down her cheeks. He made no effort to comfort her and for the first time she fully understood the magnitude of her mistake in returning to Salem after he had allowed her to leave. She knew he wouldn't allow her to leave again. And yet she was determined that she would not...could not have a child that might require the blood of others to live.

"You'll have to go stay at The Dodge House."

"I can't go. I have things to do and—"

"It wasn't a request, Erica, and it's not open to debate. You're going."

She curled her body into a ball. "Did you ever really love me, Mikhel?"

She felt his lips brush lightly against the back of her neck. "I never claimed to be in love with you. I said you were my bloodlust and that hasn't changed. That won't ever change."

She turned and looked up at him, distressed to see that his eyes still glowed and his incisors were still bared. "Oh, Mikhel! I...thought you were in love with me!" she wailed.

"I never said I was," he pointed out coolly.

Her eyes welled with tears. "Why did you do this to me?"

"Do what? You are my bloodlust and I will always cherish you as such. I would willingly die protecting you. You know that. I am becoming more vampire than half-blood every day and…I don't know if I'm capable of falling in love anymore."

She remembered that when he had described bloodlust, he had spoken of lust, desire, and need, not only for blood, but for sex with a particular person. How had she equated that with love? She pressed her lips together and closed her eyes on the tears filling them.

She turned her back to him. Somehow, she had to find a way to get away from him.

"It's too late for that," he told her softly, just as if she'd spoken her thoughts aloud. "I gave you a chance to go and you came back. I won't allow you to leave again."

She brushed her tears away and turned to face him. "Then you'll have to kill me," she spat the words at him.

"I'll tell you this for the last time, Erica, don't overestimate my feelings for you. After the baby is born, if you still want to leave…maybe I'll let you go—alone."

"What? You think I'd leave my baby for you to raise?"

"Why not? We are talking about the same baby you're prepared to abort, aren't we?"

"To keep her or him from turning into you! I hate you!" she sobbed and slapped him.

The moment her hand made contact with his face, fear filled her. What if he hit her back or worse? To her surprise, he lifted her hand to his lips and pressed a kiss into it. "Don't be afraid of me, Erica. Please," he said, his voice changing. He shook his head. "I…didn't mean to frighten you. You never have to fear me. I promise."

She could feel a difference in him. "Mikhel…what's happening to you?" she asked fearfully, although she was suddenly no longer afraid of him.

He reached out and pulled her into his arms, burying his face against her breasts. "God, help me, I think I'm becoming a full-blood."

His body shook and she could feel his fear. She wrapped her arms around him. "It's all right, Mikhel. Whatever happens, we'll face it together."

To her surprise, he jerked away from her and scrambled off the bed. "No! No!" He paced the room, raking both hands through his hair. "No. You were right to want to leave. I...I'll try not to stop you. And if you feel that you have to...I'll let you make whatever decision you deem best for the...our baby."

"Mikhel, I won't leave you like this!" She climbed off the bed and wrapped her arms around him, holding him close. "Even if you don't love me, I love you. That has to mean something." She lifted her head and looked up at him. "Doesn't it?"

"I don't know, Erica. I...I feel out of control...I want you to go away."

"But Mikhel—"

He pushed her away. "Now."

"No!" She reached out and held him again. "No. If something...bad is happening to you, I want to be there for you."

"I...I have to go home."

"I'll go with you."

"No...yes." He stroked his hand against her neck, fingering the two small wounds where he fed on her. "Yes. You come. Mother knows how I really feel about you...that I love you. I do, my Erica. She will protect you from me if need be."

Erica shivered violently. Never had she ever expected to need protection from Mikhel.

* * * * *

"Are you sure you want to do this, Rica?"

Erica turned away from the window of her apartment where she and her younger sister, Megan sat at her kitchen table, watching Mikhel put her luggage in the trunk of his car.

She nodded. "It's something I have to do, Meg."

"Look, Rica, I know he's a hunk. Hell just looking at him makes me go wet in unmentionable places."

She drank deeply from her coffee cup before answering. "Then imagine how I feel after having spent the last six weeks with him."

Meg glanced out the window and shivered slightly. "I know the sex must be great, but—"

"You have no idea," she said. "Besides, I'll only be gone for a few weeks. He wants me to meet his family."

"Isn't it a little soon to be meeting his family? I mean you've only known him for a few weeks. This is so unlike you, Rica."

She forced herself to smile. Of course she couldn't tell Meg or anyone else of her real fear—that if she didn't go, Mikhel…God only knew what he would do. As unlikely as it would have been weeks ago, the safest place for her was probably in the midst of a vampire hoard who walked around naked and liked to watch each other making love.

"So you're taking a leave of absence?"

She shrugged. "I don't know. School's out now anyway until after the New Year. After that, we'll see, but I did call the administrator and tell her I would probably need a leave."

"And the school is letting you?"

"They weren't happy, but yes."

Megan studied her face. "Are you sure? I mean, you don't really seem that happy." She glanced briefly over her shoulder out the window. "I mean if I'd met a guy like him, I think I'd be glowing a little."

What did she have to glow about? She was in love with a vampire who was becoming more menacing every day, she was pregnant with the child she'd always wanted, but now was afraid to have, and of course there was Deoctra to consider. Although Erica hadn't actually seen her again, she'd felt her presence and an ever increasing sense of menace.

"Erica? Is everything okay?"

She smiled and nodded. "Everything's fine, Meg. I know you and Mom and Dad think I've lost my mind over some young stud—"

"He is awfully young looking, Rica."

She hated that she couldn't be truthful with her own family about Mikhel. "He's older than he looks."

"So there's nothing I can say to change your mind?"

"No. I'll be fine, honey. Honest." She got up and gave Meg a hug. "Don't worry about me. Please."

She'd do enough worrying for both of them.

\* \* \* \* \*

"What's wrong with me, Mother? What's happening to me?" Mikhel went down on his knees in front of the chair where his mother sat in the living room of Dodge House. He gripped her small hands.

She pulled one of her hands free with minimal effort and stroked his hair. "Oh, my little one, I had so hoped to spare you this grief," she whispered, her dark eyes glistening with tears. "Bloodlust for a half-blood or a latent with a human can be disastrous. Bloodlust is a powerful force of nature for our kind, my little one. It's a time of great joy with the right mate, another of vampire blood. With a human, it is a time of grief, danger, and sometimes even fatal to both partners."

"Fatal to both partners?" Mikhel stared up at her. "Are you telling me there's something in me that's going to kill not only me, but Erica and our child?"

"If we are not very careful. You'll have feelings of power and vigor like never before. You will also feel as if humans are here to serve our needs. When you meet a human who disagrees, the consequences to that person can be fatal. Your need for blood and your appetite for sex will greatly increase. You will feel as if you can do as you like and answer to no one. This is how you feel. Yes?"

He nodded, remembering his treatment of Erica, the only woman he'd ever loved. He'd also treated Derri badly.

"Then it has begun."

"What has begun?"

"Your feast of indulgence."

When he was twenty, fresh out of college and fucking several women on a regular basis, Aleksei had paid one of his unexpected visits. He and Mikhel had gone out to a nightclub frequented by vampires and their lackeys. There had been one male vampire there, clearly out of control, grabbing women, human and fem alike, and fucking and feeding off them right on the dance floor, one after another.

Mikhel could remember Aleksei swearing softly under his breath that the vamp was taking the feast of indulgence to a new low.

Mikhel, who'd never heard the term before, had asked him what he meant. Although clearly surprised by Mikhel's ignorance, Aleksei had quickly changed the subject and hustled Mikhel from the nightclub. Two days later, Mikhel had learned that two of the human women the vamp had fed on had died.

Now, he shuddered at the thought that he might end up killing someone. "I don't want to hurt anyone, especially Erica. What am I going to do? How can I overcome this?"

"It will not be easy, but we will stand with you, my little one." The tears streamed down her cheeks. "You must not despair. The feast of indulgence will be rough on you, but I will not lose you or Serge. You will both survive. Yes?"

He froze. "Oh, Mother, not Serge too."

"Yes. He's in love with his Derri and he's ingested large qualities of her blood. The feast of indulgence has begun for him too."

"Then he will need me," he started to rise.

His mother gently tugged him back. "Your are such a loyal and protective big brother to Serge and Kattia, but you are in no condition to help him, my little one. You must remain here with us."

He thought of Serge, always so wild at the best of times and feared for him. "Serge is strong. He'll be all right. Won't he?"

"Aleksei and Kattia will watch over him and his Derri. Aleksei is strong and will ensure no harm comes to Serge. Your father and I will stand with you and your Erica. It is sad and frightening, but we will all survive. Yes?" She slipped from her chair and into his arms. "You must promise me you will survive. I could not bear to lose you, my little Mikhel. You will survive. Yes?"

He'd never heard her sound so frightened or unsure. As he held her small, trembling body, he knew that there was a chance that he and Serge and their loves might not survive. He shook his head. No. He was going to be a father—something he'd never dared hope for himself. Damn if he would die or hurt Erica in anyway.

"Mother, what must we do to survive?"

She lifted her head and looked up at him. "You must indulge your cravings for blood and sex."

"With Erica. It will overwhelm her. She's already so frightened."

"Not just with Erica. In her condition it is best that you stay away from her. Yes? I will stand with you to ensure you do nothing to bring undue attention to yourself. Your father will stand with her to ensure you don't hurt her."

"If I'm to stay away from Erica, how will I get this out of my system?"

"You must indulge your cravings with any and every woman who attracts you."

"But I can't do that. Erica wouldn't understand."

"She will have to understand. Yes? There is a price to pay for loving one of our kind. It is the call of your vampire blood. To try to resist it out of fear of hurting her fragile human feelings will be fatal. Give in to it, my little one. Anything less and you risk not only your life but your very sanity."

"How can I go off fucking other women when she's going to have my baby?"

"You have to do what you have to do. If she loves you, she will forgive you. Yes? Just as your father forgave me, my little one."

He looked across the room. His father stood in front of the huge fireplace, his blue eyes inscrutable. "Dad?"

His father nodded slowly. "We'll get through this, Mikhel. All of us. Your Erica loves you. She'll be hurt, but she'll forgive you because she loves you. And because to do any less would be to risk your life."

His mother put a hand against his cheek and he turned back to face her. "You are becoming a full-blood, my little one. This is a much easier process when your bloodlust is a vampire and can withstand the onslaught and even revel in your feast of indulgence."

Finally, he understood why she'd gone out of her way to ensure that they all were mated with vampires. Falling in love with Erica had not been a choice—it had just happened. He couldn't or wouldn't change it, but he would survive.

"It'll be all right mother," he told her. "Serge and I will survive. Please don't cry."

She clutched his arms, fresh tears steaming down her face. "You both must. I could not bear to lose another of my precious children to unwise bloodlust."

He stiffened. "Another? Mother? You've had other children?"

She swallowed slowly and nodded. "Yes. There have been other children before you. A long time ago. They were all lost to me...some to unwise bloodlust...some to the evils of human men."

"How? What happened? When? Why did you never tell us?"

She shook her head. "There are things about my life that I have not dared tell you, my little one. Things I cannot talk about without great pain and sorrow, even after all this time. There will come a time when we will need to talk. But I cannot talk about long dead children when the children of my heart now are in danger. You will allow me this small selfishness. Yes?"

He could see the pain and fear in her gaze. She was right. There would be another time to find out about his long dead siblings. "Yes, mother," he whispered and held her close. "It'll be all right. We'll be all right. Both Serge and I."

His father joined them on the floor and the three of them clung to each other whispering words of love and encouragement.

\* \* \* \* \*

"What are you going to do about her?"

Serge stopped pacing in front of the glass balcony doors in Katie's Society Hill Philadelphia apartment. "Nothing. I killed the full-blood stalking her and what did I get for it? Told that it was her damned duty to report it to the police. The same damned police who were incapable of protecting her from that bastard in the first place."

"Did you know him?"

"No, but he did seem familiar." He shook his head. "Not that it matters now. He's dead and that ungrateful little twit is safe."

"Serge, I liked it better when you were in love with her."

"Well, you'd better get used to this view because I've had it up to here with her jerking my chain," he said making chopping motions with the side of his hand against his throat. "She wants to fuck everything with a stiff dick, let her."

"Starting with Aleksei?"

There was a strained quality to Katie's voice. He would have questioned her about that before. Now he let it pass and shrugged. "If that's what she likes. I hope he fucks her until she can't walk anymore!"

Katie, dressed in an expensive dark dress made especially for her, crossed her living room floor and touched his arms. "You don't mean that, Serge."

"I do." He took a deep breath and looked away. "She could barely wait until I was gone before she was agreeing to let him fuck her. The silly, unfaithful bitch!"

"Serge, it's unworthy of you to speak that way about your bloodlust."

"She's a horny bitch who was only ever interested in the size of my cock!"

She threw up her hands, her eyes darkening. "I am not going to listen to this from you! She is your bloodlust and you shouldn't have left her alone with Aleksei. You know he never fucks a woman without feeding on her."

"That's her problem. I could feel her wanting his cock in her. Well, let the bitch feel his incisors too."

"Serge, you're not thinking or feeling clearly. Something is dreadfully wrong. Let's go home to Mom."

He remembered what Alex had said about his being sick. Alex was wrong. He'd never been better. Along with the rage was a sense of power that thrilled him. "Nothing is wrong. I've just finally realized that Derri Morgan is not worth my time or attention."

"Doesn't it bother you that Aleksei might go too far and bring her over?"

He moved away from Katie. Somewhere, deep inside, the thought of Alex sleeping with Derri and then bringing her over disturbed him. But he couldn't seem to break free from the rage he felt enough to care about it. Maybe that was because on some instinctive level, he knew Alex wouldn't hurt her. He'd probably fuck her until she could barely walk, but he wouldn't harm her. "It's too late to stop it," he said bleakly. "If he kills her, I'll kill him."

"And that's it? Serge, in the first place, there is no way you could prevail over him. If he hurt you, Mikhel would be honor bound to take him on and he'd kill Mikhel. Then mother would be pitted against him. Is that what you want?"

"No! Alex would never hurt Mikhel. He'd flee before he fought Mikhel."

"Fine. He might not hurt Mikhel, but what about you? Do you think we want you hurt?"

"Fine. If he kills Derri, I'll let it go. Okay?"

"No, it's not okay! Serge, she was in your care. No matter what you say now, she trusted you."

"And I protected her. I killed the full-blood stalking her and in a while I'll take care of the jackal who sent him. What more do you want from me, Katie?"

"I want you to go back there and make sure she's all right. You and Mikhel promised to protect her. First Mikhel leaves her to go chasing after his little tramp and now you leave her alone with Aleksei who can't keep his cock out of any available hole. You call that protecting her?"

"We signed up to protect her from her stalker. We did that. Now she's on her own." He turned and walked towards the door.

"Serge! Don't go like this."

He turned at the door. "I'll see you later."

She flashed across the room and stared up at him. "Where are you going?"

"To get me some pussy."

She clutched at his arm. "Serge, don't do anything crazy."

"Like what?"

"Like taking some by force." Her fingers dug into his forearm. "Promise me, Serge."

He shook his head. "The only thing I'll promise is Derri Morgan has jerked my damned chain for the last time."

"Serge, please be careful. There are some things that she as a human female will find it impossible to forgive you for. Despite what you're feeling now, I know you are going to regret this later. Bear that in mind when you leave here."

"I am finished with her. Alex is welcome to her." He narrowed his gaze. "Do you have the talisman here?"

"Yes. Why?"

He extended his hand. "Give it to me."

"No, Serge. It can be dangerous if used improperly and you have the Ebony Venus. That's enough."

"Give it to me, Kattia."

"No, Serge," she said, her eyes beginning to glow. "And don't bother taking that tone with me. I am not your little human girlfriend whom you can frighten half to death. I'm not giving it to you. You are in no condition to be in possession of both talismans."

"Give it to me, Kattia. I won't ask again."

"I'm not giving it to you. If you think you can take it from me, come try it."

He felt a surge of anger and rage rush through him. He would take it from her. Then he shook his head. No. This was Kattia, his little sister. Maybe Alex was right. There was something wrong. But damn if he would go running home like the college boy Derri was always accusing him of being. Although he wasn't sure what was happening to him, he would weather the storm alone—far away from Katie. Now, feeling afraid of the rage building in him, he pulled her apartment door open and left. He knew he was dangerously close to being out of control. As long as there was no danger to Katie, he didn't care. God help anyone else who got in his way.

Katie watched him go, her heart aching for him. She would be there when and if he needed her. In the meantime, there was something constructive she could do for him. She glanced at her reflection in the mirror in her hallway and frowned. She'd been looking forward to her "date," but now that was out of the question.

After she'd stripped off the custom made dress and slipped into a pair of designer jeans, she left her apartment. Although she told herself she was annoyed to have to make the three-hour drive to the Pocono Mountains, she was actually excited at the thought of seeing Aleksei again.

She shook her head. She wasn't going to see him. She was going to ensure that Serge's bloodlust didn't come to any harm.

# Chapter Fifteen

### ഇ

Oh, shit. Even with his eyes closed and the mother of all hangovers plaguing him, Serge knew the woman lying impaled on his cock was not Derri. *Damn. What had he done?*

For the first time in weeks, his head felt clear and the rage and need he'd felt to strike out at someone…anyone was gone. What had he done? He had left Derri, the woman he loved, alone with Alex. More, he had a vague memory of having spent the last few weeks whoring with anything in a skirt. There was just no way Derri was ever going to forgive him for this.

Oh, God, how could he have abandoned her? After doing his best to make her afraid of him? He opened his eyes and looked down at the small, slim blond asleep on him. Diane. Oh, shit!

He gave her a none too gentle shake and began lifting her off him. She moaned and came awake abruptly. When she lifted her head and looked at him, he groaned. Oh, God, he'd messed up big time. Noting how pale she was, his gaze went to her neck. He saw the telltale marks there and closed his eyes briefly.

"Serge, wait," she whispered. "I'm dry and sore."

Wanting nothing more than to be free of her so he could go in search of Derri, Serge closed his eyes, concentrated, and forcefully secreted a stream of seed and blood in her. When he felt her loosen around him, ignoring her continuing protests, he lifted her body off his and came to his feet.

He stood for a moment, looking around the strange bedroom until he realized he must be in Diane's apartment.

This was a different apartment from the one she'd had when they'd briefly dated.

He spotted his clothes in a heap by the door of the bedroom along with hers. Scooping them up, he headed for the shower.

"Serge, wait and I'll shower with you."

He turned to stare at her. She was on her feet. She looked pale and unsteady. Damn he must have come close to taking her over. He squinted as a brief memory of Alex pulling him off of Diane flashed through his mind. How the hell had he ended up with her? His last lucid memory was of leaving Katie's apartment after he'd left Derri with Alex. How much time had passed since then? "I'm showering alone," he told her and continued into the bathroom.

He stood under the cold water, trying to remember what he'd been doing besides messing up with Diane. He drew a blank. He had to get out of here and find out if Derri and Mikhel were okay.

He turned off the water, opened the shower door and found Diane, still naked, about to join him.

"What day is it?"

"What day? January second. Serge? What's wrong? You seem so different this morning. Last night and the night before you were so wild and sweet. Oh, Serge, I never knew sex could be so...wonderful while hurting so much at the same time. There were a couple of times when I thought you were going to kill me, but I loved every minute of it."

She touched his chest. "I knew if I waited long enough, you'd come back to me."

He brushed her hand away. "I haven't come back. It's still over between us, Diane."

If it were January second that meant he'd been out of it for nearly two weeks. So, it was probably over between he and Derri too.

"Serge, please. Tell me what's wrong?"

He turned to look at her. He bit back the urge to snap at her. For some reason that only God knew, he'd ended up with her when she was the last person he should have sought out. Since he had, the least he could do was make this as easy as possible for her. "Diane, I've met a woman who I'm in love with. I'm sorry, but it's over between us."

"If you're in love with someone else, why did you spend the last nine days with me?"

He snatched up a towel and began to dry himself. Nine days? He'd missed Christmas at home and New Years. His thoughts turned to Mikhel. *God, please let him be all right.*

He discarded the towel and quickly dressed. "You must have known that something was wrong with me, Diane. Why didn't you contact my family?"

"Because you made me promise not to." She shook her head. "Don't you remember anything?"

"Not much. I have to go home." He walked out of the bathroom.

She followed him through the bedroom and into the living room. "Will you call me, Serge? Please?"

He paused at her apartment door. "Look, I'm sorry, but it's over." He hesitated, then left the apartment. He could hear her crying and while it hadn't bothered him the last time he'd left her, it bothered him now. Still, he kept going. Once he'd checked on Mikhel and Derri, he would come back and do what he should have done the last time he left her — compel her to forget him.

\* \* \* \* \*

Erica sat propped up against several pillows in the bedroom she and Mikhel shared at The Dodge House. Mikhel slept with his head in her lap. She stroked a hand across his face. For the first time in weeks, his parents had allowed her in to see him. She knew he'd been with a lot of women during their forced separation. She had spent a large amount of that time with Matt Dumont, wondering how she and Mikhel could ever have a life together after this.

He insisted she went home with him, then he kept his distance from her. When she needed him most, she had to sit back and watch him fucking and feeding on every woman in sight. When she'd cried, his father had held her in his arms and told her that what was happening to Mikhel was no fault of his own. He stroked her hair and told her Mikhel's feast of indulgence had nothing to do with his love for her. He insisted that if she loved Mikhel, she'd have to understand and forgive him.

She sighed. Maybe she'd spent too much time with the Dumonts because their way of life was beginning to make perfect sense to her. Although angry and hurt, she knew she no longer had a choice. Not only was she going to have their baby, but she was also going to stay with Mikhel.

He looked so peaceful in the light of the single lamp shining onto his face. For better or worst, he was hers. She stroked his cheek again. "I love you, Mikhel. Always."

He stirred and his eyes fluttered open. "Erica?"

She saw the confusion, fear, and regret in his dark gaze. He was afraid of losing her. She smiled, her eyes filling with tears. "Hi."

He sat up slowly and touched her cheek. "Erica. How are you?"

"I'm…fine."

"And…" His voice trailed off and he touched her stomach, which was now swelling noticeably. "The baby. How is the baby?"

"Fine too. We're both fine and will be…if you are. How are you?"

"Afraid. I…" He swallowed several times and lowered his head to her shoulder. "I'm so sorry for everything. I know you must have been afraid and hating me and…"

"No!" She stroked his head. "Your father explained everything to me. I know you did what you had to do to survive. I could never hate you. I love you too much."

"I can't remember very much of the last few weeks, but it didn't mean anything to me."

"I know."

He lifted his head and stared at her. "Can you forgive me?"

She nodded. "I can and I do—for any and everything."

"I'll make it up to you, my Erica. I promise."

"Start now, by holding me. I've missed you and I need you."

He wrapped his arms around her and drew her down onto the bed. He reached out and turned off the light. His lips on hers were gentle and soft. His cock, although hot and hard felt utterly delicious as it slowly pierced her hungry pussy. They spent the rest of the night gently fucking and occasionally drinking each other's blood. When he finally pulled his cock and his incisors out of her just before dawn, she moaned happily and pressed her back against his chest.

Oh, Lord, this was the way she wanted to spend the rest of her life— with this big, handsome, passionate man that she loved more than anything else.

"All is well with you both, my little ones. Yes?"

Mikhel, already half asleep, murmured softly in response to his mother's quiet voice.

Erica opened her eyes and saw Palea Dumont standing in the bedroom doorway, watching them, her dark eyes glowing. She smiled. "Yes. All is well."

"My little Mikhel has made everything right with you? Yes?"

"Yes. Oh, yes."

She entered the room and kissed both of their cheeks. "We will have a baby in the house soon to love and cherish. Yes, my little Erica?"

The tenderness emanating from the other woman filled Erica with a sense of warmth and belonging. Palea reached out a hand and gripped Erica's in a soft, but firm one.

"Yes," Erica admitted.

"You will stay and we will all be very happy together. Yes, my little Erica?"

"Yes."

"For how long?"

"Forever," she promised.

"Forever," Mikhel echoed and brushed his lips against her neck in a caress that held a promise of love and happiness. Erica smiled and closed her eyes. She was loved and wanted by the most wonderful man in the world. She was going to have his baby, who would be surrounded and cherished by a loving, doting family. Finally, she was going to have everything she'd ever wanted out of life.

A sudden thought crossed her mind and she shivered uncontrollably.

Mikhel tightened his arms around her. "What is it?"

"I got so caught up in how wonderful it is to be with you again, I forgot about Deoctra. Is she coming back?"

"You need have no fear of her, my little Erica," Palea said softly.

"Why not?"

"Because Aleksei will try to reason with her."

None of the vamps she'd met in the community had been named Aleksei. "Who is Aleksei?"

"He's like a big brother to me," Mikhel told her.

"And if he can't reason with her?"

209

"Don't sell Aleksei short," Mikhel murmured, brushing his lips against her neck. "His talent with the ladies is legendary. If anyone can change her mind about me being her bloodlust, it's Aleksei."

"If our Aleksei can not make her see reason, we will do what we must. Yes?"

Erica shivered. Even the thought of Deoctra's death was sobering. Still, given the alternative..."I hope he can reason with her," she said, pressing back against Mikhel.

"Either way, you need have no further fear of her, my little one. Give her no further thought. Your thoughts will be on love and our precious baby growing in your belly. Yes?"

"Yes," she agreed, smiling. She'd have enough to worry about trying to explain Mikhel and his family to her family and friends without worrying about Deoctra. And even that didn't seem like the monumental task it once had. She had Mikhel back and she was going to have his baby. As long as they were together and in love, they could cope with anything life threw in their path.

"Anything," he promised.

* * * * *

Derri emerged from the bathroom, still damp from her shower with a large towel wrapped loosely around her body. She moved over to her bedroom window and looked out. It was a clear night. The view from her bedroom window was only of other high-rise buildings. Not that it mattered. Her thoughts weren't pleasant or even welcome. For some reason, the full moon made her think of Serge.

She shook her head and hugged the towel to her. The problem was, everything made her think of Serge. She took a deep breath. She had to get a grip on her emotions. She should be feeling relatively good. She was no longer being stalked and the nightmares had stopped. More, her preparations for the Smith-Barley trial were going well and when she encountered

Ralph Mariono, he no longer glared at her. Everything that had caused her grief and sleepless nights was now absent from her life. The trouble was, so was Serge.

Serge. Oh, God, Serge. She'd been nothing but a fool lately. It had been foolish to give up Karl, a man who loved and wanted to marry her. Sleeping with Serge had been the greatest mistake of her life. No, ingesting his blood had probably been the biggest mistake she'd ever made.

She did not have time to wallow in regrets. Within five weeks she would need to be in court every day as she and the prosecution would begin seating a jury for the Smith-Barley trial. Once the trial was over, she was going to head to Phoenix and try to rekindle her relationship with Karl. If he would still have her once he learned how she'd spent their time apart.

Whatever had been between her and Serge was over — had been since he'd walked out on her, leaving her with Aleksei. Thoughts of Aleksei brought a rush of heat to her body. Sometimes she felt as if she could still taste his lips burning on hers as he kissed her. Kissed her? Ravish had been more like it. Aleksei didn't make love to a woman — he consumed her. She still couldn't believe she'd actually slept with him. As she'd known, he'd been the most exquisite lover she'd ever had. So why had her thoughts immediately turned to Serge the moment Alex had pulled out of her? In truth, even while Aleksei loved her, the most elemental part of her being had wished he were Serge.

Aleksei had touched her physically as no other man ever had, but he had not touched her emotions, spirit, or heart as Serge had. She closed her eyes briefly. As Serge *did*. Sex with Aleksei had been incredible on a physical level. Sex with Serge had been that and so much more. There was something enchanting about being made love to by a man you knew was totally in love with you.

*Oh, college boy, I have to forget you. I will forget you.*

She turned from the window and caught her breath as a man emerged from the shadows in her bedroom. At first, she thought it was Aleksei. Although neither one of them had been interested in anything more than that one day and night they had spent together, maybe he'd come to see her because he was feeling horny. Well, she wasn't inclined to accommodate him. Although she'd never had a more intense sexual experience, she regretted having succumbed to the sheer, unmitigated lust between them. She now felt as if she'd been unfaithful to Serge.

"I wish you guys would learn to knock..." her voice trailed off.

It wasn't Aleksei, but Serge. Her lips parted and her heart thumped. She overcame her first instinct, to scream with delight and fling herself into his arms. The last time they'd seen each other, he'd gone out of his way to frighten her. What did he want now? She tightened her grip on the towel and backed against the window.

He shook his head and spread his hands, palms up. "Derri...I...please don't be afraid of me. I came to see if you were all right and to apologize."

"I'm fine. Now will you please leave? I don't want to see you again."

He raked a hand through his hair. "I'll go, but I need to explain."

She shook her head, averting her gaze. "I don't want or need an explanation. Aleksei spun me some line about some feast of indulgence where you had to give in to your lusts for blood and sex. He had the nerve to tell me I'd have to forgive you anything you did."

"And you didn't believe him?"

"No. Now will you please just go away? Please. Please."

He slowly closed the distance between them. "I know I hurt and frightened you and I am so sorry. Please. Just hear me out and then I promise I'll go."

"I just want you to go, Serge. Please."

He touched her cheek and sucked in a breath when she flinched. He dropped his hand. "Derri, please...please. I was...sick. You know...you must know that I would never have willingly done anything to hurt or frighten you. I was sick."

"I know that's what your sister said."

"Katie?"

"She came to the cabin the night you...left." She paused, biting her lip, remembering Katie's irate reaction to discovering her with Aleksei.

"You didn't believe her?"

"It didn't matter, Serge. You said you loved me...you almost had me believing it and then you just walked away and left me with a man who...who..."

"Who what?" His hands shot out and gripped her arms painfully. "Did he hurt you? What did he do to you?"

"Nothing I didn't want him to."

"Nothing you didn't want him..." His hands tightened on her arms. "So it's true?"

She winced. "Serge, please. I'm going to have bruises tomorrow."

He loosened his grip. "Are you saying you and he...you let him...you slept with him?"

She was aware of his watching her closely as her gaze shifted restlessly. Did he know she was considering lying to him out of fear of him? The last thing she wanted was to tell him the truth and have him freak out on her when they were alone with no one to intercede if he lost his temper. She shook her head and realized lying was unnecessary. His sister would surely have told him she'd walked in on her and Aleksei just as they finished making love for the first time.

"I need to hear the truth," he told her. She knew it took an effort for him to keep his voice level and his eyes from glowing. Thank God he hadn't bared his incisors.

"Yes," she whispered.

He made a sound like a small, hurt puppy and stumbled away from her as if she'd attempted to strike him. He balled his hands into fists and slowly slid down the wall to the floor. He covered his face with his forearms. "Why? Why?!"

"I don't know why," she admitted. "I couldn't seem to…stop myself. I…I just felt so…drawn to him…like I did with Mikhel."

"Like Mikhel?" He dropped his arms and stared up at her. "And did you sleep with Mikhel too?"

"No! You know I didn't."

He sat staring up at her. "How could you sleep with another man?"

"How could you leave me with him? What did you think would happen when you just walked out on me after all that *I love you and I'd die for you* crap?!"

"It wasn't crap!" he snapped and shot to his feet. He stormed over to her and glared down at her. "I loved you! You know I did!"

"Then why did you leave me alone when I was so afraid and needed you most?" she demanded, tears filling her eyes. "You knew I was afraid. You knew I needed and wanted you to stay, but you left anyway! You went out of your way to frighten me and then you left and he was there…he spoke softly to me, he held and kissed me when I needed and wanted you. What did you think would happen, Serge? What did you expect me to do?"

"I didn't expect you to sleep with him!" he snapped, raking a hand through his hair. "You have to understand, Derri. I was sick! I would never have done anything to hurt you if I were thinking clearly. You know that." He cupped her damp cheeks between his palms. "Don't you?"

She shook her head. "No. I don't, not anymore, Serge. I never thought I'd ever be afraid of you, but I was that day…I am now."

"There's no need! Oh, Derri!" He released her face and slid his hands down her arms. When she made no effort to pull away from him, he enfolded her in his arms and pressed his face against her hair. "I am so sorry. Please. Please try to forgive me."

She looked up at him, her eyes filling with fresh tears. "I...I can't feel you anymore, Serge. I don't know what you're thinking or feeling." She balled her hands into fists and hit his chest. "You're gone from my thoughts!"

"I know," he said bleakly. "I can't feel or hear your thoughts anymore and I feel so empty without you in my head. But Derri, you are still in my heart."

"Oh, Serge!" She melted against him and began sobbing. He lifted her in his arms and carried her to the bed. He lowered her there, pulled the towel away, stripped down to his briefs and climbed into bed with her.

Still sobbing, she turned and clutched him to her.

Serge held her in his arms while she wept nearly all night long. He felt as if his heart was being ripped from his chest as he listened to her and knew he was responsible for her pain and misery. He felt so helpless. There was nothing he could do to ease her pain—no comfort he could offer her. For the first time in his life, he regretted what he was. If he hadn't been part vampire, he would never have left her, disappointed her, or brought her to this miserable state.

*Oh, God*, he thought, casting his eyes briefly toward the ceiling. *Please, help me make it right with her.* Although he could no longer "hear" her thoughts, he could sense her fear of him. He hated that he'd done this to her—the only woman he'd ever loved. It was a sobering realization that even if she eventually forgave him, there might be long-term consequences for what he'd done.

Marilyn Lee

# Chapter Sixteen

ഔ

Serge heard Derri in the shower when he woke. He lay in bed alone, listening to the sound of the water, realizing anew how much he had lost. Before the madness that was the feast of indulgence, he would have thought nothing of stripping and joining her in the shower. Hell before the madness, he wouldn't have to strip because he'd already have been naked. Now he knew he would not be welcome.

He rolled over and buried his face against the pillow. *God, please, let her forgive me and not be afraid of me.*

"Are you awake, Serge?"

He composed his face and rolled over onto his back. She stood in the door leading from the bedroom into the bathroom, fully dressed. She had dressed in the bathroom to avoid doing it in front of him.

"Would you…are you hungry, Serge?"

He hated that she no longer felt comfortable enough with him to call him college boy or gray eyes. He remembered the spirit and fire in her that had allowed her to challenge him, even after she'd learned he was a vampire. Had he killed that spirit and fire? He sat up and extended a hand to her. "Derri? Sweetheart, please forgive me."

She remained where she was, shaking her head. "If you're not hungry, I'm just going to leave for work early. Lock up when you leave, will you?"

He allowed his hand to fall back to his side. "Derri, please…"

"Serge, you can't just walk back in my life and expect to pick up where you left off. I was ready to give my heart to you and you tossed it back at me and told Aleksei I was his to do with as he liked. Well, Serge, what if he felt like killing me?!"

"Oh, God, Derri! I know I said that, but I knew he would not hurt you."

"No, you didn't!"

"I did. I don't know how I knew, but I just knew he wouldn't hurt you. Please…"

She shook her head. "I don't want to talk about this anymore. I'm leaving now. Please leave me alone."

At the bedroom door, she paused and looked back at him. "Serge, how is Mikhel?"

"He's better, thanks." He smiled. "He's going to be a father at last."

"At last?"

"It's something he's wanted for the last twenty-five years or so."

"Then I'm very pleased for him. And Erica? How is she?"

"She's…okay…she loves him and she's forgiven him his feast of indulgence, Derri."

"Has she? Well, I'm not Erica, Serge," she said with some of her old fire.

"I know that and I wouldn't wish you to be anyone else. I love you just as you are. You know that."

She shook her head, her brown eyes filling with tears. "I don't know that I believe you love me anymore, Serge."

He spread his hands helplessly. "I do. As God is my witness, I love you more than life itself. I could not control myself. I tried, but I could not stop what was happening to me. But even when I was on the verge of madness, Derri, I came back to face the full-blood who intended to kill you. Doesn't that mean anything?"

"All that means to me is that you're capable of killing brutally with no remorse, Serge."

He sucked in a breath and fought hard to hold onto his temper. He'd hurt and disappointed her. Now she wanted to inflict as much pain on him as possible. At least that's what he told himself. She couldn't really mean she thought he was a brutal, remorseless killer.

"I need you to forgive me," he said bleakly.

"Well, I wouldn't hold my breath waiting for that to happen it I were you, Serge."

He watched her walk out of the bedroom. Shit! She was not going to forgive him. He fell back onto the bed and buried his face in her pillow, inhaling her scent. What the hell was he supposed to do now?

He felt a tingling sensation along the back of his neck. He swung around quickly, bounding to his feet and into a crouch. Alex, wearing a pale lavender suit and matching hat stood in the doorway.

"Bastard," he hissed.

Alex's blue eyes narrowed slightly. "It's good to see you too, young pup."

"What are you doing here?"

Alex took off his hat and tossed it onto the bed. "I've come to see you. How are you feeling?"

"Murderous. You slept with Derri. You bastard, you had no right. How could you touch her?" he snarled.

Alex shrugged. "If you care to remember, you left her in need of comfort. I comforted her."

"You could have done that without fucking her!"

Alex's lips tightened. "First, I did not fuck her. I made love to her and I comforted her just as Mikhel would have done. Don't stand there and try to pretend Mikhel wouldn't have made love to her under similar circumstances. We both know he would have and you would have accepted that fact."

Comparing himself to Mikhel was the last straw. Serge flashed across the room and flung a series of vicious blows at

Alex. To his amazement, they landed and Alex went down. He flung himself onto Alex's prone body.

As he closed his hands around Alex's neck, he met his blue eyes, eyes the same color as Katie's. How could he choke a man with eyes the same color as his baby sister? He released his grip on Alex's throat and staggered to his feet, confused. He didn't delude himself. He knew Alex had allowed him to deck him, just as Mikhel once had.

The question was why.

Alex bounded to his feet and brushed down his suit, his blue eyes narrowed and glowing. "That was your one and only freebie, pup. I behaved just as Mikhel would have," he said quietly.

He leveled an angry finger at Alex. "Don't compare yourself to him! He is my brother."

A long pause ensued before Alex took a deep breath and looked at him. "So am I," he said so softly Serge barely heard him.

"Liar! How dare you lie?"

"It's not a lie, Serge. Why do you suppose Mikhel and I have always been so close?"

He couldn't deny that the two of them were close. In fact, he had often resented the closeness between the two men. "Are you saying Mikhel…knows?"

"No. He doesn't *know*, but he *feels* there's a reason to be close to me. Just as you would, if you could get over the notion that I want to come between you and Mikhel."

"That's not true! Even if what you say is true, nothing and no one could ever come between us."

Alex nodded. "That's right. Nothing could change the way you two feel about each other. I'm the last one who would want to do that, but I am telling you the truth, Serge. We are brothers."

He stared into Alex's eyes and knew what he'd said was somehow true. On some instinctive level, he'd always known that Alex could be trusted—even when he'd felt as if he'd hated him. After all, he'd entrusted Alex with his most precious possession—Derri.

"How?" he finally asked.

"The usual way—we have the same mother."

He shook his head and retreated to the bed where he sat on the edge. "No. If you are her son, she would have told us."

"She doesn't know."

"That's a lie. How the hell could she not know?"

Alex's eyes narrowed into slits. "I am getting just a little tired of your calling me a liar. I'll tell you again that brother or not, I am not Mikhel. I am not prepared to take all the nonsense and disrespect from you that he does."

Serge was now a full-blood, just like Alex. Granted, the other vamp was still stronger and more experienced, but he wasn't inclined to back down. Still, he decided to let the warning pass. Derri wouldn't appreciate having her bedroom demolished by two battling vampires. "How is it possible for her not to know you're her son? It's almost impossible to hide anything from her."

Alex sighed and shook his head, looking weary. "It's a long, ugly story that I have no desire to talk about at the moment."

Serge curled his lip. "How convenient."

Alex surprised him by smiling and tossing his head, sending his hair cascading around his shoulders. "Yes, isn't it? Now I just want to give you something I've wanted to give you for a long time."

"What?" he asked wearily. Mikhel had been known to whip his ass occasionally when he felt Serge had behaved badly.

Alex opened his arms. "A hug. Come here, my angry young pup."

Serge responded as he would have to a similar request from Mikhel, he rose to his feet and returned Alex's bear hug.

\* \* \* \* \*

Derri found several dozen roses waiting for her when she arrived at work after driving aimlessly around for an hour. She walked over to her desk and lifted the card from the middle vase.

*Please. Forgive me. Your college boy who loves you so much it hurts.*

*SD.*

She sank down into her chair. How could she possibly ever trust him again, even if she did forgive him? She closed her eyes, remembering the night before. Even though she'd still been afraid of him, she'd been glad to have him there. She knew she was dangerously close to crossing the line to being in love with a vampire who was capable of killing with no remorse and equally as capable of putting the fear of God in her. How had she let this happen and what was she supposed to do if he wouldn't leave her alone? Worse was her growing fear that she didn't want to be left alone.

Besides, she hadn't been completely blameless. She had goaded him until he lost his temper. And no one had put a gun to her head and made her sleep with Aleksei. Hell, she wasn't even sure why she had. Although sex with him had been great, it hadn't been worth the risk of ruining her budding relationship with Serge.

Serge was waiting outside her apartment building that night when she arrived home. Her heartbeat sped up and she went wet just looking at him. She wanted him more than ever, but she needed to be strong.

"Serge. What are you doing here?"

He gave her a tentative smile. "The Diamonds are playing tonight. I thought you might like to come to the game with me."

She longed to go to the game with him and meet some of the boys who meant so much to him, but she'd never get over him if she didn't stick to her game plan. "Sorry, but I'm going to be working at home tonight."

He sighed and ran a hand through his hair. "Can I come see you after the game?"

Thoughts of how nice it had been to have him in her bed the previous night assailed her. Lord, it would be wonderful to have him make love to her again. It had been an eternity since they'd made love. Nevertheless, following her horny side was what had landed her in this situation in the first place.

"Serge, it's over."

"It's not over! It'll never be over for me!" he snapped, his gray eyes swirling with angry little currents. "I will always love and need you. Derri, when we fall in love, it's for keeps. Please. Let me try to atone for what I've done."

Why couldn't she just say no and walk away? Why was she so weak where he was concerned? Why was she standing there feeling his pain?

While she stood there trying to marshal the strength to walk away, he closed the distance between them and eased her against the wall of the building. He bent his head and peppered her slightly parted lips with hungry kisses.

The feel of his cock hardening against her nearly drove her into complete surrender. She shook off the desire stirring in her and shoved angrily at his shoulders. "No, Serge! No. Stop. You think I can forget everything that's happened in the last few weeks so easily? Well I can't."

His gray eyes dimmed and his shoulders slumped. He stepped away from her. "Derri. Derri, please. Please," he begged. "You have to forgive me. I couldn't help how I behaved." He went on with a long drawn out explanation. She only half listened, fully expecting him to point out that she had slept with Alex and she had no such excuse as the feast of indulgence. To her surprise, he didn't. More, she sensed he wouldn't hold it against her or throw it up in her face. If he could forgive her so readily, maybe she needed to rethink her position. Just maybe she was being a little unreasonable because the thought of him with other women was more than she could bear.

"Maybe not, but I don't want to see you again tonight, Serge. Please. Don't come back here tonight."

He stared at her for several moments in silence, his gray eyes glowing then he turned and was gone in a blur.

An hour later, two-dozen roses and a box of chocolates arrived. She sniffed the roses and ate several of the chocolates as she worked in the corner of her bedroom where she kept her computer. After a quick shower, she dried off and slipped into bed, and laid thinking of Serge.

The phone rang just as she drifted off to sleep. She reached out and lifted the receiver from the cradle and held it against her ear without sitting up. "Hello?"

"Hi."

"Serge." Despite herself, she heard her voice soften. "It's after eleven. Is something wrong?"

"Yes—we're not together. I miss you. I need you."

She closed her eyes and rolled onto her back. She bit her lip to keep from whispering that she missed and needed him too. "Serge, it's late."

"I know."

"I'm in bed."

"Are you sure I can't come over? I can be there in just a few minutes and I promise I won't try to make love to you."

"No, Serge. I have a long day tomorrow. I'd better say goodnight."

"Okay...I love you...goodnight."

"Before you go…how did the game go?"

"We kicked ass."

She smiled. He sounded part smug, part proud parent. "Congrats. By the way, what was the score?"

"Can you say wipeout?"

"Score, Serge."

"Eighty-five to fifty. We had four guys with double figures."

"Double figures?"

"Four guys scored ten or more points. Derri, the guys were on. I think we're going all the way this year," he told her.

"Serge, the season is only a few games old."

"I know, but if you had seen our guys play tonight, Derri, you'd know what I mean. They were on. Everyone was on his game and the team play and unselfish behavior was awesome. They've learned so much since last season. It's incredible…they are the greatest group of guys you'll ever meet. You have to meet them, Derri. You'll be so impressed and humbled by their hard work and determination."

She nodded. He really did care about his guys. "They sound like a great group, Serge."

"They are. If you meet them, you'll fall in love with them as I have."

Her community service minded guy. "You are one amazing vampire, Serge Dumont."

He was silent for several moments. "Is that a good thing?"

"Yes. I think it is," she admitted, then went on quickly. "I have to go."

"Okay. Good night."

She hung up and rolled onto her stomach in an effort to ease the ache in her whole body for him. The way things stood, she didn't know how long she could hold out against her need for him.

\* \* \* \* \*

"Why don't you just take the wench?"

Serge stopped pacing in front of the patio doors in Katie's living room and turned to face her. "How many times do I have to tell you that she is not a wench?" he snapped.

Katie tossed her head, sending her long hair flying around her head in a dark cloud. "Oh, please, Serge. Spare me the righteous indignation. You wouldn't be so certain if you'd seen her lying under Aleksei moaning and thrusting at him as he fucked the hell out of her! She's a cheap tramp! She's not supposed to want any other man but Mikhel!"

Serge took several deep breaths. Katie didn't know Alex was their brother. Alex had told him he wanted to tell everyone else, starting with their mother in his own time. He had agreed to keep Alex's confidence. "Katie, I'm not going to listen to you trash the woman I love. It's unworthy of you."

She sighed and threw her arms around him. "Oh, I'm sorry, Serge. Please forgive me. I didn't mean it. I know you love her and you know if need be, I would put my life on the line to protect her."

He kissed her hair and hugged her. "I know, but there are things you don't know about."

She drew away from him and looked up at him, her blue eyes darkening. "What are you trying to keep from me, Serge? What's wrong?"

"Nothing. I just needed to talk to you."

"Would you like me to have a word with her?"

"No! Thanks, but..."

"It's not right for her to make you beg for what's rightfully yours. For the life of me, Serge, I cannot imagine what you or Aleksei see in her. I think her so called charms are overrated."

He sighed. Why had he come to Katie to talk? Since she'd walked in on Derri and Alex, she'd had nothing good to say about Derri. He suspected her anger towards Derri wasn't entirely on his behalf. The sooner Alex told the rest of the family who he was, the better. He looked at Katie. He had an uneasy feeling that Katie needed to be told the truth about Alex rather quickly.

He bent and kissed her cheek. "Believe me, they're not overrated."

She stared at him coolly for a moment before giving him a knowing grin. "Good pussy?"

"That's not her only attraction," he protested, strangely unwilling to discuss their sex life. "In addition to being beautiful, she's intelligent, funny, and brave. When she thought the full-blood I dispatched was going to hurt me, she was prepared to come to my defense, even though she was scared silly. A large amount of her spare time is spent doing things for other people at shelters and soup kitchens, and alternative schools. She doesn't just write a check for charity and sit back to wait for the accolades to roll in. She's not afraid to get her hands dirty. When there's a need, she gets right in there and helps. There is a great deal besides sex about her to admire and love. And I do."

Katie's smile was genuine. "Yeah, I can see how that type of behavior would appeal to the frustrated social worker in you."

When he frowned, she rushed on. "I meant that as a compliment, Serge. Your Derri sounds perfect for you. Together the two of you can rescue all the unfortunates in the world." She touched his cheek. "In the meantime, know that everything will work out for you both in the end."

"Are you sure?"

She nodded. "Of course I'm sure. We're going to have a baby in the family and everything will be fine, Serge." She grinned at him. "Maybe we'll have two."

His heart thumped. "Two? Is Erica having twins or are you implying that Derri and I will…"

"Erica isn't having twins, Serge."

He sucked in a deep breath. The thought of fathering a child with Derri sent chills of pleasure all through him. But for all he knew Derri might not even want children—at least not with him.

"Is she…pregnant?"

"I don't think so."

God he hoped not, at least not unless that was what she wanted. He knew she wouldn't take kindly to having an unwanted pregnancy thrust on her, especially after he'd assured her she didn't need to worry about that happening.

"I'm not talking about now, Serge. It's just a vague impression that I can't pin down. But I just know everything will be all right for you and your beautiful, brave, intelligent Derri."

"She's that and more, Katie."

"Don't worry, Serge. Things will work out."

If only he could be sure she wasn't just trying to reassure him.

* * * * *

Several nights later, Derri encountered Brad Harris in the parking lot. She smiled and waved, intending to continue on her way.

He waved back and headed in her direction. He'd already tossed his overcoat inside his car. He was dressed in a dark suit with a silk tie and white shirt that contrasted nicely with his dark skin. He was a good-looking man.

"Derri. How are you?"

"Fine. You?"

"Great. Busy? How about dinner tonight?"

"Dinner? Tonight?" She should accept. He was a handsome man interested in a relationship with her. It was time she did something smart. But she didn't want smart, she wanted Serge.

"Yes," he smiled. "Tonight. I thought maybe we could…" he trailed off and looked over her shoulder. "Can I help you?"

She turned to see Serge standing less than two feet from them. Her heart thumped wildly and, as usual, she longed to rush at him and throw herself into his arms.

Serge stared at Brad, his gray eyes dark and swirling.

"Do you have a problem?" Brad sounded annoyed.

"No," Serge answered in a quiet, dangerous voice. "You're the one with the problem." He started towards them.

"Serge, what are you doing here?"

Brad glanced briefly at her. "You want me to get rid of him?"

"No, no." Before Serge could respond, she pushed her hands against his chest. "No, Brad. Thanks, but that's not necessary. I can handle him."

"Are you sure?" Brad stared at Serge. "He looks a little on the…unstable side. Look at his eyes."

"I'm positive," she said, afraid that Serge might attack Brad if he didn't leave soon. She could almost feel the rage and jealousy building in Serge. "I know him and I'll be fine."

"I don't like the idea of leaving you with him. You're sure?"

"I'm positive. Really." Go. Now. Please. She sighed in relief as Brad turned and slowly walked to his car and finally drove away. Only then did she turn back to Serge. "How dare you? Who do you think you are?"

"I know I'm the man who loves you more than life itself."

She stared at him, her lips parted in a wordless sigh. How the hell was a woman supposed to remain firm when he went and said things like that? More, she knew he meant what he'd said.

"Serge."

He bent and kissed her cheek. "I love you."

She leaned against him for several sweet moments before jerking away. "I have to go, Serge. Before I do, I want you to promise me that you won't try to harm Brad in any way."

His eyes darkened. "Is that his name?"

"Yes, and I want you to promise not to hurt him, Serge."

"Is there something between you two?"

"No!"

"Then he has nothing to worry about."

"And if there were?"

His only response was the tightening of his lips.

"If you think I'll let you frighten me into—"

"You are not the one who needs to be afraid. Any man who thinks he's going to take you from me, had better be very afraid."

"You are impossible, Serge." She got into her car and drove away. She was afraid he would follow her, but if he did, she was unaware of it. She grimaced, not that she would necessarily know if he did. After all, he had followed her for weeks without her being aware of it.

Once in bed, she lay awake for hours longing for Serge and wishing she'd allowed him to accompany her before she finally fell asleep.

The next morning she encountered Brad outside the main conference room. "Good morning, Derri. It's a relief to see you."

She shook her head. "I appreciate your concern, Brad, but it wasn't and isn't necessary. I was in no danger last night."

"I see." He paused for several moments before going on. "Are the two of you...involved?"

"Yes." Her quick, unequivocal response surprised her.

"I see. Well...in that case, I won't take up anymore of your time." He nodded slightly and walked away.

She turned and headed in the other direction.

"Ah, Derri?"

She glanced over her shoulder and saw Brad had paused near his office. "Yes?"

"Good luck with the Smith-Barley case. If I can help in any way, let me know."

"I will. Thanks." Smiling, she went to her office. She spent the morning working undisturbed. She had a salad at her desk for lunch and continued to work until the phone on her desk buzzed in the late afternoon. She flicked her intercom. "Yes?"

"Derri, there's a Serge Dumont here to see you. He doesn't have an appointment, but—"

He didn't need one. "Send him in, please. Thank you."

Moments later her office door opened after a perfunctory tap. Serge, dressed in his usual black came in. He crossed the room, leaned over her desk, and kissed her. She sucked in a breath, closed her eyes, and lost herself in his kiss. It had been ages since they'd shared a real passionate kiss and it felt as if they were kissing for the first time.

"I love you," he whispered against her lips.

She drew back, breathing quickly. "I...what can I do for you?"

He touched her cheek. "Have dinner with me."

"I...Serge, I need time. So much as happened and—"

He moved around the desk and stood at her side. "Have dinner with me...and call me college boy or gray eyes. If you call me Serge one more time, I'm gonna take hostages."

She laughed and touched his cheek. "Whatever was between us is gone. We lost it."

He clutched her hand in his and spread it over his heart. "No. It's not gone. It's still there, Derri. Have lunch with me and we can rediscover it."

"Serge…"

"The Diamonds are playing tomorrow night. Will you come?"

About to shake her head, she nodded instead. What the hell. "Yes, Serge, I'll come."

He sucked in a breath "And after the game, will you let me take you home?"

The lure of being alone with him in her bedroom again, was too powerful a temptation to keep fighting. Her desire for him, always on a slow, steady simmer was now threatening to blaze out of control. She stood up and walked around the desk and into his arms. "Hold me? Please?"

"Oh, God, thank you!" he whispered and wrapped his arms around her. "Thank you for giving me another chance with her."

A vampire who believed in and thanked God when things went his way? What were the odds? Whatever they were, she had a feeling this vampire, her vampire, was worth a second chance.

Maybe she was crazy or maybe she was just in love. Either way, she wanted a relationship with this handsome, volatile, passionate vampire. She'd already learned that there was a definite danger attached to becoming involved with him, but she'd also spent four of the most miserable weeks of her life without him. It seemed a fair trade off.

She ran her fingers through his hair. "I don't know what you've been doing or who you've been with, but now that you're back, you're mine, college boy."

He closed his eyes and buried his face against her cheek. She felt him shaking and tightened her arms around him. "You're mine," she said again. "Mine."

He hesitated briefly before he drew away from her and retrieved something from his pant pocket. When he opened his hand, she saw the small, golden talisman that had belonged to Cassy lying in his palm. "Take my hand, Derri."

She licked her lips, shaking her head. "No, Serge. It's not a good idea."

"Take my hand. It will only cause problems for people who don't love each other. That doesn't include us, my ebony beauty. Take my hand."

She knew it was a bad idea, but she felt so empty and lost without him in her head and thoughts. She licked her lips again, took a deep breath, and clasped her hand over his. A series of electric like charges immediately sizzled through her. Along with the rush of electricity, came a rush of Serge's thoughts.

"Serge! I can feel you again!" she cried, happy tears streaming down her cheeks.

Laughing, with his own eyes glistening, he lifted her off her feet and swung her around until she was dizzy, then he covered her lips with his. *God, I love you so much! I really would die for you.*

A surge of joy pulsed through her. She lifted her head and smiled up at him through tears. "I know you would, but I want you alive, my gray-eyed college boy." She touched his lips. "I'm sorry."

He frowned. "For what?"

"I shouldn't have slept with Aleksei. I don't know why I did. If you can forgive me for that, I can forgive you."

He stroked her cheeks. "About your sleeping with Alex…it wasn't your fault."

"Yes, it was."

"No, it wasn't. Alex told me he explained why you'd be attracted to Mikhel."

She nodded. "He said once a person has ingested vampire blood, they become…attracted to others who share the same blood as their vampire lover. Now I know why I'm attracted to Mikhel, even though I want you more than anything. But, Alex isn't your brother."

"Yes, he is. At least he's my half brother."

"He is?" She slumped against him. "Oh, thank God. I thought I was losing it." She looked up at him. "There's something I need to tell you."

She felt him stiffen. "What?"

She licked her lips. "I…I love you, college boy."

He sucked in his breath and she could feel his heart thumping against her. "Oh, God, sweetheart, are you sure?"

She nodded, her eyes welling with tears. "Yes. These last few weeks without you…I thought I would die for wanting of you. God, how I missed you."

He cupped her face in his hands and stared down into her eyes. *Show me. Fuck me.*

*What? Now? Here?*

*Now. Here. I want you.*

She looked around her office. "Serge, we can't. My secretary is right outside the door."

"I locked the door as I came in," he told her.

"Serge, I've worked too hard to get where I am to risk getting caught fucking in my office."

"We won't get caught," he said, hooking an arm around her waist. "It's been so long and I need you."

"We can do this tonight when I leave the office."

He brushed his lips against her neck, allowing her to feel his hard, throbbing cock. "I can't wait that long. I need you now."

Oh, God, his cock felt so damn good. She felt that uncontrollable moisture between her legs. "My secretary will hear us," she said, weakening. There didn't seem to be much point in telling herself that she could not forget where she was. She'd already forgotten everything except how much she wanted and needed him.

"We'll be very quiet."

"Serge, we can't…"

"Not only can we, but we're going to. I can't wait any longer." He lifted her in his arms and carried her into her office bathroom. While she stood trembling with desire and anxiety, he quickly undressed them both. He took her in his arms and began kissing her gently. He rubbed his hardening cock along the length of her pussy several times, before turning her around so that she faced the full-length mirror on the back of the door.

Catching her gaze in the mirror, he lifted her leg and began to greedily push his cock into her aching, dripping pussy. She shuddered with a delightful sensation of bliss and leaned back against his body. He turned them sideways so that they could both see his long, thick cock, already glistening with her pussy juices, burrowing quickly in and out of her. What a turn on. Before she lost the ability to think, she drew slightly away.

"Wait a minute, Serge. Oooh. Lord, that feels good, but not so quick," she moaned as he surged roughly into her, bringing pleasure and pain. "I don't want it to be over before I get a chance to fully enjoy having your big, delicious cock in my pussy again."

"I know, sweetheart, but I can't help it. This first time will be quick, but I'll make it up to your later. I promise."

"Oooh, Serge." She shuddered and widened her legs, trying to give him greater access to her pussy. "You're acting like you're sex starved. You can't be that hungry. Oooh. Not after spending the last few weeks fucking God only knows how many women."

"You have to forgive me for that. None of those women, whoever they were, meant anything to me," he whispered, cupping her breasts in his hands as he sank his full length into her.

The feel of his hands on her breasts sent delicious eddies of pleasure through her. "Really?" She rotated her buns against him and tightened her pussy around his cock. "And why is that?

"For several reasons. Those dark weeks are just a blurb, I couldn't control my natural urges during my feast of indulgence, and it was just meaningless sex."

"Oh, you are just full of BS," she murmured, pushing her hips back to received his cock. "Oooh, Lord. Give it all to me, gray eyes. Give it all to me. Hmm. And what is this?"

"This..." He slipped his big hands from her breasts and held her hips in his hands and he ruthlessly propelled his cock into her. "This...this is love."

Oh, God, yes, she thought, before her ability to think was severely impaired. That sounded about right. "Hmm. And just how long do you think this blissful situation is going to last?"

"I don't know sweetheart." He lifted his head and met her gaze in the mirror. "I was thinking along the lines of...forever?"

Her heart and senses were overwhelmed with the love and adoration she felt flowing into her along with his big, sumptuous cock. "Hmm," a mindless shiver shook her body.

Still, he sounded a little complacent. "Really? Well, I wouldn't get too cocky, if I were you, college boy." She laughed. "Pun intended."

She felt his shock all the way through her. "Oh, Derri, please. Please. I love you and I have to have you. Please don't tell me you're not going to stay with me."

She reached back and stroked her hands over the sides of his thighs in an attempt to soothe his rising panic. "Don't freak on me, Serge, but I'm not so sure about this."

He shuddered and his cock stopped the wonderful, sweet thrusting into her. "Why not? I know you love me. I can feel it."

"Okay, I am in love with you," she admitted. "Don't stop fucking me. It's not that."

He began a seductive movement of his big dick into her pussy, although now his strokes were slow and measured. "Then what is it? Is it the black-white thing again?"

"No." She shoved her hips back at him and squeezed his cock several times. She smiled complacently when he shuddered and cupped one big palm over her breasts while fingering her clit with his other hand. "That's out of the picture. You're my man and I'm keeping you."

"Then what does that leave?"

She gave him a sexy vampish grin in the mirror and ground her rump against him. She gloried in his helpless response. "It's just that I'm not sure," she whispered. Forever with this sweet, wonderful, totally delicious man who was not only an incredible lover, but who loved her so completely and vocally? "that forever with you is going to be long enough."

"Oh, God, Derri. I love you so much. I never dreamed bloodlust would be so incredibly wonderful."

"Oh, Lord, Serge, I love you too! More than I've ever loved any other man!"

"Oh, God, you don't know how much I've longed to hear you say that and know you mean it."

"I do mean it. I've never meant it more. I've been in love with you for weeks."

He eased out of her and drew her down to the floor with him. He settled her trembling body on top of his. She gasped and bit her lip to stifle a scream as he slowly impaled her on his hard cock.

With every inch of her creamy passage filled with his hot, pulsing length, she closed her eyes, clutched at him, and met him thrust for delicious thrust. Moments later, he rolled them over so he lay on top of her. He then began to thrust wildly into her. Her whole body shook, her heart pounded until she could barely breathe. He made love to her with a force and fury that promised the most staggering climax she'd ever had.

She titled her head and whimpered with pleasure as his incisor pierced the skin of her neck. Oh, Lord, she was about to explode! If this mind numbing pleasure was bloodlust, there was nothing in the world half as good, she thought just before she shattered into a million satisfied pieces.

# Epilogue

ଚ୨

*Okay, you are not going to cry,* Derri told herself as she stared at her reflection in the full-length mirror on one of the doors of the walk-in closet of her bedroom.

"Are you crying?"

She turned away from the mirror as Serge emerged from the bathroom. She caught her breath. He looked absolutely stunning in a cream colored tux with a black bowtie and cummerbund. He was the sexiest, most handsome, sweetest man she'd ever met. And he was head over heels in love with her.

"Oh, wow, college boy, you look good enough to eat," she said, allowing her gaze to drift down to his groin area. She sighed in relief. He was wearing the cup she'd bought him. Although she knew he didn't like it, now that she'd come to terms with the fact that they belonged together, she didn't like the idea of other women seeing the cock that belonged exclusively to her.

She smiled at the slight hint of blood staining his cheeks and crossed the room. It still amazed her that her passionate and compassionate vampire could and did frequently blush when she paid him a compliment.

She linked her arms around his neck and smiled up at him. "I love you," she said softly.

As usual, a declaration of love from her left him speechless. But she was fully aware of his love and gratitude washing over her like a warm, welcoming sea breeze on a hot, scoring day.

He slipped his arms around her waist. "We're going to a wedding, not a funeral."

"I know, but these last three weeks with you have been the happiest and most fulfilling of my life."

To her utter amazement, his beautiful gray eyes welled with tears. "Oh, God! You have no idea how much I love, worship, and adore you."

She stroked his cheek. "Actually, I do college boy. I can feel it and it's the most wonderful feeling in the world...well, short of having you ingest my blood as you make love to me."

His arms tightened around her waist and she could feel his desire stir. "Speaking of making love, how about a quickie?"

She shook her head and pushed against his shoulders. "Don't even think about that."

He reluctantly released her. "Why not?"

He sounded as if it had been weeks since they'd made love instead of just an hour earlier.

"Why not? How about because I've lost track of the number of times and places we've made love in the last three weeks. And I am not arriving at Cassy's wedding looking like I've just been fucked senseless."

He gave a long, exaggerated sigh. "Oh, all right. Speaking of weddings, why were you crying when I came in?"

She shrugged. "I always cry at weddings."

"But we haven't even arrived yet," he pointed out.

"Never mind," she told him. "I promised myself I won't cry and yet I always do."

"And in two weeks, you get to cry at Erica and Mikhel's wedding."

She grinned. "I also get to see you all decked out again. I thought you looked good in black, but in...you are the most attractive man I've ever met."

"What about Mik and Alex?"

"They are both big, handsome, charming men, but I am not wildly in love with either of them, as I am with you. Any other questions, college boy?"

He was silent for a moment before nodding. "Yes. You are clearly so happy for Erica and Cassy, when do they get to be happy for you?"

"What…what do you mean?"

"You know what I mean," he countered, his gray eyes swirling.

She did know. He'd hinted at wanting to marry her within days of meeting her. And just last week, he'd asked her what size ring she wore.

"I've been down to jewelers' row."

"Oh." She licked her lips. "Did you see anything you…liked?"

He cupped her face in his palms. "I saw and bought something I hope you will like."

Her heart thumped in her chest. They'd spent all of their free time together during the preceding three weeks. Even when she worked at home, when he wasn't at a Diamond's basketball game, he would sit silently, watching her. Occasionally when she looked up, they would exchange a silent *I love you*. Although he hadn't "officially" moved in with her, he'd spent every night with her. She'd made room in her closet for some of his clothes and given him one of her dresser drawers. He was more a part of her life than any man had ever been. And she was loving every single second of their time together.

She'd freely given him her body, her love, and her heart. Now he wanted more? Well so did she. So maybe it was now time to take the plunge.

She smiled nervously up at him. "So are you going to show it to me or what?"

He released her and stepped away. He put his hand in his pocket and produced a small, black velvet jeweler's box. His hands began to shake as he opened it revealing an exquisite diamond engagement ring.

She extended her left hand and sucked in a breath as he easily slid the ring onto her finger.

"Do you like it?" He sounded anxious.

"Of course I do."

"You're sure? Because if you want a different setting or a bigger stone, I can—"

"Serge, the diamond is huge and the ring is beyond beautiful. Thank you."

He slipped an arm around her waist. "So? Will you marry me?"

Her eyes filled with fresh tears. "Yes!!"

"Yes?" He laughed and swept her off her feet and swung her around.

She laughed and held onto his shoulders. "Serge! You're making me dizzy and you're wrinkling my dress. Put me down, you big, handsome vampire."

He gave her a quick, tender kiss before setting her gently on her feet. "When?"

"When what?" she asked, but she felt his impatience and knew what he meant.

"If you'll settle for a small, quick wedding like Cassy and Erica, we can get married two weeks after Mik and Erica."

"Forget it, Serge," she said, shaking her head. "While I am not set on a big, formal wedding, I am not getting married in four weeks."

"Why not?"

Because she wanted to get to know his family before they got married. To her surprise, his mother had flown in from Boston a week earlier to meet her. Although at first nervous, she and Palea Dumont had decided they liked each other. She grimaced. At least one of the Dumont women liked her. She didn't think Katie, who was still very cool to her, after having walked in on her with Alex, would ever like her.

"It's not that she dislikes you," Serge protested. "It's just that she has…issues with Alex and…well, her…coolness towards you has more to do with her…issues with him than they do with you. Just give her time and she'll like you, as I hope you'll like her."

She wasn't so sure she and Katie would ever like each other. But she'd worry about that later.

She gave him a mischievous grin. "Besides I want to fully enjoy being engaged to you before I fully enjoy being married to you. Can you handle that, gray eyes?"

"Exactly how long are you going to need to enjoy being engaged?"

"You are so impatient," she teased.

"I want to be your husband."

"And I want to be your wife," she admitted. "But we can't get married until after the trial."

He frowned. "That starts in three weeks?" And when she'd nodded, he went on. "How long will it take?"

She shrugged. "Roughly four to six weeks. After that, we'll sit down and talk about a wedding date. Okay?"

He nodded. "Okay. I know you'll need to concentrate most of your time and energy towards winning your client's freedom."

She liked the way he assumed she would win. "But once it's over, we'll talk wedding."

"Okay." He brushed his lips against her cheeks. "Will you do something for me, sweetheart?"

"Yes."

He arched a brow. "Don't you want to qualify that with an *if I can?*"

She shook her head. "No. If it's within my power, it's yours. So stop beating around the bush and spit it out, gray eyes."

"I know you are a highly competent, professional woman and are making a name for yourself, but will you...are you taking my name?"

She frowned. "Derri Dumont. I don't know, Serge. I love you madly, but that name...tell you what...after Cassy and Chandler leave, we'll go somewhere romantic for dinner and dancing. Then we can come back here and you can take me to bed and try to persuade me to take your name. Think you can handle that, college boy?"

He drew her into his arms and brushed his lips against hers. "I'll give it my best shot," he whispered.

Although she couldn't feel his cock through the cup, she could "feel" his desire through the bond they shared. *It's going to be a long day,* she complained.

*But an even longer, sweeter night,* he promised.

*And lifetime.*

*I will be the most devoted husband you've ever had.*

*You'll be the only one I'll ever have,* she told him. *Because once we're married, I plan to keep you forever.*

*Good because that's how long I'll love and adore you, my darling, Derri.*

His darling Derri, huh? It seemed she was destined to spend the rest of her life being the darling of handsome, adoring Serge Dumont.

*Can you handle that, sweetheart?*

Well, it's an ugly job, but someone's got to do it, she teased and pressed her lips up against his.

The kisses they exchanged were filled with a combination of love, desire, passion, and the promise of endless devotion.

Yeah, she could handle that.

# Why an electronic book?

We live in the Information Age—an exciting time in the history of human civilization, in which technology rules supreme and continues to progress in leaps and bounds every minute of every day. For a multitude of reasons, more and more avid literary fans are opting to purchase e-books instead of paper books. The question from those not yet initiated into the world of electronic reading is simply: *Why?*

1.  *Price.* An electronic title at Ellora's Cave Publishing and Cerridwen Press runs anywhere from 40% to 75% less than the cover price of the exact same title in paperback format. Why? Basic mathematics and cost. It is less expensive to publish an e-book (no paper and printing, no warehousing and shipping) than it is to publish a paperback, so the savings are passed along to the consumer.

2.  *Space.* Running out of room in your house for your books? That is one worry you will never have with electronic books. For a low one-time cost, you can purchase a handheld device specifically designed for e-reading. Many e-readers have large, convenient screens for viewing. Better yet, hundreds of titles can be stored within your new library—on a single microchip. There are a variety of e-readers from different manufacturers. You can also read e-books on your PC or laptop computer. (Please note that Ellora's Cave does not endorse any specific brands.

You can check our websites at www.ellorascave.com or www.cerridwenpress.com for information we make available to new consumers.)

3. *Mobility.* Because your new e-library consists of only a microchip within a small, easily transportable e-reader, your entire cache of books can be taken with you wherever you go.

4. *Personal Viewing Preferences.* Are the words you are currently reading too small? Too large? Too… ANNOYING? Paperback books cannot be modified according to personal preferences, but e-books can.

5. *Instant Gratification.* Is it the middle of the night and all the bookstores near you are closed? Are you tired of waiting days, sometimes weeks, for bookstores to ship the novels you bought? Ellora's Cave Publishing sells instantaneous downloads twenty-four hours a day, seven days a week, every day of the year. Our webstore is never closed. Our e-book delivery system is 100% automated, meaning your order is filled as soon as you pay for it.

Those are a few of the top reasons why electronic books are replacing paperbacks for many avid readers.

As always, Ellora's Cave and Cerridwen Press welcome your questions and comments. We invite you to email us at Comments@ellorascave.com or write to us directly at Ellora's Cave Publishing Inc., 1056 Home Avenue, Akron, OH 44310-3502.

# COMING TO A BOOKSTORE NEAR YOU!

# ELLORA'S CAVE

*Bestselling Authors Tour*

Discover for yourself why readers can't get enough
of the multiple award-winning publisher

Ellora's Cave.

Whether you prefer e-books or paperbacks,

be sure to visit EC on the web at
www.ellorascave.com

for an erotic reading experience that will leave you
breathless.

Made in the USA
Lexington, KY
14 December 2009